If You're Reading This, it's too Late

By
Pseudonymous Bosch

USBORNE

AUTHOR'S NOTE:

PLEASE READ THE CONTRACT ON THE
FOLLOWING PAGE VERY CAREFULLY AND
COPY IT OUT IN YOUR BEST HANDWRITING.
IF YOU REFUSE TO SIGN, I'M AFRAID YOU
MUST CLOSE THIS BOOK IMMEDIATELY.

P.B.

BINDING CONTRACT

I, the reader of this book, certify that I am reading this book for entertainment only.

Or to avoid cleaning my bedroom or doing my homework.

I will not try to uncover the true identities or locations of the people described in this book.

Nor will I try to contact any secret society mentioned in this book.

Although the story may concern an ancient and powerful Secret, I hereby deny any knowledge of this so-called Secret.

If I am ever asked about it, I will run from the room.

Unless I am on an aeroplane, in which case I will close my eyes and ignore the person speaking to me.

And if all else fails, I'll scream.

I will not repeat a word of this book under any circumstances.

Unless I just can't help it.

Signed,

Reader _____ *

Date _____

*NORMALLY, I WOULD ASK THAT YOU SIGN IN BLOOD. BUT LATELY I HAVE FOUND THAT KETCHUP WORKS JUST AS WELL – AND IT IS MUCH LESS PAINFUL.

PROLOGUE

The flashlight pierced the darkness

The flashlight slashed through the darkness

The flashlight beam sliced through the darkness like a sword

The flashlight beam darted – yes! – across the dark hall, illuminating a wondrous collection of antique curiosities:

Finely illustrated tarot cards of wizened kings and laughing fools...glistening Chinese lacquer boxes concealing spring traps and secret compartments... intricately carved cups of wood and ivory designed for making coins and marbles and even fingers disappear... shining silver rings that a knowing hand could link and unlink as if they were made of air...

A museum of magic.

The circle of light lingered on a luminous crystal ball, as if waiting for some swirling image to appear on the surface. Then it stopped, hesitating on a large bronze lantern – once home, perhaps, to a powerful genie.

Finally, the flashlight beam found its way to a glass display case sitting alone in the middle of the room.

"Ha! At last!" said a woman with a voice like ice.

The man behind the flashlight snickered. "Who was it that said the best place to hide something was in plain sight? What an idiot." His accent was odd, ominous.

"Just do it!" hissed the woman.

Grasping the heavy flashlight tight in his gloved hand, the man brought it down like an axe. Glass shattered in a cascade, revealing a milky white orb – a giant pearl? – sitting on a bed of black velvet.

Ignoring the sharp, glittering shards, the woman reached with a delicately thin hand – in a delicately thin white glove – and pulled out the orb.

About the size of an ostrich egg, it was translucent and seemed almost to glow from within. The surface had a honeycomb sort of texture comprised of many holes of varying sizes. A thin band of silver circled the orb, dividing it into two equal hemispheres.

The woman pushed aside her white-blonde hair and held the mysterious object to her perfectly shaped ear. As she turned it over, it whispered like an open bottle in the wind.

"I can almost hear him," she gloated. "That horrid monster!"

"You're so sure he's alive? It's been four, five hundred years…"

"A creature like that – so impossible to make – is al

the more impossible to kill," she replied, still listening to the ball in her hand.

A small red bloodstain now marked her white glove where one of the glass shards had cut through; she didn't seem to notice. "But now he can escape us no longer. The Secret will be mine!"

The flashlight beam fell.

"I mean ours, darling."

Beneath the shattered display a small brass plaque gleamed. *The Sound Prism, origin unknown,* it read—

AAAAAAAAAAAAAAAAA
AAAAAAAAAAAAARRGH!

I'm sorry – I can't do it.

I can't write this book. I'm far too frightened.

Not for myself, you understand. As ruthless as they are, Dr. L and Ms. Mauvais will never find me where I am. (You recognized that insidious duo, didn't you – by their gloves?*)

No, it's for you I fear.

I had hoped the contract would protect you, but now that I look the matter square in the face – it's just not enough.

What if, say, the wrong people saw you reading this book? They might not believe your claims of innocence. That you really know nothing about the Secret.

I regret to say it, but I can't vouch for what would happen then.

Honestly, I would feel much better writing about something else. Something safer.

Like, say, penguins! Penguins are popular.

---

*If not, you were probably lucky enough not to read my earlier book, Cass and Max-Ernest and the Mystery of the Secret Spa. Also called Cass and Max-Ernest and the Curse of the Not-So-Ancient Pyramid. You may know it as The Name of This Book Is Secret – a title that is so confusing I seldom use it myself. To find out who Dr. L and Ms. Mauvais are, and to catch up on the story so far, turn to page 402. Or better yet, keep reading in ignorance – in this case, a much safer course.

No? You don't want penguins? You want secrets?

Of course you do. Me, too... It's just, well, what if I were to tell you that, after all, I was just the teensiest bit scared? For my own skin, I mean.

Let me put it this way: the monster Ms. Mauvais spoke of – that wasn't a figure of speech. She meant *monster*.

So how about giving me a break? Just this once.

What's that – it's too late? You signed a contract?

Gee. That's nice. I thought we had a friendly arrangement, and now you're threatening me.

Oh, sure. I know how it is. You want to laugh at my jokes. Maybe shed a few tears. But when it comes to having real sympathy for a terrified soul like me – forget it, right?

Readers, you're all the same. Spoiled, every last one of you. Lying there with your feet up, yelling for someone to bring you more cookies. (Don't tell me they're chocolate chip because then I'll be really mad!)

I'm sorry, I didn't mean that – this whole writing business is making me crazy.

Let's be honest – I'm stalling.

In a word: Procrastinating. Putting off. Postponing.

I'm draaaagggggginnnnnnggggg myyyyyy feeeeeet.

You're right – it's only going to make my job harder in the end.

Better to jump back in.

Never mind how cold the water is. Or how deep. Or how many man-eating—

The only way to write is to write and I'm just going to—

Wait! I need a second to settle my mind.

Two seconds.

Three.

There. I'm standing on the edge, pen in hand, ready to take the plunge.

And here I—

HEY, DID YOU JUST PUSH ME?!?!

WELL, I GUESS IT HAD TO HAPPEN.
BY NOW, WE ALL KNOW I CAN'T KEEP
ANYTHING TO MYSELF - NO MATTER HOW
DANGEROUS OR ILL-ADVISED.

AND THE TRUTH IS:

IF YOU'RE READING THIS, IT'S TOO LATE.

CHAPTER THIRTY-THREE*

A Bad Dream

*YOU WILL NOTICE THAT I HAVE NUMBERED THE CHAPTERS IN THIS BOOK BACKWARDS. LIKE A COUNTDOWN FOR A ROCKET LAUNCH. OR A BOMB. WITH ANY LUCK, THE BOOK WILL EXPLODE AT THE END, AND I WON'T HAVE TO FINISH IT.

A graveyard at night.

On a mountainside. By a lake.

Our vision is blurred. Rain falls in sheets around us.

Everywhere there is water. Dripping. Dripping.

A strange song starts to play. It sounds far away, yet impossibly close.

Like the singing of fairies or sylphs.

Like the ringing of a thousand tiny voices inside our ears.

Above us, a crow flaps its wings against the rain and, screeching, disappears into the dark.

Lightning briefly illuminates the tombstones at our feet, but they are so old that no trace of name or date remains. They are no longer grave markers; they are just rocks.

What lies beneath is a mystery.

A mouse scurries between the stones, frantic. As if he's trying to get out of a maze. A deadly trap.

Soon he is joined by others of his kind. They swim against a tide of mud. Clawing at each other in their desperate attempt to escape.

Automatically, we look in the direction they are running from. There is a burial mound with a broken tombstone on top. Its jagged edge silhouetted as lightning strikes a second time.

*The strange, eerie song wafts through the wind –
until it is drowned out by a crack of thunder.*

*As we watch, the broken stone topples – and lands
with a thud in the mud. A gaping hole is left in the
ground. Clods of dirt erupt. A mud volcano.*

*First one hand, then another – both very, very large
– emerge out of the hole, grasping at the mud to find
a hold.*

And then: a nose.

*At least, we think it's a nose; it could be a
cauliflower—*

"Cassandra...!"

*We look down. A lone, stranded mouse is calling to
us – as if from a great distance.*

"Get up, Cass – it's late!"

He sounds oddly like our mother—

Shivering, Cass lifted her head off her pillow.

She was a member of a dangerous secret society
now, the Terces Society, she reminded herself. Or she
would be soon. She couldn't let a little dream scare
her.

What had Pietro, the old magician, said in his
letter? That once she and Max-Ernest had sworn the
Oath of Terces, they would "face the hazards and the

hardships". And that they must "obey all the orders without the questions".*

If she couldn't face her own dreams, how could she face real enemies like Dr. L and Ms. Mauvais? Like the Masters of the Midnight Sun.

Even so, the strange song lingered in her mind, haunting her.

Again.

Each night a different dream. But always the same song.

Why?

"Cassandra!"

Her mother was calling up to her from downstairs. Cass couldn't hear every word but she knew what her mother was saying:

Get up – it's late! I'm off to work (...or to yoga...or to a meeting). There's oatmeal on the stove (...or granola on the counter...or a waffle in the toaster). Don't forget you have your maths quiz (...or book

---

*IF YOU'VE NEVER SEEN THE LETTER, I RECOMMEND YOU READ IT YOURSELF. IT WAS WRITTEN IN CODE AND SIGNED *P.B.* PIETRO BERGAMO. CASS AND HER FRIEND MAX-ERNEST FOUND IT ETCHED ON A FOGGY WINDOW. BUT YOU WILL FIND IT AT THE END OF THE LAST CHAPTER OF MY FIRST BOOK, *CASS AND MAX-ERNEST AND THE SECRET OF THE ROTTEN EGG SMELL*, OR WHATEVER IT'S CALLED. WHETHER YOU READ THE WHOLE BOOK FIRST (WHICH IS THE HONOURABLE THING TO DO) OR JUST SKIP TO THE LETTER AND THEN PUT THE BOOK BACK ON THE SHELF (WHICH IS BASICALLY LIKE STEALING) IS UP TO YOU.

report...or oboe lesson). Love you!

These days, Cass's mother ended nearly everything she said to Cass with *Love you!* – kind of like it was a punctuation mark or a nervous tick.

"Love you!"

See.

The front door slammed shut; her mother had left.

Unwilling to get up, Cass stared at the wall facing her bed.

Cass's Wall of Horrors, her mother called it.

Hundreds of magazine and newspaper clippings covered the wall – all describing disasters, or potential disasters:

Earthquakes. Volcanoes. Tsunamis. Tornadoes.

There were pictures of seabirds blackened by oil spills, and of starving polar bears standing on shrinking icebergs. There were mushroom clouds and poison mushrooms, killer bees and killer mould.

Posters and diagrams showed How to Treat Frostbite... THE HEIMLICH MANOEUVRE... Three Signs That You Have a Third-Degree Burn... The ABCs of CPR...

And in the centre of the wall: an article about a bear haunting campers in the mountains. BEAR OR BIGFOOT? the headline read.

Most people – people like Cass's mother – would

find a wall like this very disquieting. Cass found it comforting.

Usually.

As a survivalist, she liked to be prepared for the worst at all times. She could face anything, she felt, if she knew it was coming.

Hurricane? Board up the windows. Drought? Save water. Fire? Don't panic, avoid smoke inhalation, look for a safe way out.

And yet these were all *natural* disasters. What would she do, she couldn't help wondering now, if she ever confronted a *supernatural* disaster?

That was what upset her about her dreams. They were strange and irrational. *They didn't make sense*, as her friend Max-Ernest would say. (Max-Ernest talked compulsively, but he was *always* very logical.) An earthquake might not be totally predictable but at least it obeyed the laws of nature.

Most of her dreams involved a monstrous creature and a spooky old graveyard. How do you prepare for *that*?

Not that she thought her dreams were going to come true; she wasn't superstitious. It was just that they felt so real.

"There must be something in the graveyard you want," Max-Ernest had said when she finally told him about the dreams. "A dream is the fulfilment of a wish. That's what Sigmund Freud says. How 'bout that?"*

"But why would I wish for a monster?" Cass had asked. Max-Ernest's parents were psychologists – so she figured he knew what he was talking about.

"Well, I don't know if it means you wished for it, exactly. I think dreams are like things you can't admit you want because you feel guilty or embarrassed or something. It's called the unconscious," Max-Ernest had concluded. "It's kind of confusing."

Still in bed, Cass thought about what he'd said. She reached under her pillow, pulling out the small stuffed creature she'd hidden beneath it.

"Who are you? What are you?"

Cass's sock-monster was a little, odd-shaped thing made out of old socks and scraps from her grandfathers' antiques store. She'd sewn it together in a kind of fever one day, obsessed by the creature from her dreams. It was green and purple and troll-like with a big, sock-heel nose, bulging bottle-cap eyes, and floppy ears made from tennis-shoe tongues. Cass liked the

---

*FREUD WAS THE INVENTOR OF THE FREUDIAN SLIP – WHICH IS NOT SOMETHING YOU WEAR UNDER A DRESS, BUT IS WHEN YOU INTEND TO SAY ONE THING, THEN ACCIDENTALLY SAY SOMETHING ELSE THAT WAS ON YOUR MIND. SO CHEESE – I MEAN, *PLEASE* – TAKE EVERYTHING HE SAID WITH A GRAIN OF SALT (OR AT LEAST WITH A SLICE OF CHEDDAR). PERHAPS HE MEANT THAT A DREAM WAS THE FULFILMENT OF A *FISH*!

ears especially – ears almost as big but not nearly as pointy as Cass's own.

Since it was one hundred per cent recycled, the sock-monster was a super-survivalist, and Cass found that if she held him tight she absorbed his survival powers.

Sometimes.

Other times, he just felt good to hug.*

Maybe, thought Cass, her bad dreams would end when her new life – her secret life, her life with the Terces Society – began.

Like any serious survivalist, Cass followed a rigorous routine every morning:

As soon as she was on her feet, she pulled her backpack out from under her bed and double-checked its contents. The backpack was a custom-made model that Pietro had sent her; it had special secret capabilities, like converting to a tent or a parachute. Even so, Cass kept some of her old survivalist supplies in the backpack – like chewing gum, for its sticking value, and grape juice, which she liked to use as ink.

---

*YES, I AGREE. HUGGING A SOFT TOY – EVEN A RECYCLED SOCK-MONSTER – DOESN'T SEEM VERY SURVIVALIST-ISH. CASS WOULD BE RATHER UPSET THAT I MENTIONED IT. PLEASE FORGET ABOUT IT – AS WELL AS ABOUT EVERYTHING ELSE I TELL YOU, OF COURSE.

She didn't know what her first Terces Society mission would be – all she knew about the society was that it was dedicated to protecting the Secret – but she would be ready.

Next, Cass examined every corner of her house to see if anyone had entered overnight – whether friend or foe.

She checked:

1. The tiny threads of dental floss she tied to the handles of her desk drawers so she'd know if anybody ever opened them.
2. The dried bee corpse she'd discovered one day and left strategically on her window sill.
3. All the windows and mirrors and doors to see whether someone had written a coded message in dust, toothpaste, or shaving cream.
4. And a few other places I won't give away, in case the wrong person reads this.

Only after she was sure that nothing had changed upstairs did she allow herself to go downstairs, where her first stop was usually the kitchen cupboard. Cass had a hunch she might find the next secret message from the Terces Society in a particular old box of alphabet cereal.

But this morning, when she walked through the kitchen door, Cass let out a very un-survivalist-like gasp of excitement: the magnets on the refrigerator had been moved. They weren't arranged the way she'd left them the night before (by colour rather than letter); she could tell from the doorway.

She covered the distance in two leaps and stood breathless in front of the refrigerator, ready to decipher a coded message or to read directions to a secret meeting place or to take instructions about a new mission. Or all three.

Then her heart sank.

The magnets spelled: LOVE YOU

Clipped underneath was a handwritten note:

7 a.m. Off to work. There's a waffle — the wholewheat kind — in the toaster. Don't forget you have your field trip to the tide pools tomorrow — do you know where your windbreaker is? I can't find it. M.

M being for Mom or Mother. But also for Mel.

Mel being short for Melanie, her mother's name.

Hardly a secret code.

Cass crumpled the note in her hand, despondent: why did her mom have to be such a mom?

And when was the Terces Society going to come?

CHAPTER THIRTY-TWO

The Nuts Table

T*he Xxxxxxxxx School. City of Xxxxx Xxxxxx. Lunchtime.*

I'm sorry – I still cannot tell you the name of Cass's school. Or where the school was located. Or what it looked like. Or almost anything else about it.

Of course, I trust *you*. But there's always the possibility that, through no fault of your own, you will toss this book out the window and it will fall into the wrong hands.*

I can tell you this: it was a school that lived by strict rules.

There were, first of all, the principal Mrs. Johnson's rules, which were strict enough, but usually understandable. Like no skateboarding in the hallways, for example. Or no wearing your underpants outside your clothing.

But there were also many other, unspoken rules that were made by nobody in particular, and that made no sense at all.

One of these pointless rules was that you ate lunch

---

*WHILE I'M ON THE SUBJECT, YOU DO REMEMBER THAT ALL THE NAMES IN THIS BOOK ARE MADE UP, DON'T YOU? CASSANDRA. MAX-ERNEST. ALL OF THEM. YES, I'M RECKLESS AND IRRESPONSIBLE, BUT THERE'S A LIMIT – EVEN FOR ME. I WOULD NEVER TELL YOU MY CHARACTERS' REAL NAMES. IF SOMEBODY READING THIS BOOK – *SOMEBODY*, I SAID, NOT YOU – WERE ABLE TO TRACK ONE OF THEM DOWN, WELL, I DON'T EVEN WANT TO THINK ABOUT THE CONSEQUENCES.

at the same table and with the same people every day; if you changed tables it could only mean that you were in a fight or something truly drastic had happened.

The lunch tables were clustered outside in a part of the school yard known as the Grove (even though there weren't any trees nearby). At the centre table sat Amber and her friends. Amber, you may remember, was the nicest girl in school, and the third prettiest. At least, that's what everybody said.

Other tables spread out from there – like planets orbiting a sun.

Cass and Max-Ernest, I am sorry to report, did little to rebel against this system. In fact, their table, located on the very outermost fringes of the Grove, was so well known it had a name: the Nuts Table.

"The name doesn't make any sense," Max-Ernest complained almost daily. "It should be the No Nuts Table, since it's for kids with nut allergies."

"I think people think the Nuts Table sounds funnier," Cass told him.

But she stopped short of a full explanation: if Max-Ernest didn't understand that the other students thought that the kids at the Nuts Table were, well, nuts, then good for him.

Cass had no allergies herself; nonetheless, her diet was very restricted. Because she saw lunch as part of her survivalist training, everything she ate had to be capable of lasting for months without spoiling, whether in an underground bunker or an outer-space escape pod. Thus fresh fruit was prohibited, but fruit gums were permissible. Sandwiches were out, but cup-o-noodles was okay.

Trail mix was the most ideal food of all; it was a whole meal in one.*

Today, however, Cass hesitated before digging into her trail mix. A handwritten note was sitting on top.

Cass grimaced in annoyance. She hated it when her mother put notes in her lunch – it was *so* embarrassing. Not to mention, the notes usually consisted of lists of not-very-fun things Cass was supposed to do or remember.

She pushed the note back into her reusable waterproof lunch bag. She would read it later. Maybe.

Unlike Cass, Max-Ernest did have several nut allergies (to which nuts he was never sure) as well as a host of other food-related ailments. But what was more remarkable, he always brought two lunches to school: one made by his mother, and one by his

---

*DON'T WORRY, AS CASS OFTEN POINTED OUT TO HER NERVOUS LUNCH TABLE COMPANIONS, THERE WERE NO NUTS IN HER TRAIL MIX – JUST PEANUT-BUTTER CHIPS, AND THEY WERE ARTIFICIALLY FLAVOURED. FOR CASS'S PATENTED "SUPER-CHIP" TRAIL MIX RECIPE, SEE BOOK I, APPENDIX.

father; he was always careful to eat the same amount from each. Max-Ernest's parents were divorced, and everything in his life was doubled or divided. (When Cass first visited his house, she couldn't believe it: the house was split down the middle, each side designed and decorated differently, with neither parent ever stepping onto the other parent's side.)

Today, he didn't seem to be in a hurry to eat *either* of his lunches.

"So, I learned a new trick. Wanna see?" he asked, already laying out his playing cards. "It's called the Four Brothers."

Max-Ernest had been reading up on magic for several months now, not just how-to books but also histories and biographies of famous magicians. Every time Cass saw him he had a new story about an Indian sword-swallower or a nineteenth-century flea circus or an essay on the first time a magician made an elephant disappear.

For today's trick, Max-Ernest removed the four jacks from his deck and fanned them out in front of Cass. "See these four jacks? They're brothers and they don't like being separated."

He gathered up the jacks and placed them in different places in the deck, separating them – or seeming to. Then he cut the deck.

"Now, watch how the jacks all come back together..."

He riffled through the deck and showed her how they'd moved next to each other – or seemed to. "How 'bout that?"

He was getting better, thought Cass. But not that much better.

It didn't help that Max-Ernest had a big pimple on the tip of his nose. Between the pimple and his spiky hair – each strand, as always, cut exactly the same length – he looked more like a hedgehog than a magician.

"Pretty good," said Cass diplomatically. "But I think I've seen the trick before – only with kings. And they weren't brothers, they were friends."

"That doesn't make sense. Four kings would never be friends – they would be rivals, fighting over their kingdoms. And even if they weren't fighting – I doubt they would have that many friends. It's not very realistic—"

Cass was about to point out that sometimes *brothers* could be rivals. Like Pietro and Dr. L. They were twins – but also mortal enemies. At the same time, plenty of people had four friends or even more. Amber, for instance. Amber considered herself to be friends with their entire school.

But Cass decided not to say anything. You had to choose your battles with Max-Ernest. Otherwise, you would be arguing all day.

Besides, neither of them had very many friends; in that respect, he was correct. In fact, she was Max-Ernest's only friend. And, as much as she hated to admit it, he was *her* only friend as well. (Unless you counted their old classmate, Benjamin Blake. But his parents had put him in a special school this year. And he'd never said that much anyway – at least that you could understand.)

"Well, I still wish you would concentrate on training for the Terces Society instead of magic tricks," she said.

"We don't even know what we're training for!" said Max-Ernest, a little exasperated. "Besides, Pietro was a magician, wasn't he?"

"You mean, he *is* – he's still alive, remember?"

"We don't know for sure. Somebody else might have written the letter who had the same initials. Or who was pretending to be him. Or maybe he died *after* writing it. I mean, it's been four months. Why hasn't the Terces Society contacted us again, if they even—"

Cass gave him a look. She hated it when he suggested that Pietro might be dead. Or that the Terces

Society might not exist. She'd spent too much time preparing to contemplate such a thing.

"The letter said that Owen would come get us, and he will!" she said with more confidence than she felt.

Owen was the man who'd helped rescue them from the clutches of the Midnight Sun. He had a habit of switching identities, so for months Cass and Max-Ernest had scrutinized every face they encountered. But they'd never detected a single false moustache or fake accent. Or even any suspicious car accidents. (Owen was a terrible driver.)

"Well, maybe he already came," Max-Ernest offered conciliatorily, "but it was like an abduction. We actually took our oaths under hypnosis, and now we're operating under secret instructions—"

Cass laughed. If nothing else, Max-Ernest was always willing to consider all the possibilities.

"Was that funny?" he asked in surprise.

Cass nodded. He grinned. "How 'bout that?"

(To Cass's chagrin, Max-Ernest's magical aspirations had done nothing to diminish his previous, even more unlikely desire: to be a stand-up comedian.)

"Is that from your mom?" Max-Ernest asked, changing the subject. He was looking at the note still sticking halfway out of her lunch bag.

Irritated, Cass pulled it out. This is what it said:

Cass, here's the grocery list for tomorrow —
MEAT — no need for A quality
DUCK (3) — tell butcher you owe —
he'll understand
12 Potatoes, Mashed
Peanut Butter

Mother

Now that she was looking at the note, it seemed strange to Cass for several reasons:

First, her mother had gone to the grocery store yesterday.

Second, they'd never had a duck in her house – let alone three.

Third, her mother always bought potatoes whole, then mashed them at home. Cass wasn't even sure you could buy pre-mashed potatoes if you wanted to.

Fourth, her mother never signed her notes "Mother". Usually, she just signed "M". If she was feeling especially loving or playful she might write "Mommy". Sometimes, when she wanted to show Cass she was treating her like a grown-up, she signed "Mel".

But *Mother*? Not that Cass could remember.

A little feeling of excitement started tingling in her

toes, bubbled through her stomach, then burst out of her mouth:

"Hey, look at this..." she whispered to Max-Ernest.

"It's from them. I know it. It's in code. Can you believe they got it into my lunch?! It was only in my locker for an hour! Do you think Owen is here right now?"

She looked around. The only person she didn't recognize was an Asian boy sitting at the next table, plugging his guitar into a little portable amplifier.

A frown appeared on Max-Ernest's face as he studied the note.

"What – you don't think it's in code? It has to be. It's definitely not from my mom."

"No, I agree – it looks like it's in code. It's just kind of weird..."

Surreptitiously, Max-Ernest pulled out what looked like a game player of some kind from his pocket. Sent to him by Pietro, the hand-held device was actually the ULTRA-Decoder II. Specially designed for decrypting codes, it contained over a thousand languages and even more secret codes in its memory.

Holding the grocery list under the table, Max-Ernest pointed the Decoder at it and scanned.

"I dunno, the Decoder doesn't pick up anything," he whispered. "If it's in code, there's, like, no system to it..."

Cass sighed. Could the note be from her mother after all?

"The Skelton Sisters gave it to me as a prize when I joined the Skelton One Hundred," said a familiar, sugary voice.

It was Amber, walking by with her friend Veronica (the second prettiest girl in school, and not even the fourth or fifth nicest). As far as Cass knew, neither girl had yet turned thirteen. But somehow, over the summer, they'd aged by several years. It was the glittery make-up, Cass decided. (She couldn't believe Mrs. Johnson let them wear it – never mind their mothers.) And the tight clothes.

Amber held up a sparkling pink cellphone decorated with a big red heart. "The ringtone automatically changes to a new Skelton Sisters song each time!" she bragged loudly enough so the entire school yard could hear. "So I'll know all the songs by the time I go to the concert. If I get in – it's almost sold out."

(Romi and Montana Skelton were teenage twins who'd risen to fame on television and video but who now commanded a vast commercial empire – twin♥hearts™ inc. – that produced everything from fuzzy pink backpacks to stinky sticks of lipgloss. Cass had a particular hatred for them – partly because Amber had a particular love for them.)

"Here, listen..."

Amber started pressing buttons on her phone, but before she could make it ring, the school yard was filled with the sound of feedback – and the twisting, sliding whine of an electric guitar. It was the new boy at the next table – channelling Jimi Hendrix.*

Cass laughed aloud. The timing was perfect – interrupting Amber just as she was about to subject them all to some awful Skelton Sisters song.

She looked over at the young guitarist. He was strumming and staring out into space, as if he were alone in a garage and not in school with hundreds of other people. He was tall for his age and he had a thick mop of long black hair that fell over his eyes. He wore bright green tennis shoes and a T-shirt bearing the words:

---

*If you ask your parents, they will probably tell you that Jimi Hendrix was the greatest rock guitar player who ever lived. What they might not tell you is that he also liked to wear wigs. Feedback, by the way, is that high-pitched squealing you get when a microphone picks up sound from a loudspeaker (a sound which, if you think about it, came from the microphone in the first place!). Before Hendrix, most people thought of feedback as trash noise. But he turned it into music.

ALIEN EARACHE
We rock so hard they hear it on Mars!

"I bet that's that new kid – from Japan," Cass said to Max-Ernest. "Remember Mrs. Johnson made that announcement?"

Cass's laugh, meanwhile, had not gone unnoticed by Amber.

"Hey, Cass...are you okay?" asked Amber, stopping at Cass's table – but not without taking a good look at the guitar player first.

"Uh, yeah, I think so..."

"Oh, good!" said Amber sweetly. "I was worried maybe that guitar hurt your ears—"

"No..." Cass didn't like where Amber was heading.

"I just thought they would be really sensitive 'cause they're so – you know."

"No, we don't know!" said Max-Ernest hotly. "Her ears are totally normal, Amber. She hears the same stuff you do."

Cass's ears, as everyone knew, were a sore subject for Cass. Not only were they big and pointy, like an elf's, they also tended to turn bright red when she was angry or embarrassed or in any way upset.

Or when people talked about them.

At the moment, they were turning a violent shade of scarlet.

"Oh, hi, Max-Ernest!" said Amber, as if she'd only just seen him. "I totally didn't mean it as an insult. But that's so sweet the way you defend her! Are you guys, like, a *couple* now?"

Max-Ernest choked on the two identical carrot sticks he was eating. And then he turned very pale.

Amber glanced covertly at the guitar player to see if he was taking this all in. He didn't seem to be.

"We are *not* a couple," Cass said as calmly as she could – considering so much blood was rushing to her ears it felt like a firestorm. (The difference was, she had an asbestos blanket to ward off a *real* firestorm.)

"Oh, that's too bad. You guys make such a cute couple," said Veronica. "C'mon, Am—"

Stifling laughs, they sauntered away.

"Sorry. Forgot to check the volume, yo!" said the guitar player, sounding decidedly un-Japanese. He reached down to disconnect his instrument from his amplifier and turned his head towards the Nuts Table. "I heard that girl Amber was the nicest girl in school. Didn't really seem like it."

"Yeah, that's kind of f-f-funny, huh," stammered Cass, trying to cover her ears with her hair (which was very difficult because her hair was braided). "Anyway, don't worry about it. I thought your playing was –" she searched for the word – "cool."

"Thanks," he said with a big smile. "I'm Yoji. You know, the new guy."

"Yeah, we kind of guessed," said Cass, desperately hoping her ears were turning back to normal.

"You can call me Yo-Yoji. If you want. That's what my friends call me…"

"Okay. Hey, um, Yo-Yoji, I hate to break it to you, but you may have a little more apologizing to do—"

She nodded towards the principal, who was striding across the yard in Yoji's direction, her big yellow hat flapping with each step.

Yoji made a face of exaggerated fear. "Uh-oh… Well, it was nice knowing you. Or meeting you – or whatever."

"Yeah, nice to meet you, too… Oh, I forgot – I'm Cass. And this is Max-Ernest… Say hi, Max-Ernest."

She tugged on her friend's sleeve.

"Hi, Max-Ernest," said Max-Ernest, who'd been stewing in tormented silence ever since Amber had asked if he and Cass were a couple.

Before Yo-Yoji could reply, Mrs. Johnson arrived at his table.

"Up!" she said. "Now march—" She pointed in the

direction of her office. Yo-Yoji shrugged and headed off, guitar on his back.

Cass watched him go, wondering how this new, unexpected element might change the carefully controlled social environment of their school: did she need to take any precautions?

Suddenly, Max-Ernest sat up very straight. "That's it!"

"What?" asked Cass, distracted.

"*Meet*. Look at the note. See how it says 'Meat – no need for A quality'? What if that means no need for letter *A*? Because *meat* means *meet*. With an *E*."

"So we have to meet somewhere? I knew it!" said Cass, forgetting all about Amber and Yo-Yoji and even her red ears. "What about the next line – 'Duck (3)'?"

"'Tell butcher you owe'," Max-Ernest finished for her. "Well, that could be about the letters, too, I guess. If *you* was the letter *U*. And *owe* was *O*."

"So then it's *MEET DOCK 3*?"

Max-Ernest nodded. "And the rest is easy: '12 Potatoes, Mashed' has to be 12 *p.m.* And Peanut Butter – that must be *P.B.*"

"Pietro Bergamo!"

"How 'bout that," Max-Ernest said. "But I still think it's weird he didn't use a more normal code. There's not even really a key."

"So what – you figured it out, anyway! Just like I knew you would."

Max-Ernest nodded, smiling, and wrote the decoded message next to the grocery list.

Meet Dock 3, 12 p.m., Pietro Bergamo

CHAPTER THIRTY-ONE

The Tide Pool
Caper

"S *ick!"* said Yo-Yoji.

Ankles underwater, he was gently poking a large sea anemone with a stick – and the anemone's translucent tendrils were closing tight in reaction.

Cass, Max-Ernest, Amber and a few other students you probably wouldn't recognize stood watching on the wet, moss-covered rocks.

"Sick? I think it's neat-looking," said Max-Ernest. "Kind of like an alien—"

"I think he means sick in a good way," said Cass.

"Oh, yeah," said Max-Ernest, a little confused.

"Well, I think it's disgusting – in a bad way," said Amber. "It looks like dog butt!"

Cass knew better than to argue, but she couldn't resist. "It's not disgusting. It's natural. It's a defence mechanism."

"Actually, I think it thinks the stick is food," said Max-Ernest. "The tentacles have poison on them, and they pull little fish and stuff into its mouth."

"Actually, you're all right – even Amber," said their teacher, Mr. Needleman, stepping up to them. "Because a sea anemone's mouth is also its anus. It eats out of its behind."

"Eeew!" said Amber. "Eeew! Eeew! Eeew!"

"Well said," said Mr. Needleman. "Now, Yoji, stop

poking him, please. Cass, I'm surprised at you! – letting your new classmate torment the sea life like that."

"Sorry," said Cass, although she wasn't sure why her teacher was making her apologize for somebody else. "Anyway, he wasn't hurting him – I was watching."

"Okay, but I want you guys all to be more careful. See those..." He pointed to the spiky purple balls that lined the rocks like so many little porcupines. "Those are sea urchins. Please don't step on them. Very painful. For you *and* the urchin." Mr. Needleman chuckled. "But if you do happen to squish one by mistake, let me know – they make very good sushi."

The kids all groaned.

Mr. Needleman had a flame-red beard and a flaring temper to match. He'd arrived from New Zealand that autumn, and Cass had been very excited to meet him because environmental science was her favourite subject and New Zealand was her favourite country. (She'd never been there but she'd read about it in her mother's travel books: rainforests, glaciers and volcanoes – all in one place!) But instead of treating her like a favourite student as she'd hoped and even sort of expected, Mr. Needleman had from the beginning singled her out for harsh treatment.

Cass didn't know why exactly, except that their perspectives on the world were so different. Mr. Needleman considered himself a "proud sceptic" and a "debunker". Which as far as Cass could tell meant that he made a lot of snide comments about global warming, or as he called it, "Global hokum".

"Have you ever watched a weatherman on TV?" he asked whenever the subject came up. "Those kiwi-heads can't predict the weather next week – how do you expect them to predict the weather in fifty years?"

As you can probably guess, this infuriated Cass, who considered herself an expert on all weather-related catastrophes.

But was *that* why he called on her whenever she drifted off for a second in class? Was *that* why he always claimed he was disappointed in her work?

Max-Earnest said Mr. Needleman just had high expectations because he respected her, but it certainly didn't feel that way.

It was a cold and drizzly day, and the water was very rough.

By now, half the class had slipped on the rocks or stumbled into puddles; most of the others had been pushed into the ocean.

Cass and Max-Ernest had managed to stay dry – Cass because she was such a good rock hopper, Max-Ernest because he kept as far away from the water as possible. (As Cass had discovered at an especially inconvenient moment during their adventures at the Midnight Sun Spa, Max-Ernest didn't know how to swim.) But they were irritable for another reason.

They'd been walking around the tide pools for over half an hour and they still hadn't found a way to get away from the group.

Cass had intended to say she had to pee; after she left, Max-Ernest would say the same. But Mr. Needleman insisted that the teacher's aide escort anyone who wanted to go to the bathroom; so that plan was out. Cass considered saying she was seasick and asking if she could walk back to the bus, but Max-Ernest, who was expert in all kinds of illness, pointed out that seasickness was something you got on a boat – it is a kind of motion sickness – and not something you got on the beach.

Beginning to grow frantic, Cass interrupted Mr. Needleman in the middle of an explanation of red tides and asked if their class was going to be allowed any free time to explore. "You're always telling us to think for ourselves – how are we going to do that if we're following you the whole time?"

Not many grown-ups would take that argument seriously. Mr. Needleman, however, seemed to have a sudden change of heart towards Cass. "You know, you're absolutely right," he said. Just like that.

Cass was so surprised she almost continued arguing.

Mr. Needleman told the class they could have a few minutes of freedom so long as everyone stayed within sight and no one poked the sea life.

Cass looked at her watch. It was ten minutes until noon.

Ten minutes until they were supposed to meet Pietro Bergamo, the long-lost magician.

Ten minutes until their lives as members of the Terces Society would officially begin.

They could just see a wharf – with three docks – on the opposite side of the bay, separated from the tide pools by several large rock outcroppings.

"Walk slow and pretend you're just looking around," Cass whispered to Max-Ernest.

As they approached the rocks, the tide pulled out, leaving a narrow strip of beach between the rocks and the churning water.

"C'mon!" said Cass.

Max-Ernest wavered. "But I—"

"Would you rather swim?"

By the time the tide returned, they were standing on a small patch of sand surrounded on all sides by jagged rocks – safe and dry, for the moment.

There was only one problem: Yo-Yoji had followed them.

"Yo, dudes, where you going?" he asked, wading through the surf.

Max-Ernest looked at Cass: now what?

Cass glanced at her watch: they had six minutes.

"Hey, Yo-Yoji. I know you don't really know us very well, but...can you do us a huge favour?"

Yo-Yoji agreed to act as lookout, on one condition: that they tell him where they were going.

"Okay," said Cass quickly. "But can we tell you afterwards?"

Without waiting for an answer, Cass nudged Max-Ernest forward.

Yo-Yoji watched, at once irritated and intrigued.

"Don't forget the three-point rule!" he called after them.

"What's that?" asked Max-Ernest.

"Always make sure that two hands and one foot, or two feet and one hand, are touching the rock beneath you," said Cass, flashing a smile at Yo-Yoji.

She thought she was the only person who knew that!

And then she started up the rocks.

Max-Ernest waited only until the tide came in and splashed his ankles.

As they ran along the beach on the other side of the rocks, they found their way blocked by a crumbling shack – an old tackle shop – decorated with a lifebelt that looked like a shark had taken a bite out of it. A hand-painted sign advertised "Live Bait".

Cass and Max-Ernest both wrinkled their noses: the scent of rotten fish filled the air.

They walked around the shack as quietly as possible. But when they got to the other side, it was boarded up; nobody in sight.

Until they heard a familiar New Zealand accent: "Cassandra? Max-Ernest? I know you kiwi-heads are out here!"

The two kiwi-heads just had time to slip under a mound of fishing nets before Mr. Needleman's ankles came into view.

Flies buzzed around their noses and unidentified crawling things started investigating their legs. It was excruciating.

"Come out now and nobody will know," shouted

Mr. Needleman. "Otherwise, I'm warning you – I'll have you suspended!"

How had Mr. Needleman known where to look for them? Cass wondered. If it was Yo-Yoji, she was going to make him pay!

Mr. Needleman picked up a fishing spear that had been leaning against the shack and held it aloft. With his bushy red beard, he looked almost like a Viking. Or some threatening sea god.

Did he plan to have them suspended or did he plan to impale them right then and there?

Cass felt a tapping on her shoulder. She looked over at Max-Ernest in annoyance; why would he risk movement at a time like this?

He tapped her again: Two long taps. Three short.

Morse code.

Cass knew three short taps represented an S. (Everyone knows SOS is three short, three long, three short.) But what did two long taps represent?

Then she remembered that she and Max-Ernest had once taught themselves the Morse code for *Morse code*. It started with two long.

Two long was *M*.

MS.

Midnight Sun! Of course! thought Cass, feeling a wave of nausea come over her. Max-Ernest was saying that Mr. Needleman was part of the Midnight Sun.

Now that Cass was looking at her teacher (or at least at his legs) in this light it seemed so obvious. His sudden appearance at their school. The way he singled her out.

Was *that* why he'd arranged the field trip? Was *that* why he'd so easily let them have free time to explore?

And now he planned to murder them without any witnesses.

Well, if so, he wasn't going to succeed – yet.

Mr. Needleman took one more look around and started walking away.

A low, rusting metal gate blocked the way to Dock 3. A chain lock hung loose, swinging in the wind and clanging repeatedly.

"Maybe we should wait here," said Max-Ernest nervously.

"Where Mr. Needleman can see us?"

Cass pulled open the gate, revealing a rotting wooden stairway that looked like it might collapse if anyone stepped foot on it.

Which Cass proceeded to do without pause.

Gingerly, Max-Ernest followed.

The long, narrow dock was deserted – save for a few small, barnacle-encrusted boats. Other than the cries of seagulls and an occasional splash when the tide pushed a boat into the deck, there was total silence.

Max-Ernest shivered. "It's like a ghost town. Only with boats. I really think we should go—"

"Would you just be quiet for a second?" whispered Cass. "Look out there—"

A large ship was pulling into the harbour. She (you always refer to a boat in the feminine) had four tall masts and a dozen billowing square sails – like an old Spanish galleon in a pirate movie.* Yet the ship sparkled like new, its black hull so glossy it reflected the water. While they watched, the sun broke through the clouds, illuminating the sails and turning the ship a brilliant gold.

As the ship came closer, sails were lowered to slow its speed, and a man was suddenly visible standing near the prow. (For anyone who has as much trouble with directions as I do, the prow is the front of a ship – as opposed to the stern, which is the back.) They couldn't see his face, but he looked like a

---

*ACTUALLY, IT WAS NOT A GALLEON, BUT RATHER A NINETEENTH-CENTURY SCHOONER – A SIMILAR BUT SLEEKER VESSEL. BUT I THINK THE WORD *GALLEON* HAS A MORE ROMANTIC AND ADVENTUROUS RING TO IT, DON'T YOU?

picture-perfect yachtsman. He wore a white hat, a navy jacket, and…was he looking at them?

Yes – better yet, he was waving at them.

Cass looked at her watch. Noon exactly.

She broke into a smile. Could this be it? Had this fantastic ship come just for them? Was *this* how they were going to go meet the Terces Society? How grand!

"Where do you guys think you're going?!"

They turned to see Mr. Needleman striding towards them, diving spear in hand.

Cass grabbed Max-Ernest by the hand and they started running down the dock.

Behind them, Mr. Needleman picked up his pace.

A gangplank had been lowered for them (the wide kind with arm rails, not the narrow kind you see in movies, although I agree that would have been more dramatic) and Cass and Max-Ernest ran up it without stopping.

Until they saw the man standing at the top.

Then they froze no less instantaneously than if he had some terrible superpower that turned his victims into ice sculptures on a giant seafood buffet.

It was the last face on earth they'd expected to see.

The last face on earth they'd wanted to see.

Cass and Max-Ernest looked over their shoulders; running back towards Mr. Needleman suddenly seemed like an attractive option. But he was gone.

Worse, the gangplank was starting to rise and crewmen were already casting off. They would never make the jump.

They turned back to confront this new seafaring version of their old enemy – Dr. L.

The man laughed, seeing their expressions.

"Why so shocked? Did you not remember that Luciano – that Dr. L – and I are twins? I am Pietro. Welcome aboard!"

Half laughing, half crying with relief, Cass and Max-Ernest each shook the man's hand and then scrambled onto the boat.

They were safe!

CHAPTER THIRTY

At Sea

"Hard alee!"

The ship tacked to the left and leaned precipitously.

Cass and Max-Ernest grabbed each other, laughing, as a spray of water hit them in the face.

Around them, the crew hoisted and foisted. Sails whipped in the wind – until they caught and went taut. And everywhere the ship's brass fittings flared in the sun.

"Don't worry, this ship is sound!" shouted their host, leading them onto a wooden deck so swabbed and polished that it shined like glass. "She may be two hundred years old, but she's armed with all the latest technology!"

"We're not worried!" Cass shouted back. How could they be? The ship was glorious to behold.

And yet, she couldn't help noticing, she couldn't help feeling, this man so closely resembled Dr. L it was unnerving. He had the same perfect silver hair that seemed frozen in some kind of eternal wind. The same perfect tan skin and perfect white teeth that made him look more like a photograph than a person. The same distinctively indistinctive accent.

How was it that in Cass's imagination Pietro hadn't resembled his brother in the least? Usually, she'd pictured a long, snowy beard, twinkling eyes and a wizard's cloak – or, sometimes, a tuxedo and a top hat. Occasionally, she'd imagined an old adventurer in a pith helmet. But never *him*. Never *this*.

She shook off the thought. Here at last was *her* adventure. The one she'd been waiting for for so long. Enjoy it, she told herself.

"Cassandra, Max-Ernest – can you tighten this line for me?" their host asked. "That's a winch. You crank it this way—"

He started the job for them. Then said, "I've got to get something below. Back in a minute," and he headed away.

Thrilled to be given a task, Cass tossed her backpack aside and joined hands with Max-Ernest. Together they began to tighten a line to the ship's rearmost sail.

And then, suddenly, the line went slack.

Before they knew what was happening, the rope was looped around them and they were pulled off their feet. They fell together onto the hardwood deck and slid across the polished surface.

"Hey!" said Cass.

"Ow!" said Max-Ernest.

Roughly, a deckhand began to tie Cass and Max-Ernest to each other back-to-back.

"What are you doing?!" Cass cried. "Pietro! Where are you?"

"Stop that! That hurts!" protested Max-Ernest.

"You won't struggle if you know what's good for you!" threatened the deckhand. He tied their hands together for good measure, then left them lying in shock on the deck.

"You think this is like a test – to see how we would act if we were captured?" asked Cass, fighting back tears.

"Maybe, unless – oh no! Look—" Max-Ernest nodded upwards with his nose.

From their new vantage point, they could see for the first time the flag flapping in the wind on top of the boat's tallest mast.

I wish I could tell you it was the flag of the Terces Society. Or, for that matter, the flag of the Royal Navy or the merchant marine. Or even that it was a skull and crossbones – surely a pirate ship would have been preferable to the reality.

Alas, the flag was none of those things.

Rather, it showed a white sun emblazoned on a black background.

The flag of the Midnight Sun.

Although tied back-to-back and unable to see each other, Cass and Max-Ernest shared the same expression of despair.

They were prisoners. Again.

And nobody – not even the Terces Society – knew.

"What are *those*?"

A minute later, two skeletally skinny girls – twins – hovered over Cass and Max-Ernest, eyeing the ship's new captives with lazy curiosity.

Aside from their differently coloured hair (one was blonde with pink streaks, the other brown with purple streaks) and differently coloured bikinis (one was pink with purple polka dots, the other purple with pink polka dots), they looked nearly identical.

Judging by their faces, they might have been about sixteen or seventeen, but I wouldn't try to guess their real ages. They were, after all, part of the Midnight Sun. As Cass and Max-Ernest could tell immediately by the gloves on their hands.

"Those what?" asked the purple-er one.

"*Them*," said the pinker one, pointing with a curl of her toe. She moved with an odd jerkiness – as if she were a marionette on a string.

"Oh, *those*," said the purple-er one.

"Yeah, Elf Ears and Electro Hair," said the pinker one.

Only now did Cass and Max-Ernest realize that it was they who were being spoken about. In the third person.

"I'm Cass. This is Max-Ernest," said Cass, forcing

herself to speak boldly. "There was a terrible mistake. Please, could you—"

"Elf is a Cass. Electro is a Max-Ernest," said the purple-er one, ignoring Cass.

"Oh. Well, what's that, then?"

"I just told you – it's a Cass."

"No, *that* – that *thing*!" said the pinker one.

She pointed her toe at Cass's sock-monster, hanging from Cass's backpack – a metre or so out of Cass's reach.

"Oh, *that*. That is so cute. I so want it!"

"Well, I so want it more!"

"But you said you don't know what it is…"

"Neither do you!"

"So?"

"So there."

"Hey, that's my sock-monster, and you can both have him – *if* you untie us," said Cass, desperate. "I'll even make you another one."

The girls stared at Cass as if she had just levitated or turned into a frog.

"No way! I think it just told us to do something!" said the purple-er one.

"No way! I'm taking that thing. Just to show it a lesson."

"No way! *I'm* taking it—"

They both lunged for Cass's sock-monster – and slammed into each other. Their bony bodies toppled to the ground, right on top of Cass and Max-Ernest. Their suntanned skin was unexpectedly clammy and cold – and made Cass and Max-Ernest's skin grow cold in turn.

"It's mine!"

"No, it's mine!"

The ghoulish girls each pulled on one of the sock-monster's tennis-shoe-tongue ears, trying to tear the sock-monster away from the other.

"Hey, leave us – I mean them, I mean *it* – alone!" said Max-Ernest, sounding unusually brave and forceful, if a little confused.

"Having fun, children?" asked an icy voice that will be unmistakable to readers of my first book, but that would, I think, send chills down the spines of anyone unlucky enough to hear it.

Even the two sisters seemed to feel it; they shrank away from Cass and Max-Ernest, leaving the sock-monster lying on the deck.

Yes, I'm afraid the voice belonged to Ms. Mauvais.

In contrast to the loud, clacking sisters, she walked towards Cass and Max-Ernest with an almost preternatural calm.

Although dressed for the sea in gleaming white,

Ms. Mauvais seemed to carry with her a kind of darkness. No friend of the sun, she exposed hardly a speck of skin to the elements. To shade her face, she wore a hat with a brim so broad she appeared to be sprouting wings. To shield her eyes, she wore a pair of mirrored sunglasses so enormous they gave her head the look of a space alien or maybe a gigantic fly. And to cover her ancient clawlike hands, the sight of which Cass and Max-Ernest remembered with such horror, she wore long white gloves that made her arms look like the limbs of an albino praying mantis.

Of Ms. Mauvais herself, you could see only a mouth – admittedly an exquisitely beautiful and evermore youthful-looking mouth – and even that she'd covered with a frosty white lipstick that glittered with an unnatural phosphorescence.

"Ah, Max-Ernest, darling! And my dear Cassandra," cried Ms. Mauvais, circling her captives so she could get a good look at both of them. "To happy reunions!" She raised her cocktail glass, ice tinkling in tune with her voice.

I wouldn't call it that, Cass thought grimly.

"I see you've met Romi and Montana Skelton."

So these were the famous Skelton Sisters? Cass marvelled. What a sick joke! Max-Ernest had been right months ago when he mistakenly referred to them as the *Skeleton* Sisters. Had Cass not been tied up on an enemy ship far out at sea and been certain to die any moment, she might have laughed.

"I'm afraid I still don't see the family resemblance." Ms. Mauvais chuckled drily.*

"Well, have they told you where he is?" asked Dr. L, emerging from below decks – for of course it had been he, not Pietro, who'd welcomed them onto the ship.

"Not yet, darling. I was just getting to it," Ms. Mauvais answered.

How could she have let this awful, plastic man convince her he was Pietro? Cass wondered.

True, he and Pietro were twins. But, as Cass and Max-Ernest well knew, Dr. L had gone to great, even murderous lengths to stay so young, so handsome. Even if he wasn't the bearded wizard of her fantasies, Pietro would have looked much older by now. Older and wiser. Older and kinder.

Come to think of it, would a Terces Society boat look anything like this shiny ship? A Terces vessel, Cass suddenly felt sure, would be smaller and scrappier, fit for stealthy missions and dangerous adventures.

---

*I BELIEVE MS. MAUVAIS WAS REFERRING TO THE TIME CASS PRETENDED TO BE A SKELTON SISTER IN ORDER TO GAIN ENTRANCE TO HER SPA. A RATHER MEAN JOKE, IF YOU ASK ME.

This Midnight Sun ship was better fit for a pleasure cruise.

Or maybe a television ad.

She'd been so desperate to join the Terces Society that she'd been willing to believe anything.

Ms. Mauvais turned back to Cass and Max-Ernest. "Well?"

"Well...w-w-what?" stammered Max-Ernest.

"Where. Is. He?" asked Ms. Mauvais, stone-faced.

"Where is who?" asked Cass, confused. "Pietro?"

"The homunculus, fool!"

"The hom – *what*?" asked Max-Ernest.

"THE HOMUNCULUS! I'm warning you, don't play with me."

"Believe me, we would never play with you," said Cass.

"We don't even know what a homunculus is," said Max-Ernest. "Well, I don't know what it is. And if I don't know, I doubt she knows. Not that she doesn't know things that I don't know, but this kind of—"

"Silence!"

Ms. Mauvais picked up Cass's battered sock-monster and dangled it in front of them as if it were a dead mouse. "What, pray tell, is this?!"

"My sock-monster – I made it."

"I see. And *whom* was it modelled after? Tell me that!"

"Nobody. He's just made from a sock." Cass certainly wasn't about to say he was modelled after a creature in her dreams.

"You expect me to believe this thing isn't supposed to be a homunculus? You must think me very dumb."

"Hey, give that to us!" / "Yeah, give it to us!" said Romi and Montana, who'd perked up as soon as the sock-monster was mentioned.

Ms. Mauvais eyed them in irritation. "Don't you girls have a concert to prepare for?"

She tossed the sock-monster to them, and they chased after it like two ungainly puppies after a ball. Cass watched sadly – now she'd never get her sock-monster back.

"You needn't bother pretending," said Dr. L. "We know you're members of the Terces Society now. Or have you forgotten how we got you here?"

"But we're not pretending!" cried Cass.

"If you tell us where the homunculus is, we'll give you a lifebelt when we toss you over, and there's a chance – a small chance – that someone will save you. Otherwise—"

"Otherwise, our chef is very eager to make shark fin soup, but so far all we've been able to catch is tuna," said Ms. Mauvais.*

She gestured towards three deckhands who were wrestling with an enormous tuna. It thrashed wildly until one of the men slit its belly with a knife. Guts spilled onto the deck.

"We've been looking for the right bait," said Dr. L. "If you don't tell us, we'll make sure you're both dripping plenty of blood before we drop you in the ocean."

Cass and Max-Ernest gripped each other's hands.

"Did you know sharks smell blood from over a kilometre away?" continued Dr. L. "It's a unique evolutionary feature."

"They also sense electricity and movement," said Max-Ernest, unable to stop himself. "They call it shark sense. How 'bout that?"

"Very good," said Dr. L, not looking like he particularly meant it. "So try not to splash when you hit the water."

---

*IT DOESN'T SURPRISE ME THAT MS. MAUVAIS'S CHEF WOULD WANT TO MAKE SHARK FIN SOUP; IT IS A SOUP FOR THE HEARTLESS. IN ORDER TO MAKE IT, A FIN IS RIPPED OFF A LIVE SHARK – THEN THE SHARK IS THROWN BACK INTO THE WATER. UNABLE TO SWIM, THE SHARK DROWNS – OR BECOMES PREY FOR OTHER FISH.

"Unfortunately, we don't have time for marine biology lessons," said Ms. Mauvais. "The Midnight Sun has been waiting five hundred years for the homunculus to rise. We will not wait any longer."

She waved to one of the deckhands chopping up the tuna. "You there – take these kids below!"

Then she turned back to Cass and Max-Ernest. "You destroyed our lives once," she said with a voice as cold and smoky and unnatural as dry ice. "But with your help we're going to live for ever."

Not bothering to wipe the fish guts off his hands, the deckhand grabbed Cass and Max-Ernest by their ears and dragged them away – right past the Skelton Sisters, who were lying on deckchairs in the sun, Cass's sock-monster perched between them.

CHAPTER TWENTY-NINE

An Itch

Max-Ernest had an itch. It was under his toe.

The second toe – counting from the outside – of his left foot, to be exact. And Max-Ernest was always exact.

No, wait, that was wrong.

The itch was under his middle toe. Yes, the middle toe. That was it.

Max-Ernest tried to wiggle the toe without wiggling the others. But before he'd managed a proper wiggle, the itch had – oh no! – moved under his fourth—

No, darn it. It had moved again. Up this time. To the top of his big toe. No, to the top of his foot. It was, Max-Ernest had no choice but to admit now, a *travelling* itch.

The very worst kind.

His brain instructed his hand to scratch his foot – but for some reason he couldn't move. His hand was stuck behind his back.

He opened his eyes. The room was dark, but even so he could tell he wasn't in either of his two bedrooms. The smell was different.

Sort of a musty, dusty smell. But also salty. Like the sea.

Where was he?

"Max-Ernest," Cass whispered. "Are you awake?"

Oh, he thought, relieved. He must have slept over

at Cass's. But, then, why would her room feel like it was swaying?

"What time is it?" he answered. "I have this really bad itch. It feels like a bug is crawling up my leg. Or maybe I have a rash. Or eczema. But I don't usually get eczema on my foot, so—"

"Shh! Forget eczema! Have you forgotten that we're stuck on a boat in the middle of the ocean and they're going to feed us to—"

"Hey, we're tied up!"

"Duh! And stop moving, it hurts my hands!"

"Sorry." Now that he was thinking about it, Max-Ernest realized his hands hurt as well. In fact, his whole body hurt. He wasn't sure what was worse – the pain or the itching.

"So what do you think we should do?" asked Cass.

"Me? You're always the one with the escape plans."

"Well, I don't have one now. And my backpack is over there in the corner. I can't reach any of my supplies."

"So we're just going to die?"

She didn't answer. She didn't have to.

They sat for a moment in scared silence.

Then Max-Ernest had an idea...

"I told you, stop moving!"

"I know – I'm just checking for slack. I've been reading this book by Houdini and—"

"Houdini?"

"Yeah, Harry Houdini, the escape artist. Most famous magician of all time."

"I know who he is!"

"Well, he says the mistake people make when they tie someone up is that they use too much rope. Then there's always slack. See—"

He tugged on the rope to show her.

"Now, take your shoes off."

"What? How?"

"You know, push them off with your feet. It'll be easier to get out of the ropes. Houdini always took his shoes off before trying one of his escapes."

"I can't believe you're trying a Houdini act," muttered Cass, but she pushed her shoes off just as he instructed. A little, just a little, impressed.

Max-Ernest explained that in his escape acts Houdini never used magic or illusions; he used strength – and a few tricks like swelling up his chest in a special way. Usually, Houdini could escape faster than the time it took to tie him up.

It took Max-Ernest much longer than it would have taken Houdini – twenty-seven minutes. For one thing, he wasn't a trained escape artist. For another, Cass kept counterwriggling his wriggles. Until finally, he told her to keep still.

Just as the rope was beginning to loosen—

Footsteps.

Quickly, they retied themselves and pretended to be asleep.

A deckhand shone a flashlight at them from the doorway – then, thankfully, he walked away.

Eventually, the rope dropped to the floor. Breathing heavily, they staggered to their feet.

"We did it. How 'bout that?" Max-Ernest whispered.

"*You* did it. How 'bout *that*?" said Cass. "Guess those magic books weren't such a waste of time, after all." She smiled in the dark.

Max-Ernest smiled back. It wasn't often that Cass admitted she was wrong.

Cass picked up her backpack and started gathering all the survivalist supplies that had been left strewn across the floor.

When her hand found her flashlight, she immediately turned it on.

The room, they saw now, was some kind of cargo

hold. Around them sat piles of what looked like plundered treasure – as if they were in a pirate ship, after all.

Here an archaeologist might have been able to reconstruct the history of the Midnight Sun.

There were Egyptian statuettes with the heads of jackals and large Greek vases decorated with scenes of battle. Medieval helmets and suits of armour. Gothic paintings and crystal goblets.

Along one wall sat the remnants of a sixteenth-century laboratory: old test-tubes and decanters, weights and scales. And along the opposite wall sat remnants of an eighteenth-century *library*: old maps and globes, and stacks of books of all shapes and sizes.

Many of the books were charred around the edges – as if they'd been pulled out of a fire. And, indeed, they had – the fire at the Midnight Sun Spa. The fire that Cass and Max-Ernest themselves had set while rescuing their classmate Benjamin Blake.

"We should get out of here – while it's still dark outside," said Cass.

"I know – just give me some light for a second."

Max-Ernest held a large leather-bound volume in his hands. Emerald green and embossed in gold, it was entitled *The Dictionary of Alchemy*.

As Cass trained the flashlight on the pages, he flipped through them until he found the entry he was looking for.

"Look..."

HOMUNCULUS

To most people, a homunculus is just a small man or dwarf. But to an alchemist, the word has a special meaning: a man-made man.

In the Middle Ages and later, many alchemists believed that — if they only found the right recipe — they could create a miniature human being in a bottle. A few notorious alchemists even claimed to have succeeded.

Reports varied as to what ingredients worked best. But it was commonly understood that the bottle had to be buried in mud or dung for the homunculus to grow...

Our two friends stared, dumbfounded, at the page in front of them.

No doubt they were startled to read about a miniature man grown in a bottle. But it wasn't only the *definition* of the word that shocked them; it was also the *illustration* that accompanied the definition.

It was just a black-and-white drawing small enough to fit on a box of matches. Nonetheless, they could see the same bulging eyes and floppy ears, the same big nose and little body.

There was no mistaking it: the homunculus looked just like Cass's sock-monster.

"Have you seen this before?" whispered Max-Ernest.

"No – I swear."

"Then how come...?"

"I don't know – I don't understand."

It was true – she'd never even heard of a homunculus before. She was just as surprised as he was.

Cass replayed her dreams in her head: how was it possible?

She shivered as the eerie graveyard tune came back to her unbidden.

Then, suddenly: voices.

Cass turned off her flashlight.

"Are you so certain we must catch the homunculus? There's no other way?"

Dr. L.

He sounded so close – it was as if they were in the same room.

Cass and Max-Ernest crouched behind a large trunk, hardly daring to breathe.

"*Yes, I'm certain! Am I ever not?*" Ms. Mauvais responded shrilly.

"Where are they?" Max-Ernest whispered in Cass's ear.

Cass clamped her hand over his mouth. He nodded, pushing her hand off: *I get the message.*

"*You were certain that thing would help us find him – the Sound Prism. And has it?*"

"*No one else knows where the grave is!*" said Ms. Mauvais, ignoring the question. "*The homunculus is the key.*"

They couldn't be in here, Cass thought. There'd been no footsteps. No door opening. And yet—

"*What about those kids?*"

Max-Ernest gestured in the darkness to the trunk in front of them: Dr. L's voice seemed to be coming from inside!

They both put their ears up against it.

"*What about them?!*" Ms. Mauvais hissed. Her voice also seemed to come from inside the trunk. "*They obviously know nothing...*"

Shaking, Cass turned her flashlight back on. If they were seen, it would all be over. But she had to know.

No. They were alone. She and Max-Ernest both exhaled, relieved.

The trunk was dark and heavy-looking and long enough to hold, well, a lot of things.

"Go on," Max-Ernest, whispered. "Open it."

"No, you..." said Cass, uncharacteristically reticent.

Max-Ernest shook his head vigorously.

Cass shrugged – and sprang the latches.

I'm not sure what they expected to find inside the trunk – Dr. L and Ms. Mauvais lying like vampires in a coffin? – but what they saw was:

Nothing. Nobody.

Just a ball sitting on a blanket. Or that's what it looked like to them. You would have recognized it as something else.

(And while I'm on the subject, will you please congratulate me for writing about the Sound Prism, not to mention Dr. L and Ms. Mauvais, without even blinking? I think I've acted quite courageously, thank you very much.)

The voices continued, louder:

"At least they won't trouble us again...right, my darling doctor?"

A cruel laugh. *"Let's make sure of it."*

Cass looked behind the trunk – there wasn't a mouse,

let alone an evil doctor or a scarily ageless woman.

"You think there's some kind of ventilation system that carries their voices?" she asked.

"Highly unlikely. This is a boat, not an office building. And I don't see any vents. Or even any windows. Unless—"

"It has to be the ball," said Cass, leaning in closer to look at it.

"You mean, like, it's some kind of eavesdropping device? Like a baby monitor? Or a walkie-talkie? But that doesn't really make sense – it doesn't even look like it has a battery. It just looks like a bunch of straws bundled together..."

Cass picked up the ball and illuminated it with her flashlight; it was strange and beautiful and unlike anything she'd ever seen.

"*I* think it looks like it comes from the sea."

"Like it was part of a tropical reef or something? I guess I can see that," said Max-Ernest. "With hundreds of tiny fish darting in and out of those tiny holes."

Cass held the ball to her ear and started turning it in her hand. Sure enough, all kinds of sounds immediately flooded her senses: Max-Ernest breathing next to her. The lapping of water against the sides of the boat. Even a whale call far out in the sea.

It was like spinning a radio dial and hearing different frequencies come in and out of range.

Was the ball really an eavesdropping device? It seemed too beautiful for such a criminal purpose.

"Listen to this—" She held it up to Max-Ernest's ear.

"What? Is it supposed to sound like the ocean? Only conch shells do that. It comes from the way air passes through – oh wait, wow!"

"I'm taking it with us," said Cass, pulling it away from him.

"But that's stealing!"

"So what. They kidnapped us. They're murderers. For all we know, we're saving somebody's life by taking it."

"Hmm, I don't know if that makes any sense," said Max-Ernest, but he made no move to stop her.

They tiptoed out of the cargo hold and crept cautiously up the stairs to the stateroom level. There they walked down a long narrow hallway with a thick white carpet and gleaming mahogany walls lit by small yellow lamps.

As they passed a row of closed doors, Cass held the purloined ball to her ear, listening to the snoring of the crew. Silently, she gave Max-Ernest the okay sign.

The hall ended in a luxurious living room, furnished entirely in white and built in a circle around a glossy black floor.

Glancing down at her reflection, Cass remembered an awful moment at the Midnight Sun Spa. She'd been looking in the mirror when Ms. Mauvais had crept up on her and commented cruelly on her ears, guessing correctly that Cass's mother's ears were much prettier.

Where, then, Cass wondered fleetingly now, did she get hers? From the father she'd never met?

Max-Ernest grabbed her arm, snapping her out of her reverie: beneath them, a long, undulating jellyfish was briefly illuminated, swimming under the ship's hull. The floor was glass.

A loud gurgling startled them. The jellyfish?

"I think somebody just went to the bathroom," Cass whispered, listening with the ball to the sound of a toilet flushing.

They waited a moment, tense. There were footsteps – but they faded away. Nobody appeared.

Still on tiptoe, they headed for the spiral staircase that led up to the deck.

It was a clear, starry night. The anchored boat swayed gently.

They scanned the horizon – there was no land in sight, nor a single other ship. Cass turned the ball around in her hand but it didn't pick up anything beyond the cry of seagulls and the crashing of waves.

"My backpack floats – and it's waterproof," whispered Cass as she carefully placed the ball inside it. "You think we can survive out there until help comes? I have some trail mix—"

"You want me to go in the water? Did you forget I can't swim!? Plus, what about dehydration? And hypothermia! And that jellyfish!"

"Okay, so then what, Houdini?"

"Don't you think there's a life raft or something?"

As quietly as they could, they walked the length of the vessel, looking for a raft.

They stopped at the captain's deck where, as if turned by an invisible hand, a steering wheel rotated back and forth in time with the rocking of the ship.

Behind them, a light went on—

Ms. Mauvais was visible in silhouette. "Who's out there? Romi? Montana?"

Cass and Max-Ernest inched into the shadows. Then stood frozen for what seemed like for ever but was really less than a minute – until the light went out.

Exhales.

They crept back down the other side of the ship but didn't see a raft – or even a life jacket.

"Look..." whispered Max-Ernest.

Cass followed his gaze – and shuddered.

Two large hands were grasping the side of the boat – just like in her dream! Could it be...?

As they watched in fearful fascination, a dripping man pulled himself over the rail and onto the deck.

"Mr. Needleman?!" exclaimed Cass.

He nodded, smiling mischievously under his wet beard. "You guys are really holding up the class."

"But how did you get here?"

Mr. Needleman put his finger to his lips. "Later. Right now I want you to get ready to jump."

"Are we in big trouble?" asked Max-Ernest.

"Jump!" Mr. Needleman commanded, pointing over the side of the ship. "Or do you want to wait until somebody sees you?"

They looked over the edge. The ocean was dark and foreboding – and awfully far down. A few metres from the ship, an empty speedboat rocked back and forth in the water.

"Now!"

Mr. Needleman grabbed each of them by the wrist and – before Max-Ernest could explain that he was afraid of heights or that jumping made his nose bleed or even that he couldn't swim – they jumped off.

Plunging feet first into a cold black ocean in the middle of the night isn't like diving into a warm swimming pool in the middle of the day.

Just in case you thought it was.

Max-Ernest, of course, hadn't experienced either before. He'd never been underwater.

He thought he was dead.

Not dying. Not drowning. Dead.

Why else would he not know which direction was up? For what other reason would he feel so much pressure on his chest and in his ears? In what other state would he be so totally and completely cold?

Never mind that he was safe in Mr. Needleman's grip the entire time.

"I'm alive!" he cried when they surfaced. "I'm alive!!!"

"Shh!" said Cass, coughing for air on the other side of Mr. Needleman. "Do you want them to hear?"

The small boat nearly capsized as they climbed aboard. It wasn't made for passengers.

"Thanks, guys," said Mr. Needleman when they'd all managed to sit up – clothes drenched, teeth chattering, but, as Max-Ernest so succinctly put it, alive. "We couldn't have located the Midnight Sun without you. Congratulations!"

"F-for w-what?" asked Cass, confused. She'd just noticed that Mr. Needleman had lost his New Zealand accent.

"For completing your first Terces mission, of course."

As Cass and Max-Ernest watched in astonishment, Mr. Needleman reached up to the side of his face and ripped off his beard.

"Ouch!" he exclaimed, wincing.

It was Owen.

CHAPTER TWENTY-EIGHT

Owen?!

Did you see that coming?

Did you have your hand up – *oh oh oh oh oh oh!* – dying to say who it was? Or were you surprised when he pulled off his beard?

Don't be ashamed. I was almost surprised myself, and I knew Mr. Needleman was really the Terces Society spy all along.

As for Cass and Max-Ernest, they nearly fell off the boat, they were so shocked.

In the past they'd known Owen as a shy stutterer, a cocky surfer, and a mischievous Irishman. But their science teacher? Cass's tormentor?!

They would have barraged the former Mr. Needleman with questions, but his speedboat made so much noise nobody could hear a thing. He drove so fast that the fan of water behind them rose thirty metres in the air – well, three metres in the air, anyway. (Since Max-Ernest was there, I'm afraid to exaggerate.)

Thanks to Owen's nautical skills, or perhaps just to his recklessness, the *Midnight Sun* never caught up with them.

But the coastguard did. And that was nearly as frightening.

Less than an hour after escaping from the *Midnight Sun*, and still a long way from shore, they found themselves blinded by a searchlight.

"You, there! Stop!"

Owen quickly threw a tarp over Cass and Max-Ernest before slowing down the speedboat.

They waited. Huddled together like a couple of sardines from the day's catch.

"Are we in a pu-pu-puddle?" Max-Ernest shiver-whispered to Cass.

"Doesn't ma-matter when your clothes are already we-wet."

"But wh-what about hypothermia?"

Cass touched her arm in the darkness.

She thought a minute. "Can you touch your thumb with your little finger?"

They both could.

Cass gave Max-Ernest a thumbs up. Safe. Momentarily.

A coastguard officer explained over a booming loudspeaker that a couple of students named Cass and Max-Ernest had gone missing. Their school was afraid that they might have stolen a boat from the harbour, then got lost at sea. "When I get my hands on those two punks, I'm going to wring their little necks. I haven't had a wink of sleep all night, thanks to them!"

"I don't know anybodies by the names of Lass or Mack Sernis," Owen shouted back. "But if they're still out heaya, they're wicked lucky to be alive!"

"Well, if you see anything, call us on the radio!"

After the coastguard boat had disappeared, Owen pulled the tarp off the young stowaways.

"The Midnight Sun will eat those guys for dinnah," he said, grinning.

"What kind of accent is that?" Cass asked, remarking on the sudden change in Owen.

"Boston. Can't you tell? I'm a lobstah fisherman."

Cass laughed through chattering teeth.

It was dawn by the time they reached land.

Owen swore up and down that he'd never intended for Cass and Max-Ernest to board the Midnight Sun's ship, only for them to lure the ship to the docks – so he could put a tracer on the hull. But just in case the field trip was unexpectedly prolonged, he had stashed his car nearby.

Cass and Max-Ernest groaned when they saw the old VW bug: another wild ride lay ahead.

As they climbed in, Cass pulled the bungee cord belt she was wearing off her cargo pants. She strapped herself to the side of her door, and then to Max-Ernest.

"Just a precaution. The percentage of traumatic brain injury related to car accidents is staggering."

Max-Ernest grinned; the survivalist was back in action.

"Hold on, Lass and Mack!" The car exploded into drive.

Lass and Mack both came close to regurgitating the dinner they never had.

"So are you taking us to meet Pietro now?" Cass shouted over the roar of the engine. "Aren't we supposed to go to a meeting?"

Owen looked over his shoulder. "First rule of the Terces Society – no meetings. Too boring!"

"Really?" asked Max-Ernest.

Owen laughed. "No. The reason is we don't like too many members in one place at once. Less chance we'll all be killed."

"Grilled?"

"KILLED!"

"Oh. Right." Max-Ernest gulped.

Owen slowed the car just enough so they could hear.

"You'll meet Pietro soon enough. For now, just keep an eye on each other. If you think you see the Midnight Sun lurking around, report back to us right away."

"But what about our next mission?" Cass asked. "What about the Oath of Terces?"

"Later."

Cass felt as if she'd been demoted – like a police detective taken off the street and given a desk job.

Worse: Owen said he wouldn't be going back to school with them. Now that the Midnight Sun had seen him, he would need a new disguise; Mr. Needleman was no more.

"Probably some awful teacher's going to replace you," Cass complained when they were nearing home. "Somebody who's really mean, not just acting that way."

"Sorry, I've got another job now." After he checked in with his Terces colleagues, Owen told them, he was going right back to sea in search of the Midnight Sun.

"They stole something, and I have to get it back. That's why we put the tracer on their boat."

"What did they take?" asked Max-Ernest.

"The Sound Prism. One of the Terces Society treasures... It's a...ball. About yea big—" He held out his hand.

Cass and Max-Ernest looked at each other apprehensively; he had to be talking about the ball in Cass's backpack.

Max-Ernest poked Cass in the side. Wasn't this their cue?

Cass shook her head imperceptibly.

Max-Ernest opened his mouth, but Cass pleaded

with her eyes. They had one of those silent arguments that make you look like a monkey mimicking people at the zoo – until Max-Ernest shrugged and relented. He wouldn't say anything, but Cass could tell he wasn't happy about it.

She made a mental note to thank him later. In a highly functioning survivalist team, there had to be a leader. You didn't have to agree with her all the time. But you couldn't get to the top of Everest if someone wasn't the lead on the rope.

Owen insisted on circling their neighbourhood, then dropping them off a few blocks away from home – just in case anyone was staking out the territory.

"No time for tearful goodbyes. If there's an emergency, you can reach us at the Magic Museum."

"Where's that?" asked Cass.

"You don't need to know."

Cass rolled her eyes.

The VW ripped away, leaving them standing under a telephone pole. They both started talking at once – having the argument aloud that they'd had silently in the car.

I won't try to untangle the entire conversation, but it boiled down to this: Cass didn't trust Owen.

"The Sound Prism is all we have," she said. "We already gave ourselves up to Dr. L, thinking he was Pietro. And Owen let us fall right into the trap!"

"I still think we should have showed him the Sound Prism. He *did* save our lives," Max-Ernest pointed out.

Cass hesitated, then relented. "Okay, fine – we'll give it to them. But only if I can give it right to Pietro."

Max-Ernest, who was very hungry and very tired and very much missing both of his beds, figured she meant sometime in the sort-of-distant future. But Cass had another idea. They should go find Pietro now. While they still could.

"We're in trouble no matter what. What's the difference if we're missing a few hours longer?"

"But our parents probably think we're dead—"

Cass nodded. "That's why we should go now – dead people have more freedom!"

Max-Ernest shook his head – just when you thought you'd won an argument.

"Good," said Cass. "Now all we have to do is figure out where the Magic Museum is."

"Oh, that's easy." Max-Ernest reached in his pocket. "I found this on the floor of Owen's car…and, well, it had the word *magic* on it, s-s-so, anyway," he stammered, embarrassed.

He held out a book of matches.

The address was on the back.

"How 'bout that?"

Cass looked stern. "Max-Ernest, that's stealing!"

He paled.

"Joking!"

He laughed. Sort of.

CHAPTER TWENTY-SEVEN

I'm terribly sorry
but I lost this
chapter.

I wrote it on a napkin in a diner late last night and...

You know how it is – one minute you're banging on a broken vending machine, hoping just this once it will have pity on you, the next minute you're tearing through the countryside, looking for anyplace, for anyone that will offer you a little bite of chocolate.

Okay, *bites*.

I fell asleep in my car halfway through my twelfth Hershey bar. (Why can't you ever find any decent imported dark chocolate in the middle of the night?) By the time I checked back at the diner, well, that napkin was wiping off anybody's chin but mine.

Don't worry – you're not missing anything. The chapter didn't contain anything important.

Oh, except that I finally revealed the Secret.

Or did I?

Actually, if you want to know the truth, my head's a bit fuzzy at the moment – not to mention a bit funky, considering all the chocolate stuck in my hair. I don't remember *what* I wrote on that napkin. I hope I didn't write anything I shouldn't have because it could be anywhere by now. And anyone could be reading it.

Well, there's nothing to be done. The whole thing is out of our hands – out of mine, anyway.

Why don't you skip ahead to the next chapter? I'll be with you in a minute.

Ahem...
　　Cough...cough...

If you don't mind...

Perhaps I didn't make myself clear enough:
　　Move on. Now. Please.
　　I'm in desperate need of a shower.

CHAPTER TWENTY-SIX

Members Only

I t took six dollars, three buses, two hours, and one last bag of trail mix to get there.

But where?

Cass had told herself not to expect a medieval castle. But a mini-mall?

"Well, at least we can get Slurpees before we go back," said Max-Ernest, looking at the convenience store that stood where the Magic Museum should be. There was also a dry-cleaner's and a pet grooming salon called Shampooch.

At first, they thought they had the wrong place. But when they walked around the side of the building by the bathrooms, they saw a stairwell leading to a basement door.

Next to the door was a small sign:

THE MAGIC MUSEUM

MEMBERS ONLY

"Members only?" Max-Ernest was disconcerted.

"Well, we are members – in a way. Terces members. At least, almost."

"True," Max-Ernest reflected. "And it doesn't say you have to be a *museum* member – you could be a member of anything!"

Cass tried the handle and the door swung open with surprising ease.

They found themselves in a small waiting room that looked like it belonged in a Victorian mansion rather than under a mini-mall. Persian carpets were piled haphazardly on the polished wood floor. On the walls, portraits of famous magicians – some in tuxedos, others in robes and turbans – hung from satin ropes. And in the corner, perched on a brass stand, an iridescent green parrot preened in front of a full-length mirror.

An attractive but aloof-looking woman wearing black-framed glasses and a black satin suit sat behind a cluttered desk. Above her, flyers advertising museum events were posted on a bulletin board:

The Magical Mimes: Quietest Magic Show on Earth

NEXT MONTH:

THE OLE TIME TRAVELLING CIRCUS REUNION

She smiled coolly at the two young people in front of her. "I'm sorry, the museum is closed to the public," she said.

"Members only! Members only!" the parrot squawked.

"Owen told us to come," said Cass, suddenly aware for the first time how they must look in their muddy clothes and ocean-washed hair.

"Does Owen have a last name?" asked the receptionist, expressionless, consulting her computer.

Cass shook her head hesitantly.

"Well, he probably does," Max-Ernest corrected. "We just don't know it. We don't even know if Owen is his real name. Sometimes he calls himself Mr. Needleman."

"Sorry, that name doesn't ring a bell, either. If you'd like to come back – we offer tours on the third Sunday of every month."

"What about Pietro Bergamo?" asked Cass. "He's a magician – don't you know him?"

The woman shook her head.

"Members only!" the parrot repeated, as if speaking for her.

A youngish man with longish hair and a shortish goatee on his chin walked in from outside. He wore round wire-rimmed glasses, and his eyes flickered briefly over the kids before he nodded at the receptionist.

Then he looked directly at the parrot. "Password

please," he said in a precise English accent.

"Make a spell. But don't try very hard," replied the parrot.

The Englishman thought for a moment. Then he said:

"Abraca-dabble."

The parrot's eyes glowed red and he spread his wings with the squeak of a hinge.

"I thought the parrot was real," Cass whispered.

"I think it is – or was. It's taxidermy," Max-Ernest whispered back.

Behind the parrot, the full-length mirror swivelled on its axis, revealing a dark hallway. Without another word, the Englishman strode through the opening. The mirror closed behind him.

"Well, if you have no further questions, it's time for my break now," said the receptionist, standing. The kids expected to be ushered out but instead the receptionist smiled at them and exited the building, leaving them alone inside.

"I can't believe she just left us like that," said Max-Ernest.

"I think she did it on purpose," said Cass. "I don't know why. Like, she knows we're not allowed but she wants us to get into the museum anyway... Either way, let's try to get in fast."

Cass walked up to the parrot and looked it in the eye. "Abraca-dabble!" She stepped towards the mirror but the parrot didn't move – and neither did the mirror.

"I bet the password changes every time," said Max-Ernest. "That's why he had to ask for the clue."

He looked at the parrot and said, "Password please."

"Demand entry," said the parrot. "But don't forget to feed me."

"What kind of clue is that?"

"I think we're supposed to put two words together – you know, like *Shampooch*," said Max-Ernest. "*Abracadabble* is *abracadabra*, which was the spell part, plus *dabble*, which means not trying very hard."

Cass looked sceptical. "So we need a word that means *demand entry*, and then one that means *food for the parrot*?"

"Yeah…maybe."

"How about, 'let me in…parrot food'?"

Max-Ernest scrunched his face. "Um, that's kind of the idea. But the words should fit together."

"Open up. Pizza delivery for a parrot!" said Cass.

"We're not thinking about this right," said Max-Ernest. "What do birds eat?"

"Birdseed," said Cass. "How about, 'open birdseed'?"

"That's it – you got it!" said Max-Ernest excitedly.

"I did…?" She looked at the parrot, but the parrot didn't blink.

"Well, not exactly…but I know what it is now."

Max-Ernest stepped in front of the parrot and said: "Open sesame seed!"

The bird's eyes glowed red.

It took a moment for their eyes to adjust to the darkness.

The only light in the hallway came from the display lights above the old magic show posters that lined the walls:

PROUDLY PRESENTING
MONSIEUR HENRI
THE HUMAN SALAMANDER.
He will pass a red-hot bar of iron through his tongue…

COMING TO YOU FROM
THE EXOTIC EAST...

CHUNG CHOW
THE CHINESE
CONJUROR

WATCH BAMBOO GROW FROM
HIS FINGERS!

HURSTON
THE MASTER OF MYSTERY
VANISHES
BEFORE YOUR
VERY EYES

At the end of the hallway, they walked under a sign
that read *Magic – A History of Disappearing, or a
Disappearing History?* and they entered a large room
displaying numerous magical antiques.

Max-Ernest excitedly explained to Cass what they were looking at – at least the things he recognized from books. Ingeniously hinged cages designed to conceal birds before they were released onto a stage... folding tables with hidden holes in which to drop rabbits...secretly marked playing cards and unevenly weighted dice...

"And that's Houdini—"

Max-Ernest pointed to a black-and-white photo of a bare-chested man that hung above an exhibit of his locks and chains.

Cass didn't say it, but she thought Houdini looked fairly undignified, less like a world-famous magician than a short man in a Tarzan outfit.

What, she wondered, would Pietro look like? Surely, he didn't look like the white-bearded wizard of her imaginings. Or wouldn't she ever get to see him, after all?

Max-Ernest nudged her: in the middle of all the displays was an empty black pedestal bearing a small brass plaque: *The Sound Prism*. A few tiny shards of glass missed by the vacuum cleaner remained on the floor beside the pedestal.

The scene of the crime.

Spooked, they looked at it for a moment – for some reason, it felt as though Dr. L and Ms. Mauvais were about to pounce on them – and then they continued on.

The next room was round and covered in striped fabric – an indoor circus tent.

SIDESHOW...**SIDESHOW**...**SIDESHOW**...blinked a sign made of tiny, popcorn-style light bulbs.

Here they found old photos of grinning Siamese twins. Saucy dancing girls. Surly bearded ladies. Tattooed fire-eaters. And – "Ow!" said Max-Ernest – an Indian fakir lying on a bed of nails.

They stopped to examine a fading circus poster in a peeling gold frame. It showed two identical young boys in tuxedos, one blindfolded, standing over some kind of fiery cauldron. Smoke curled up around them. "The Amazing Bergamo Brothers and their Symphony of Smells," it read.

Pietro and Luciano at age eleven.

Our two friends turned and looked at each other, eyes shining: now they knew they were in the right place!

"Uh, Cass, what do we do now?" asked Max-Ernest a moment later. He nodded towards the end of the hallway, where a man in a grey suit sat at a small table writing a note.

"Just act like we're supposed to be here... Excuse

me, mister," Cass said, raising her voice. "Do you know where we can find..."

The man didn't look up, and when they got closer they could see why: he was not real, he was mechanical. And the note he was writing was simply a phrase written over and over in his jerky but precise hand:

Loose lips sink ships. Loose lips sink ships. Loose lips sink...

"Kind of creepy, don't you think?" asked Cass.

"Not really. I think he's cool," said Max-Ernest.

"He's an automaton. Kind of like an old-fashioned robot. I read about them. In the old days, magicians used to perform with—"

Before Max-Ernest could finish:

Thwang! Thunk!

The two kids jumped as one: an arrow whizzed by their heads and landed right next to them amid dozens of arrows on a large target.

"Hey, you could have killed us!" Cass shouted.

But when they turned to see who'd nearly shot them, they saw only another automaton: this one holding a bow, a quiver full of arrows on the floor beside him.

As they looked around the room, they saw other

automata playing games of cards or chess; watering fake flowers; telling fortunes over crystal balls. There were also mechanical animals: rabbits, chimps, birds. It was quite a collection. Most of the automata looked very old and some of them creaked very loudly or seemed to be broken altogether.

Apart from all the mechanical people, there didn't seem to be a soul around. They thought they heard someone playing the piano – but when they followed the music to its source, they saw an old player-piano, unaccompanied by anyone human or otherwise, its keys moving up and down, seemingly of their own accord.

"You think they're just not here? Do we have to come back?" asked Max-Ernest. "Where did that guy with the glasses go?"

Before Cass could answer, a scrawny cat darted in front of them, then started scratching herself against what looked like a cabinet or booth of some sort with a curtained opening. "Hey, isn't that—"

"Pietro's cat?" Cass finished Max-Ernest's thought. (They'd met – or at least, seen – the magician's shy feline when they visited his house in their last investigation.) "Yeah, could be. She's just as skinny and has the same colour, or multicolours – what's it called?"

"Tortoiseshell."

As soon as Max-Ernest pronounced the word, the cat stepped into the booth and seemed literally to vanish before their eyes.

"Hey, where'd she go?!" Cass exclaimed.

As Max-Ernest watched, she stepped into the booth after the cat – and vanished just as quickly.

It was then that he noticed the glittering sign above the booth:

GATEWAY TO THE INVISIBLE

"Cass? You there?" Max-Ernest took a cautious step towards the booth Cass had disappeared into.

"Yeah, I'm right here! Can't you see me?"

"No, it's just black. It must be an illusion – you know, like for a stage show," said Max-Ernest, trying to sound confident. "Are there mirrors inside?"

"Um, yeah, but I can't really…wait, I think there's some kind of door – it's in the floor…okay, I'm going down just to look—"

"Wait – don't go without me!" said Max-Ernest.

But by the time he entered the booth, she was gone – and light streamed up at him from the hatch in the floor.

CHAPTER TWENTY-FIVE

The Invisible Man

The basement of the Magic Museum was occupied by a large workshop that, for the most part, looked like it could have been anywhere in the world: normal hammers and wrenches and saws hung from hooks on the wall. Normal scraps of wood and metal lay on the floor. A normal scent of sawdust and glue filled the air.

But whereas in a normal workshop you might find someone making a chest to keep blankets in, the chests made here were meant to be sawed in half – with somebody inside. And whereas in a normal workshop you might have found a wardrobe cabinet designed for coats, here the wardrobe cabinets were designed for making tigers disappear.

In short, it was a magician's workshop.

As Cass and Max-Ernest walked in, they saw an old man standing behind a workbench. He looked up at them briefly, then returned to the large silver vase in his hand. It had two handles and looked something like a trophy cup. He seemed to be fixing the bottom with a screwdriver.

He wore no velvet cloak – just old work clothes and a leather apron. He had no long white beard – just curly grey hair and a bushy moustache that snowed sawdust whenever he moved. And if he resembled a man from a fairy tale, it wasn't the noble wizard Cass had imagined, it was that humble Italian woodworker, the father of Pinocchio, Gepetto.

Still, Cass knew who he was right away. As if she had known him for ever.

"Um, excuse me, are you Pietro?" she asked, her heart beating hard in her chest. "Or Mr. Bergamo, I mean," she corrected herself, remembering they'd never actually met before.

"Pietro will do," he said by way of answer, not looking up from his work. His voice had a timbre similar to Dr. L's. But Pietro's voice retained more of his native Italian accent. And more of his native humanity.

The resemblance to his brother was uncanny, but not in the usual way of twins. It was more like seeing an old portrait of a friend's ancestor – a portrait that looks exactly like the person you know but in a different era and at a different age.

Unlike Dr. L's smooth and ageless face (a better word might be *facade*), Pietro's face bore all the marks of time: scars and spots, wrinkles and veins. It was imbued with that ineffable sense of history, of life lived and of experience gained, that only the best and oldest faces possess.

He could have been Dr. L's father, even his grandfather. Maybe an uncle. Anything but a twin brother.

"We, I mean, I am Cassandra," she stammered. "This is Max-Ernest."

Pietro remained silent. Max-Ernest felt compelled to jump in: "We're the ones who saved Benjamin Blake from the spa last year. The ones who Owen—"

"Yes. I know," said Pietro gently.

At last, Pietro finished doing whatever he was doing to the vase and looked up at the two intruders. "So. You have found me at work on my new stage."

"What stage?" asked Max-Ernest, confused.

"My favourite stage – *off*stage."

Pietro smiled to show he was making a joke. "I mean I have retired from being a magician. I was never the great entertainer – that was my brother. So these days, I only make the magic – I no longer perform it. Here—"

He placed the vase on the table in front of them.

"Each of you take a handle and pull. But gently! It's very old and I don't want to have to fix it again."

They pulled – and for a moment nothing happened.

Then a little silver leaf sprouted above the lip of the vase. Its stem grew taller and taller, as if drawn upwards by some invisible sun. Soon, other branches were growing from the central stem, leaves sprouting on each of these. Until a little silver tree stood in front of them.

One by one, delicate golden flowers budded and bloomed all over the branches.

"Whoa," said Cass.

"Double whoa," said Max-Ernest. "I've never seen one of those before. Even in books."

"You can imagine what people thought a hundred and fifty years ago – before the movies and the computers and the special effects."

As they spoke, a glittering gold canary emerged out of the top bloom and began to sing a lovely—

Screech!

Before the canary could get out a second note, its voice turned to a shrill whine and the whole tree started to smoke.

"Is that supposed to happen?" asked Cass nervously.

Pietro laughed. "Not at all. It's supposed to sing a Mozart melody. Now if I were on the stage, I would have to pretend like I wanted it to smoke all along."

He gestured to the loose gears and half-restored automata around him. "What I meant about making the magic – I create the illusions. I design them and I build them – but I do not use them so much any more. And now you can see why."

"Wow, so you're a...well, what do you call it? I've

never heard of what you do," said Max-Ernest as if that made such a job impossible.

"There's no name for it – because nobody's supposed to know that it is done. We like magic to be a mystery, no? You don't want to know somebody is standing behind the curtain, playing with mirrors. That ruins the whole thing."

"We call him the Invisible Man," said a voice from the back.

A tall, pinched-looking man with a pen behind his ear walked towards them.

"William Wilton Wallace III, certified public accountant, at your service," he said, handing each of the newcomers a business card.

"Mr. Wallace is an accountant by day, but he is the Terces Society archivist by night," Pietro explained.

"Nice to meet you," said Cass.

"Oh, we've met before, when you were in diapers," said Mr. Wallace with an expression of distaste – as if he could still smell the diapers in question. "I did the books for your grandfathers' store until I gave up on them. Far too disorganized. Absolutely hopeless, those two. But I expect you feel the same?"

"No, well, I..." Cass trailed off, wanting to defend her grandfathers, but not wanting to pick a fight.

"And this is Lily Wei. I think you have met her

upstairs." Pietro nodded as the beautiful, black-suited woman entered the room. "Of course, she is not just our receptionist, she is a master of the Chinese music."*

Lily smiled modestly. "Master is a relative word."

"Will you play for them?" asked Pietro, indicating the collection of exotic instruments hanging on one wall.

Lily tilted her head in assent. Then picked out an odd, violin-like instrument with a horse's head carved at the end of the neck where a scroll should be.

"This is the morin khur. From Mongolia. Close your eyes..."

Cass and Max-Ernest obeyed, and suddenly, they heard the sound of a horse galloping. The horse whinnied, then stopped short right next to them.

The effect was so startling they opened their eyes.

Lily laughed softly, still playing. "In the old days, they made the morin khur from the skull of a horse. They say you can still hear the horse's ghost."

---

*READERS OF MY PREVIOUS LITERARY EFFORT MAY REMEMBER A YOUNG CHINESE GIRL MENTIONED IN PIETRO'S NOTEBOOK. A VIOLIN PRODIGY, SHE WAS KIDNAPPED BY MS. MAUVAIS AFTER A CONCERT. YES, LILY WEI IS THE VERY SAME GIRL, NOW GROWN UP. AS YOU CAN IMAGINE, HER YEARS WITH THE MIDNIGHT SUN WERE HARROWING, AND HER ESCAPE EXHILARATING – BUT THAT, I'M AFRAID, IS A STORY FOR ANOTHER TIME.

The music became lovely and mournful and then—

She moved so swiftly that they never saw her pull the long, needle-like sword out of her violin bow. By the time they grasped what was happening, the sword was tickling Max-Ernest's throat.

"Wha—!" he gasped.

Lily dropped the sword just as quickly.

Cass stared, pale.

"I forgot to tell you, Lily is also a master of defence," said Pietro, enjoying their reaction, "our, what is the term? *Muscle*."

The kids looked suitably impressed.

"You will always be safe when I am nearby," said the demure receptionist, sheathing her sword back in the bow.

"So then – you knew it was us all along?" asked Max-Ernest, still quivering from the shock.

"I suspected. But I had Owen take a look just in case."

"Owen? Is he here?" Cass looked around in surprise.

"Right here."

Everyone turned to see the goateed Englishman sitting quietly in a chair by the wall. He removed his glasses.

The kids groaned. How could they not have guessed?

"The question is: why are you here?" said the English Owen. "I seem to remember dropping you off at home."

"Give them a second. They'll tell us in a moment," said Pietro.

"How can you always look so different?" Max-Ernest asked. "Is that even your nose?"

"Of course it's mine!" said Owen, offended.

He pulled on his nose – and it stretched like putty.

"I paid good money for it!"

Everyone laughed. And Cass felt a sudden surge of happiness.

The members of the Terces Society might not be the Knights of the Round Table any more than Pietro was Merlin, but, at the moment, she wouldn't trade them for anyone. Even Owen.

"So, then, is this...everybody?" she asked.

At this, Mr. Wallace coughed and looked at Pietro with raised eyebrows.

"They will turn up when we need them, you will see," Pietro said defiantly.

"I'm sure they'll put on a fabulous show," sniffed the archivist. He was obviously sceptical that they would turn up – whoever *they* were.

"The Terces Society has many friends," said Pietro, turning back to Cass and Max-Ernest. "But it is well that we do not all know each other… Speaking of this, have you two figured out our name?"

"Max-Ernest figured it out over the summer – he's really good with stuff like that," said Cass, in case anybody didn't know.

"It's *secret* backwards, right?" asked Max-Ernest.

"Exactly right," said Mr. Wallace, sounding faintly disappointed. "The early members found that whenever they said the word *secret*, it aroused too much interest. They called themselves the Terces Society so the riff-raff would stay away." He looked hard at their young guests.

Cass and Max-Ernest each took an involuntary step backwards.

They had a thousand questions about the Terces Society, but they sensed this might not be the time to ask them.

"And now, perhaps you will tell us why you're here," said Pietro. "You took a great risk."

Cass looked at Max-Ernest – he nodded – and she removed her backpack from her back. Silently, she unzipped it and pulled out the Sound Prism.

Pietro twinkled. "Ah, I knew you would have a good reason for coming." He shot a look at Mr. Wallace – as if to say, *Told you so!*

Owen laughed and shook his head ruefully. "You

sneaks! Not even mentioning it in the car!"

"Showed you up, did they, Owen?" asked Lily slyly.

Cass and Max-Ernest glanced at each other, unable to hide their proud smiles.

"We heard this was stolen," said Cass.

"It was, indeed," said Pietro. "You have done a very great thing – and, who can say? Averted much tragedy."

Cass was about to hand him the Sound Prism, but he held up his hand, stopping her.

"And now – how do they say it on the television? I have a mission for you, if you choose to accept it."

They nodded eagerly. Cass gripped the Sound Prism in excitement.

"Good. I think maybe you have heard of the homunculus?"

"Yeah, but he can't be real," said Max-Ernest confidently. "You can't grow a man in a bottle. It's not possible."

"The Midnight Sun thinks it's possible," said Pietro.

"Yeah, but...you don't...er, right?"

The old magician let the question hang. In a room like this, with half-built illusions all around, who could say what was possible?

"And that's why they want him?" asked Cass,

after a moment. "Because they think he's one of these man-made guys? And they want to make another one?"

"We think they want something from him," said Pietro. "Something he has or knows where to find."

"Like what?" asked Max-Ernest. He still wasn't ready to believe the homunculus existed – let alone that it knew anything.

"The grave!" said Cass, remembering the conversation they overheard on the boat.

Pietro nodded. "That would be Lord Pharaoh's grave. The alchemist who made the homunculus, he called himself Lord Pharaoh. Assuming this thing exists..." he added for Max-Ernest's benefit.

"Isn't that redundant? Like calling yourself King King," said Max-Ernest.

Pietro laughed. "Redundant, yes. And vain. But those were not his worst crimes. The Midnight Sun, they believe he knew the Secret."

Max-Ernest and Cass fell silent, treating this information with the gravity it deserved. Pietro put a warm, calloused hand on each of their shoulders.

"You must find the homunculus before the Midnight Sun. It is of the utmost importance."

Max-Ernest stammered in surprise. "Us? But—"

"But they're only children!" protested Lily.

"It does seem dangerous," said Owen. "Not that I'm volunteering..."

"Pietro, this is insane – even for you!" said Mr. Wallace, red-faced.

"Yes, isn't it?" He smiled broadly at Cass and Max-Ernest.

Cass tried to smile back and show she was brave. She wanted to ask more about the homunculus. About why they were being given this task. But all she could get out was: "How...?"

"With that—" Pietro pointed to the Sound Prism. "After all, it belongs to you."

Before she could ask why, he continued, "It's the only tool that we have. And you, Cassandra, are the only one who can use it."

Cass looked at the ball in her hand as though she'd never seen it before.

As though it were a stranger looking back at her.

CHAPTER TWENTY-FOUR

Grrrrrounnnnded

A lake at dawn. It is very cold.

A familiar eerie song starts to play.

Clouds of fog cling to the surface of the water. We can hardly see through the air, it is so wet and clammy.

Dark, hulking trees move in and out of view like shadowy hunters stalking prey. In the background, jagged mountain peaks rise out of the mist like giant jaws ready to clamp down on the entire picture.

A single bright spot interrupts the gloom. It is an orange triangle that, from a distance, looks like one of those safety cones used to divert traffic.

Looking closer, we see that the triangle is not a cone but a lone camping tent standing on the otherwise empty lake shore.

Two boys are talking and their voices can be heard all across the lake – although, oddly, they are not shouting. From the sound of it, they're maybe eleven or twelve years old, thirteen at the most.

"Oh man! That freakin' stinks!" says one.

The other boy laughs. "Chill out, dude. Everybody does it!"

"Not again!" says the first boy. "If you don't get out of the tent right now, I'm going to kill you!"

A few blades of grass block our view of the lake as

we listen to the boys in the tent, taking note of their presence, but not making a sound.

We are like a crocodile, or a snake. A predator lying in wait.

A boy – the farter, we're guessing – steps out of the tent. "Hey, where's Tommy?" he asks.

"Hiking with my parents," says the boy inside.

"But your dad told you to watch him—"

"He did?!"

Suddenly, we lift our head and disappear into the undergrowth.

Darkness.

What a creepy dream, Cass thought. It was almost like she was the homunculus. Waiting.

But for what? Not to eat those kids?

Automatically, she reached for her sock-monster. Then remembered that Ms. Mauvais had tossed it to the Skelton Sisters. Sigh.

Why did the homunculus come to her in her dreams? When she had no idea how to find him in reality.

"This is your job and you cannot fail. It would

be...a catastrophe," Pietro had repeated before saying goodbye.

It had taken all her courage to ask why she was the only one who could use the Sound Prism. "You will see," was Pietro's cryptic reply.

He'd hardly been more forthcoming when she asked how to use it. "Ah, I wish I could tell you. But I do not know."

Of course, even if she'd known exactly where to find the homunculus, or how to use the Sound Prism, it wouldn't have done her much good anyhow. She couldn't leave the house.

How often did Terces Society members get grounded? she wondered bitterly. I'll bet Pietro didn't think of *that* when he gave us our mission.

Grounded.
   Such a
       heavy
          word.
              Grrrrrounnnnded.
Say it out loud.
It sounds almost onomatopoeic, doesn't it?*

---

*IF YOU DON'T KNOW WHAT ONOMATOPOEIC MEANS, WELL – DING-DONG-CLICK-CLACK-BUZZ-QUACK! – LOOK IT UP.

In the past, Cass had experienced the word only as a threat. Being grounded was something that happened to other kids, to *bad* kids, not to her. Even when Cass and Max-Ernest had run off to the Midnight Sun Spa, her mother had been so relieved that her daughter had returned home safe that she'd barely reprimanded her. She figured Cass had learned her lesson.

But evidently Cass had *not* learned her lesson.

"You know who *has* learned her lesson? Me!" said her mother, who, now that she was no longer worried about Cass being lost at sea, was absolutely furious.

"I don't know who you think you are that you can keep running away like that, but this time you're not getting off so easy. I don't care whether this is some kind of plea for help or premature teenage rebellion or you're trying to get back at me for every wrong I've ever done to you or you just like boats a lot. You, young lady, are grounded for the rest of the year!"

Other than being confined to your house, being grounded often means losing privileges of various kinds. The problem for Cass's mother was that Cass didn't seem to mind having things taken away. Or at least she didn't let on if she did. (Cass knew she was going to be punished; she figured she should just grin and bear it.)

They were in the kitchen when her mother set down the rules – Cass eating cereal at the counter, her mother opening, and then slamming shut, cabinet doors at random.

The conversation went something like this:

Mom: "And there will be no extracurricular activities of any kind!" Slam.

Cass: "Fine."

Mom: "I'm taking away your cellphone!"

Cass: "Fine."

Mom: "And no television!"

Cass: "Fine."

Mom: "No internet!"

Cass: "Fine."

Mom: "Nothing fun whatsoever!"

Cass: "Fine."

Mom: "And no dessert!"

Cass: "Fine."

Mom: "No Thai food – not even pad thai!"

Cass: "Fine."

Mom: "Okay, fine – then no dinner at all!"

Cass: "Fine."

Mom: "All you get is gruel!"

Cass: "Fine."

Mom: "I'm taking away your bed!"

Cass: "Fine."

Mom: "You'll sleep on the floor in chains!"

Cass: "Fine."

Mom: "Fine!"

Cass: "Fine."

Mom: "Fine! Fine! Fine! Is that all you can say? Fine – then you know what, you can just leave this house right now! And don't come back!"

Cass: "So then you mean I'm not grounded?"

Mom: "Oh, you are so grounded! You can't believe how grounded you are! You're not leaving this house ever!"

The transition from screaming fight to mutual mother-daughter silent treatment was nearly instantaneous. An unrelenting quiet fell over the house like a miserable spell of weather. And it seemed it would never lift.

They both sought distraction wherever they could find it – anything to relieve the tedium that overtook their household.

Before Cass was grounded, when salespeople had called, Cass's mother always hung up or shouted a few choice invectives into the phone; now she engaged salespeople in long conversations about the weather in India or the Philippines or Macao, while Cass tried to eavesdrop and pick up information about the world without letting her face show any interest.

In an effort to make her time more productive, Cass pretended being grounded was a Terces Society survivalist training exercise.

Although her mother never made good on her threat to take away her bed, Cass slept on the floor anyway. What food she ate she ate standing up – and with her hands. And in her spare time, she taught herself the entire alphabet in Morse code: she didn't want to be caught unawares the next time Max-Ernest tapped her on the shoulder with an emergency message.

Indeed, she became so proficient at Morse code that she decided that from here on in, all Morse communications with Max-Ernest should be backwards: *Esrom code*, they could call it.

That is, if she ever got to communicate with Max-Ernest again.

One evening after dinner, not long after the grounding began, Cass told her mother – truthfully – that she was going upstairs to study. What she didn't tell her mother was that she meant *study the Sound Prism*.

She sat on her bed and turned it around in her hand, tracing the silver band with her finger and peering into the hundreds of little holes. How was this ball of sound supposed to help her find the homunculus? Was it as simple as listening until she heard him? How would she recognize the homunculus's voice when she did?

If he even had a voice.

Suddenly, she overheard her mother talking. The walls in their house were quite thick, and normally any sounds coming from downstairs were muffled and unintelligible. But Cass could hear her as plainly as if they were in the same room:

"*I always meant to tell her,*" her mother was saying, "*but it never seemed like the right time. And now she's getting older, and I'm so afraid of losing her... I know she's a smart girl – she'll figure it out, and what then?!*"

Her mother sounded frantic.

Grandpa Larry, Cass thought. She's talking to Grandpa Larry on the phone.

And almost at the same time, she thought: my father! She's talking about my father. What else could it be?

"*But I can already hear the sounds of a rebellious teenager,*" her mother protested. "*I can only imagine what she'll be like next year – you know how daughters get with their mothers. And if I tell her, she'll just have one more excuse to hate me... Sure, she loves me*"

NOW – *you don't think anything can change that!"*

Could anything change that? Cass wondered. What was her mother's secret? Was her love for her mother so strong that it would survive anything?

What if her father was a mass-murderer and he was in jail for life?

Or what if – what if her mother had killed her father? They could have had a fight, and it was self-defence. Or maybe it was just an accident. Either way, her mother wouldn't have wanted Cass to know.

It fitted the facts – you had to admit that.

No, she was being ridiculous: her mother wasn't a killer. And for all she knew, her mother's secret had nothing to do with her father.

Cass glanced with trepidation at the Sound Prism. She would have to be more careful about what she listened to in the future; some things you just didn't want to hear.

Later that night, when she was sure her mother was sound asleep, Cass snuck out the back of her house.

The night air was surprisingly warm for the time of year, and she enjoyed the newfound sense of freedom as she walked along their high wooden fence to a certain patch of dirt behind the remains of an old doghouse.

She hadn't visited this spot in a few years, but when she was younger it had been a frequent hideout. She called it the Barbie Graveyard because it was where, one night when she was nine years old, she'd ceremoniously buried every single doll she had. She'd marked the site with a melted Barbie toaster.

"They all died in an electrical fire," she told her mother sombrely. "I couldn't save them."

That next day she'd declared herself a survivalist.

Now, she had something else to bury.

It had occurred to her that the Sound Prism might not be safe in her bedroom. What if the Midnight Sun broke in while she was asleep and she never had time to hide it?

She tossed the Sound Prism back and forth in her hands as she looked for the best place to dig. At first, she barely heard the sound the Sound Prism was making. But when she held it still, she noticed that the sound stopped as well.

She tossed the Sound Prism between her hands again. And there was the sound. Like singing. Why was it so familiar?

Growing excited, Cass tossed the Sound Prism high into the air...

As it spun, the Sound Prism emitted a strange and wonderful sort of music – music that sounded impossibly close and yet seemed to come from far, far away.

Like the singing of fairies or sylphs.

Like the ringing of a thousand tiny voices inside your ear.

As soon as the Sound Prism fell back into her hand, Cass tossed it into the air again.

She stared, listening.

It was the song from her dreams.

CHAPTER TWENTY-THREE

Unavoidably Detained

A note from a teacher can get you out of a myriad of difficulties – tardiness, say, or PE.

Sadly, when it comes to a serious crime – like running away from a field trip – a note only helps if it absolves you of the crime; it doesn't do you much good if it blames you for the crime.

The note that Mr. Needleman (aka Owen) sent to Mrs. Johnson did not excuse their misadventure on the ocean. On the contrary, it explained that Cass and Max-Ernest had taken advantage of his good nature to escape from their class.

Mr. Needleman claimed that he'd suffered "severe emotional trauma" while pursuing his "reckless" and "renegade" students. He was checking himself into a mental health facility; therefore, unfortunately, he did not expect to return before the end of term.

He ended by saying he was considering suing the school for criminal negligence and suing Cass's and Max-Ernest's parents for raising criminals.

Cass was horrified. She couldn't believe Owen would write a letter like that. They would probably be suspended. Or even expelled! She'd been right not to trust him, after all, she told Max-Ernest.

But Max-Ernest pointed out that Owen had only done what he had to do. "If he just talked about how great we were, Mrs. Johnson would think we forged it.

And what would be the point of that?"

As it turned out, Mrs. Johnson did not suspend the juvenile delinquents otherwise known as the heroes of this story.

"Match the punishment to the crime, that's my motto," she said, staring imperiously at them from under a new royal-blue hat, as they stood against the wall in her office like prisoners awaiting a firing-squad. "Why should I give you time off from school for running away from school? Does that make sense to you?"

Instead, Mrs. Johnson chose a far less pleasant course: detention.

For the rest of the year.

"Does that mean the whole year or just the school year?" Max-Ernest asked. "Also, do we have to sleep here, or do we get to go home at night?"

Mrs. Johnson didn't deign to answer.

Cass tried to hide her smile.

Detention.

It was just like being grounded. Only at school.

Cass and Max-Ernest had detention at lunch, free period, and even recess. There was no more arguing about their investigations at the Nuts Table. No more sneaking off to share secrets behind the gym.

Even environmental sciences felt like detention now – because Mrs. Johnson had decided to save money by filling in for Mr. Needleman herself. "After all, managing this school is just like running a zoo – and zoology is an important part of environmental sciences," she said, as if that somehow qualified her to teach the class.

Despite her professed passion for zoology, Mrs. Johnson had removed all the animals from Mr. Needleman's classroom as soon as she moved in. Hence Cass and Max-Ernest didn't even have any gerbils or frogs to entertain them, only empty cages and terrariums.

On their first day of Johnson Jail, as they called it, Mrs. Johnson made them chisel off all the wads of gum from under the desks. (The hard wads were easy to remove; it was the sticky ones that were hard.) On the second day, she made them lick envelopes.

The envelopes contained copies of Mr. Needleman's letter, along with a second letter from Mrs. Johnson that made doubly sure everyone understood that Cass and Max-Ernest, and not their principal, were to blame for the "tragedy at the tide pools".

There was one envelope for every student (except in the case of siblings and divorced parents) – which,

Max-Ernest calculated, amounted to 312 individual licks.

"Why don't you send e-mails?" Cass asked Mrs. Johnson. "All that paper – it's killing trees for no reason. I thought you were the Principal with Principles."

"I am. And one of my principles is that students never talk back to their principal," the principal predictably responded.

When Mrs. Johnson finally left them alone, Max-Ernest told Cass he didn't mind licking all the envelopes. He liked the taste.

"Great!" Cass handed him her pile, and he started right away, attempting to lick as many envelopes in one minute as possible.*

"It's so frustrating. I know the song means something – I just don't know what," Cass said, returning to a conversation they'd started on the bus that morning. "It's like singing, but not with words. At least not in English or any other language."

"'ould be 'ome 'ind of 'usical 'ode 'aybe," Max-Ernest said, not stopping licking.

---

*I WILL LET YOU, DEAR READER, DECIDE WHETHER CASS DID RIGHT IN LETTING MAX-ERNEST DO ALL THE WORK, OR WHETHER – JUST POSSIBLY – SHE WAS HIDING BEHIND HER ENVIRONMENTAL SENSITIVITIES TO AVOID A TASK SHE DIDN'T WANT TO DO IN THE FIRST PLACE.

"What? Take that out of your mouth."

"I'm trying to lick for both of us, so I have to go double fast," said Max-Ernest, putting the envelope down. "I said, it could be some kind of musical code... Do you have it with you?"

"The Sound Prism? I buried it in my backyard. Why? Could you use the Decoder to see?"

Max-Ernest shook his head. "No music recognition software. But maybe if we could figure out the notes—"

Before he could finish his thought, they were interrupted by the reappearance of Mrs. Johnson and the words: "Yo, what's up, dudes?"

For a second, it seemed like it was their principal who had greeted them in this fashion. Then Yo-Yoji emerged from behind Mrs. Johnson.

"I regret to say you two will be having company," said the principal. "Your colleague here has been downloading music in the library, despite the fact that rules about internet usage are written in black-and-white above the computers. Perhaps I need to have them translated into Japanese..."

"I don't read kanji," muttered Yo-Yoji, taking a seat across from Cass and Max-Ernest.

Mrs. Johnson slapped a fresh stack of envelopes on the table. "I noticed a typo. We'll have to start over," she said, and walked out without another word.

Max-Ernest stared glumly at the stack, not quite as eager to lick as he was before.

"So what happened at the tide pools?" asked Yo-Yoji. "You guys better tell me – you owe me that much."

"What do you mean – we owe you? We got into big trouble 'cause of you," said Cass.

"I didn't say anything – I swear."

"Then how did Mr. Needleman know where we went?"

Max-Ernest looked at Cass in confusion. "What are you talking about? Mr. Needleman was following us."

Cass gave Max-Ernest a warning look. "Why would he follow us? He's just a teacher."

"Oh, I guess you're right," said Max-Ernest, back-pedalling fast. "It's not like he's a spy!"

"Why are you dudes acting so weird?" asked Yo-Yoji. "I knew you were hiding something!"

"What's to hide? We went to practise rock climbing," said Cass.

"Yeah. Then we got lost," said Max-Ernest. "That's all. I mean, it's not like we were looking for something, or looking for someone, or, like, trying to meet someone – I mean, who would that be? Members of some secret society? That would be ridiculous!"

"You guys suck as liars," said Yo-Yoji. "C'mon – what was behind the rocks?"

"Nothing." / "We can't tell."

"Well, which is it – is it a secret or was nothing there?"

"Both." / "Neither."

Yo-Yoji laughed. "It's a good thing you guys aren't really part of some secret society – you wouldn't last a minute, yo."

"Hi, Yo-Yoji!"

While they'd been talking, Veronica had entered the classroom. She smiled at Yo-Yoji, ignoring the others. "I have a message from Amber. She's waiting outside and she wants to know if you want to be in a band with her. You know, for the talent show – because you're so good at music?"

"Um...I kind of already have a band with these guys in Japan." Yo-Yoji turned to Cass and Max-Ernest. "We're trying to keep it going online. That's why I was downloading stuff before—"

"You mean you don't want to have a band with Amber?" Veronica was so appalled she couldn't bother to hide it.

Yo-Yoji shrugged apologetically. "Yeah. I mean, not really."

Veronica ran out to tell Amber the shocking news

– and returned in less than a minute with another message for Yo-Yoji: "Amber says she was watching and she knows you got in detention on purpose," she said breathlessly. "Because you have a crush on Cass!"

Cass's ears instantly turned red.

Max-Ernest looked like he'd been hit by a truck.

"That's not true! And, I mean, that's not why I wanted detention," said Yo-Yoji, blushing. "I just wanted to ask about the tide pools," he whispered to the others.

Mrs. Johnson stuck her head, or at least her hat, through the doorway; she didn't look happy. "Veronica – out, now! And the rest of you – is this detention or social hour?"

Veronica scurried out, looking extremely pleased with herself.

Cass, Max-Ernest and Yo-Yoji all sat, stunned, as silent as the empty animal cages around them.

"You know, you don't really sound like you're from Japan," said Max-Ernest finally. The way he said it, he might have been accusing Yo-Yoji of murder. Or at the very least of stealing his allowance.

"I'm not. We were just there for a year—"

"What were you doing there?" asked Cass, still

recovering from the unexpected, unwanted and apparently untrue news.

"My dad was studying pollution on Mount Fuji."

Cass's eyes lit up. "What kind of pollution?" Even as rattled as she was, the topic couldn't fail to interest her.

Max-Ernest, on the other hand, seemed about as interested in hearing about pollution as he was in breathing it. At least, if it meant hearing from Yo-Yoji.

"All kinds. He does all these tests on snow. We go backpacking all the time so he can take samples."

"Wow, your father sounds really cool," said Cass.

"He's okay, I guess. Sometimes it blows having to go to the mountains all the time because my parents have this rule about no electronic devices. So you can be all at one with nature or something. Do you ever go backpacking?"

"Are you kidding? My mom hates nature."

"What about you, Max-Ernest?"

"My parents aren't a couple," he answered, not looking at Yo-Yoji.

"So?"

"They're divorced. We don't do stuff like that."

"Oh, okay. Right. I get it," said Yo-Yoji, clearly not getting it at all.

Rather than offering any clarification, Max-Ernest

started relicking envelopes, soothing himself with the satisfying taste.

Unwillingly, Cass found her mind going back to what Veronica had said. Obviously, Amber was just mad because Yo-Yoji wouldn't be in a band with her... right?

Cass dismissed the thought. There was a more important question to answer:

"Hey, Yo-Yoji, do you know how to read music and stuff?"

"Um, pretty much."

"Do you think if I hummed some notes you could tell what they were?"

Max-Ernest looked at Cass in alarm. "Cass, you can't—"

"So what – it's just a song... So, can you?" she asked Yo-Yoji.

"Well, I can try... Actually, the choir teacher at my old school said I had perfect pitch—"

"You know, there aren't many people who really have perfect pitch," said Max-Ernest. "It's very rare."

"Let him try at least!"

Max-Ernest shrugged. He didn't approve but he could tell Cass couldn't be stopped.

"So, what is this song, anyway?" Yo-Yoji asked. "Wait, don't tell me, it's a secret!"

Cass nodded.

Yo-Yoji laughed. "Yeah, whatever. Go ahead—"

"Okay. My voice isn't very good, but hopefully you'll get it..."

Cass began to hum the song of the Sound Prism – at least her best approximation.

Yo-Yoji made her repeat the song. Then he concentrated, humming the tune to himself. "It's kind of hard because there are a few sharps and flats... but I think it goes C – A – B – B – A – G – E – F – A – C – E."

"*CABBAGE FACE*?" Max-Ernest pronounced. "You're saying the tune spells *cabbage face*?"

"If you're trying to insult me, I've heard worse things – better insults, I mean," said Cass, her ears reddening again.

Well, one thing was clear: he didn't have a crush on her. That made life simpler, anyway. But she still needed to know what the notes meant.

"Why would I want to insult you? I didn't even notice what the notes spelled."

Cass searched his face to see if he was telling the truth. "Well, then, thanks, I guess. It's just kind of weird..."

"What's wrong with Cabbage Face? I think it would be a sick band name! Good band names are really hard to think of. My band's called Alien Earache. I came up with it – well, the earache part."

Could that really be what the song was saying? Cass wondered. All those nights. All those dreams. And all the while the song so beautifully calling... *Cabbage Face*?

Lost in thought, she didn't notice the expression on the face next to her: Max-Ernest's glare would have been enough to make any cabbage wilt.

CHAPTER TWENTY-TWO

On The Bus

66 I still can't believe they don't have seat belts on school buses," said Cass that afternoon, sliding into her usual seat next to Max-Ernest (eleventh row, left-hand side). "I think we should boycott until they start following safety codes. What use is an education if you're brain-dead because you went flying through the windshield?"

"We're all the way in the back of the bus. I doubt we would make it that far," Max-Ernest replied. He was sitting with his legs folded against the green vinyl seat-back in front of them and he didn't look like he was flying anywhere. "I bet we wouldn't even break an arm—"

"You know what I mean! Why do you have to be so...logical?"

"Because I have a brain and I use it. I thought you didn't want us to be brain-dead—"

"Okay. You're right," said Cass, who was feeling rather cheerful despite her morbid thoughts.

The bus lurched into gear – and Cass and Max-Ernest both rocked dangerously in their seats, Cass's braids swinging. But Cass refrained from pointing it out.

"Hey, I was thinking we should have some kind of signal for emergencies," she said, lowering her voice so the other students on the bus wouldn't hear. "You know, since my mom took my cellphone away. Maybe you could call my house, ring once, hang up quick, call back, ring twice. 'Cause that would be like one short two long – which is E M in Esrom code, which is M E in Morse code. For Max-Ernest, get it? Then I'll know to meet you in my backyard at midnight."

She couldn't tell whether he liked the idea or not. "That's our signal then, okay?"

He nodded. Vaguely.

"So that was pretty cool, the way Yo-Yoji could tell the Sound Prism notes like that," said Cass.

"Yeah, it was sick."

In the solemn, matter-of-fact way Max-Ernest said this, he might as well have said "The cat is sick" or "I'm holding a stick".

"Sick?" repeated Cass with a laugh.

"It means, like, cool – right? Isn't that what you said?"

"Yeah, it's just – never mind." She couldn't believe Max-Ernest had used Yo-Yoji's word. If it were anybody else, she would have thought he was being sarcastic.

"Anyway, I was sure the Sound Prism was saying *something*, but...Cabbage Face? It's like something somebody would call you at school..."

"Call *me*?" asked Max-Ernest. "Why would they call me that?"

"No, duh. Anybody. It just sounds like a mean name... You think it's another name for the Sound Prism? Because it's round like a cabbage?"

Max-Ernest shook his head. "Then it would be *Cabbage Head* or just *The Cabbage*."

"Yeah, you're probably right," said Cass agreeably. "Besides, the Sound Prism is too pretty to have a name like that."

She took a notebook out of her backpack and opened it to a page on which she'd written *CLUES – CABBAGE FACE* in big capital letters.

"What about some kind of warning or prophecy?" she asked.

"Like, if you don't watch out your face will look like a cabbage? That doesn't sound like much of a warning – *yo*," he added. With all the flatness of "I must untangle my yo-yo" or "I will now be singing my so-lo".

Oh no – not *yo*, too! Cass groaned to herself.

"Max-Ernest, can I tell you something, as your friend? Don't say *yo*. Or *sick*."

"But Yo-Yoji says them—"

"That's different. He's...Yo-Yoji. You...sound silly."

Usually, because Max-Ernest was bad at emotions, you could say something like that without worrying about hurting his feelings (at least that's what Cass told herself), but he looked so stricken that she immediately added, "I mean, Yo-Yoji sounds kind of silly, too."

"But you said he didn't! That's what you meant, anyway." Max-Ernest turned away from Cass and faced the window.

Cass studied the back of his spiky-haired head. What was wrong with him today?

"So have you tried putting Cabbage Face in the Decoder yet?" she asked.

Max-Ernest shook his head, still not looking at her. "I didn't think you wanted me to. Yo-Yoji already figured it out, didn't he?"

"That was just the notes – what about the words? I tried different combinations but I don't think any of them work."

Cass tapped Max-Ernest on the shoulder and he glanced at her notebook briefly.

Cabbage Cafe
A Cab Cafe Beg
Beg a Cab Face
Ceca Fa Be Bag

"Well, I guess you don't need me then – did Yo-Yoji do those with you?"

"No, I did them myself! I haven't even seen Yo-Yoji since you did."

"It doesn't matter – none of them are right, anyway."

"Yeah, I didn't think so. I was just showing you."

Max-Ernest nodded and started looking out the window again. What was so fascinating out there? Not the dry-cleaner's they were driving past. Cass couldn't remember him ever being this quiet.

"So it's Wednesday – are you coming to my grandfathers'?" she asked. "My mom said I could go even though I was grounded if I walked Sebastian. 'Cause that was kind of like a job."

"No, I got stuff to do."

"Oh." She didn't ask what stuff.

Were they in a fight? It sure seemed like they were, but with Max-Ernest, it was hard to tell.

"Besides, why don't you just ask Yo-Yoji to come?"

"What do you mean?"

"Well, you're a couple now, right?"

"What are you talking about?"

He turned to face her. "Aren't you?"

"No!" Cass had never said the word more forcefully in her life. But Max-Ernest didn't seem to hear it.

"Well, anyways, I was thinking, maybe you guys should be collaborators instead of us. He knows all about the three-point rule and backpacking and everything. I'll bet Pietro would let him in the Terces Society if you asked. I'll even give you guys the Decoder if you want. Do you want it?"

"No."

"Okay, I'll keep it then. It could be helpful with homework, I guess."

"Max-Ernest, why are you being like this?" Cass thought she knew the answer. It was just that it was so surprising it was hard to believe.

"Like what?"

"Like...crazy. Are you mad at me?"

"What do you mean? You're the one whose ears are all red," said Max-Ernest.

"Great. Thanks a lot for telling me," said Cass. Unlike Max-Ernest, she knew how to be sarcastic when she wanted to be.

What she didn't know how to do was make things right. A jealous Max-Ernest was a disaster – natural or unnatural, she wasn't sure which – that she was altogether unprepared for.

CHAPTER TWENTY-ONE

Upside Down

For as long as Cass had known them (which was as long as she'd been alive), Grandpa Larry and Grandpa Wayne had lived in an old fire station, but Cass had never once seen a fire engine there. This is not quite as surprising as it sounds because the fire station no longer operated as a fire station; rather than firefighters the station housed only Cass's grandfathers and their antiques store, the Fire Sale.

But that afternoon, when she arrived to walk Sebastian, Cass saw not only a long red fire engine, but also paramedics and policemen and emergency workers of every stripe. They spoke into walkie-talkies. They took photographs. They bandied about phrases you usually only hear on television like "securing the perimeter" and "talking to witnesses".

Normally, the sight of so much emergency activity on the quiet tree-lined street would have excited Cass, and she would have pummelled the paramedics with questions about CPR techniques, or at least complained to the firemen about the seat belt situation on her school bus.

But it was different knowing her grandfathers were inside.

Had someone been hurt? Had the firehouse caught on fire? Cass looked around, her heart beating in her chest. The sky was clear. She didn't smell smoke.

Cass ran up the steps and found Grandpa Larry right inside the doorway, deep in conversation with a woman in a police uniform.

As it turned out, nothing terrible had transpired – except a rather minor burglary. The reason all the emergency vehicles had come was that Larry had been so distressed when he called the emergency number that he wasn't able to get a word out, and the dispatcher had assumed he was choking or worse.

"They just turned the place upside down!" Larry was saying now.

"Yes, I can see that," said the expressionless policewoman, looking at the piles of junk on the floor. There was stuff everywhere: the store was bursting at the seams. The only relief from the chaos was a shiny brass fire pole that disappeared into a hole in the floor above.

"Oh no…those piles are from when we started doing inventory three years ago. Big mistake!" Larry shook his head, remembering.

"I see… So those shelves, then?" The policewoman nodded towards the open shelves: books and crockery and old machinery and knick-knacks, all tumbled out of the shelves very much as if someone had upended them.

"Are you kidding?" Larry huffed. "We just organized

those shelves last month! It took days. They've never been so neat."

"Right… Then what exactly…?"

"Well, those drawers, of course! And the cabinets over there! Can't you tell? Those bloody so-and-sos just tore them apart!" Larry pointed across the room.

"Uh-huh," said the policewoman, straight-faced. There was no way to tell what had been torn apart and what hadn't. "But they didn't take anything at all?"

"That's the worst part – how dare they not take anything! They couldn't find anything they wanted? Those laptops, for example – perfectly usable. And they left the Staffordshire! A chip here and there maybe, but stunning just the same…"

"Could be someone's angry at you. Or playing a joke. Unless you're playing one on me…?" She looked at him sharply.

"No. No. I never…oh Cass, I didn't see you!" said Larry, agitated. "Sweetheart, could you do me a favour and take Sebastian on a little walk? All this nuttiness is making him…nutty."

Larry gestured towards his blind basset hound, lying a couple of metres away. Sebastian, it must be said, looked a lot calmer than Larry. But Cass didn't argue.

Grandpa Larry might not have known what the

burglars wanted, but she did. Well, she suspected. As far as Cass was concerned, there was only one thing they could be looking for. And it wasn't at the firehouse, it was at *her* house.

"Uh, no...I'll take him. Right now!" She grabbed Sebastian's leash and he started to roll—

That's right. *Roll*.

You see, over the last few months, Sebastian had lost his ability to walk. Oh, he could shuffle a little bit. But his back had got so painful, and his belly had fallen so low to the ground, that he couldn't move more than a couple of metres without exhausting himself to the point of collapse.

Sometimes, he looked more like a rug than a dog; indeed, more than one customer in Cass's grandfathers' shop had stepped on him only to be surprised by the loudest yelp they'd ever heard.

Grandpa Wayne (as you know *if* you've read my first book, and if you haven't, what can I say, there are risks to everything) was a retired auto mechanic and a constant tinkerer. He had dealt with Sebastian's disability by rigging an old skateboard for the dog's use. The skateboard was outfitted with a seat belt (to prevent Sebastian from falling off) and a leash (with which to pull the skateboard). Everybody was happy with the contraption, even Sebastian, until an obstacle became apparent: how was Sebastian supposed to "do his business" if he was strapped to a skateboard?

Hence Cass's grandfathers had taken to wrapping Sebastian in a towel – oh, let's call it what it is, a diaper – with a hole cut for his tail.

If you've never seen a dog in a diaper, let me tell you there are few sights sadder. Unless it is the sight of a blind, near deaf, and virtually paralysed dog in a diaper.

"It's a good thing he can't see himself," was all Cass could say the first time she saw Sebastian in his new get-up.

As brave as Cass was, I must admit that it occasionally embarrassed her to walk Sebastian in this condition. Today, however, she didn't give a thought to the way he looked.

She ran down the street with Sebastian practically flying behind her.

When they reached her house, Cass walked right past – and down another block.

Partly to look for suspicious activity. Partly to screw up her courage.

When they returned, she still didn't let herself in – she went around to the back.

With Sebastian standing guard (or *lying* guard, anyway) she dug until she could verify that the Sound Prism was still there, wrapped in a Mylar space blanket, just the way she left it. Then, relieved, she quickly reburied it.

She entered the house as silently as she could considering she was pulling a dog on a skateboard behind her.

Inside, the house was quiet – and apparently untouched. The couches had not been torn apart. Bookshelves and drawers had not been upended. The cupboards had not been ransacked.

Could she have been wrong? Was it possible her grandfathers' burglars hadn't been looking for the Sound Prism after all? Was it possible the Midnight Sun had never been to the firehouse? Wouldn't they have checked her house first?

She was almost disappointed. She'd been so certain.

Cass felt a tug on Sebastian's leash. He'd been acting anxious ever since they'd arrived at her house. But now he was wriggling on his skateboard and barking frantically.

"What's wrong, Sebastian? Better not be your diaper because I'm definitely not changing it!"

Maybe he just wants to get off the board for a minute, she thought.

As soon as Cass untied him, the blind, near deaf, and physically ailing dog leaped off the skateboard, sending the board shooting backwards. And then he bolted towards the stairs with the energy of a dog half his age.

Astonished, Cass followed Sebastian upstairs, where he ran unhesitatingly all the way to her closed bedroom door.

Which he proceeded to paw furiously.

When Cass opened the door, he bounded into the room and, trembling with excitement and exhaustion, fell in a heap in front of her bed.

Cass stared at the dog: "What has got into you? Are you...trying to tell me something?"

Cass knew from experience that Sebastian had a keen sense of smell – and of danger. Not for nothing did they call him Sebastian, the Seeing-Nose dog. For him to act so peculiarly, there had to be a reason.

Nervous, Cass went through her regular checks.

At first she didn't notice anything unusual – but when she glanced at her window sill, she stopped short: the dead bee was gone.

She looked down: there it was on the floor, a little way from the wall.

Somebody had opened her window.

When she checked her drawers a second time, she saw that the dental floss had been retied rather sloppily.

Somebody had looked in her drawers.

Somebody had been in her room.

And that's when she saw it sitting on her bed. Her sock-monster. What was once her sock-monster, anyway.

It had been ripped to pieces and was now a pile of scraps:

A few torn socks

bottle caps
and
tennis shoe
tongues

some loose
threads

loose recycled
cotton stuffing

So the Midnight Sun had come, after all.

They'd even left her a gift of sorts. A warning.

Of course, now that she'd established she was right, Cass wasn't so excited about it.

In fact, she was rather frightened.

CHAPTER TWENTY

Max-Ernest
the Magnificent

After the bus dropped him off that afternoon, Max-Ernest went home – or, as he sometimes thought of it, he went *homes*.

Perhaps I should explain:

As you may possibly remember, Max-Ernest's parents had divorced almost as soon as Max-Ernest was born. But they'd kept living together so that Max-Ernest would grow up with both parents in the house.

In principle, that might have been a good idea. In practice, however, it was very stressful for all of them – especially because Max-Ernest's parents insisted on living entirely distinct lives, each keeping to his or her half of the house and never speaking to the other.

Recently, thankfully, Max-Ernest's parents had made the sensible decision to separate.

"Isn't this what you always wanted?" asked his mother. "A nice, normal divorced family?"

"Now we can be like every other divorced family on the block," said his father. "Wouldn't you like that?"

(Max-Ernest's parents had an odd habit of repeating each other's words without acknowledging that the other parent had spoken.)

Their separation was quite real; they literally cut their house in two. With chainsaws. Max-Ernest's mother's half of the house (the modernist-style half) stayed where it was, while Max-Ernest's father had his half (the cosier, woodsier half) hauled to an empty lot across the street.

I'm sure I don't have to tell you how unusual the half-houses looked. However, both half-houses were boarded up on the sides where'd they been severed – so their interiors were not exposed to the elements and you could live in them more or less "normally".*

In their new mood of common-sense compromise, Max-Ernest's parents worked out a custody arrangement for their son that made them both equal partners in parenting. They called the agreement "half-and-half".

For the first half-hour of every hour, Max-Ernest was expected to be at his mother's half-house, for the second half-hour, his father's. Exceptions included mealtimes, which were broken into fifteen-minute segments so Max-Ernest would never miss a meal

---

*JUST TO BE CLEAR: A HALF-HOUSE HAS NOTHING TO DO WITH *HALF-LIFE*, WHICH IS A WAY OF MEASURING RADIATION RESIDUE AND OTHER THINGS THAT DISAPPEAR OVER TIME. NOR IS A HALF-HOUSE ANYTHING LIKE A *HALFWAY HOUSE*, WHICH IS A PLACE WHERE PEOPLE STAY AFTER THEY'VE BEEN IN JAIL. TO THE BEST OF MY KNOWLEDGE, NEITHER OF MAX-ERNEST'S PARENTS WERE EVER CRIMINALS. AS FOR MAX-ERNEST HIMSELF, I CAN'T ANSWER FOR HIS FUTURE ACTIONS, BUT SO FAR, HIS RECORD IS CLEAN!

with either parent, and sleeping hours, which were spent at alternate half-houses nightly.

By now, Max-Ernest was used to the arrangement; I might go as far as to say he'd mastered it. His watch was programmed to beep every half-hour, but he'd got to the point where his internal sense of time was just as accurate as his watch, and usually he was stepping through the doorway of his mother's or father's half-house (whichever was next) by the time his watch beeped.

Today was different.

The bus had dropped him off at an awkward time, 3:47, and he had trouble remembering whether he was supposed to go to his mother's or his father's first, and whether he was supposed to stay with parent number one until 4:00 (thus cheating parent number one of seventeen minutes) or 4:30 (thus cheating parent number two of thirteen). It didn't matter that neither of his parents would be home yet; it was a point of honour that he abide by the agreement even in their absence.

As he stood in the middle of the street debating which way to go, his mind went back to his conversation with Cass on the bus. His questions, he thought, had been very sensible: If Yo-Yoji had a crush on Cass, why *wouldn't* they be a couple? If Yo-Yoji was good at climbing, why *shouldn't* they be collaborators?

And yet, for some reason, his feelings didn't make so much sense.

Scccrrrrrrrrrrrrrrrrreeeeeeeeeeeeeeech!

A truck braked, blaring its horn; Max-Ernest jumped out of the way and wound up in front of his mother's half-doorstep.

His mother's half-house was very stark, almost empty inside. Nevertheless, movement was sometimes difficult because of where it had been split from his father's half-house. Usually, Max-Ernest ran up the stairs to his room without a problem, his body remembering exactly when and where he had to dart to the side to avoid hitting the plywood wall that bisected the stairway.

This time, he hit the wall twice, scraping his shoulder and elbow.

Was he mad at Cass, like she said? Was that why he was so upset?

It was strange losing a friend. As strange as it'd been to make a friend in the first place. But much worse. He almost wished he'd never made a friend at all.

Once safely in his bedroom, almost as a test, he tried throwing some things around in his room, which is what he imagined someone angry would do. Yo-Yoji, for example. *He* would probably break something. Like a guitar.

But it was no use. His model rocket didn't fly any further than when he tried to launch it properly. The frisbee bounced off the wall and hit him in the face. He couldn't even bring himself to throw the specimens from his rock collection.

I must not be very mad, he thought. Or else maybe I'm just not good at it.

Then he noticed the brown-paper package on his desk. Max-Ernest had received packages in the mail before – kits for building aeroplanes and spaceships, mostly, and boxes of books – but only when he'd ordered them. This one was a surprise. As was the name written on it:

"Max-Ernest the Magnificent."

Repeating the name with a sense of wonder, he sat on the floor and opened the package, revealing a large cardboard box. The box was decorated with a top hat and a magic wand, as well as the words, **THE MAGIC MUSEUM'S HOME MAGIC SHOW**.

When he lifted the lid off the box Max-Ernest saw a classic magic set arrayed in moulded plastic. There was a wand. A deck of cards. A rope for rope tricks. A cup and ball set similar to the ones he'd pointed out to Cass. And a few other things I won't give away because I don't want to ruin anybody's magic show.

Now all I need is a hat – how 'bout that? Max-Ernest thought.

A small card was paper-clipped to the manual:

Try the cone trick.
It's a good place to start.
P.B.

Following instructions in the manual, Max-Ernest made a cone out of black construction paper. The cone was designed so that it looked empty when you opened it up for your audience, but it had a secret compartment that you could pull a scarf out of. The idea was to make it seem like you were pulling the scarf out of thin air.

Max-Ernest's first idea was that he would practise the scarf trick a few times, then try it on Cass the next day. Then he remembered he might not be talking to her ever again. Perhaps instead he could try the trick out on his mom and dad (separately, of course). If it went well, he could make it part of his magic comedy routine for the talent show.

After all, Cass wasn't the only person in the world – just his only friend. At least, she had been.

The manual suggested practising in front of a mirror. So he took his paper cone into the bathroom along with a bandanna left over from the one day four years ago that he'd tried being a Cub Scout.

"Ladies and gentlemen," he pronounced, addressing the mirror. "I, Max-Ernest, the Magnificent, have in my hand a normal piece of paper folded into a cone. Look, it's totally empty and—"

Max-Ernest was certain he'd made the cone correctly, but as the minutes passed, he got more and more frustrated. No matter how hard he tried, he couldn't make the cone look empty; he kept seeing the corner of the bandanna poke out. He decided to look in the manual again; maybe he'd missed something earlier.*

Thumbing through, he noticed that a particular passage had been underlined in red.

The passage explained that diversions help set up tricks:

For example, you might hold up your wand and say, "Watch my wand closely – I promise there's nothing tricky or magic about it," before tapping your magic

---

*PERSONALLY, I THINK THE PROBLEM WAS THAT HE WAS USING A BULKY BANDANNA INSTEAD OF A PROPER MAGICIAN'S SCARF. IF YOU'D LIKE TO MAKE YOUR OWN MAGIC CONE, YOU CAN FIND INSTRUCTIONS IN THE APPENDIX. AND PLEASE TRY IT WITH A "SILK", AS MAGICIANS CALL THEIR SCARVES, NOT A BANDANNA.

cone with your wand. That way your audience will
think the secret of your trick lies in the wand, not in
the cone.

Strange, thought Max-Ernest. It was almost as
though the words had been underlined just for him.

He took the wand out of the magic set and tried
the cone trick in front of the mirror again. But he was
so frustrated by his earlier failures – and, I suspect, so
angry at Cass – that instead of gently tapping his cone,
he flung the wand across the room.

Almost as if he was good at being angry, after all.

As the wand hit the wall, its white cap flew off
– and a tightly scrolled sheaf of papers slid out. Max-
Ernest picked them up and unfurled them with a sense
of nervous excitement.

On the first page, there was a note in pencil:

Dear Cassandra and Max-Ernest:
I have persuaded Mr. Wallace that as long as
you have the Sound Prism, you should have this
file as well. Share these pages with no one. And
please return them when your mission is complete.
Or I will be in big trouble with Mr. Wallace!
Regards,
P.B.

The first page also had a carefully typed label:

Sound Prism:
Notes, Stories, Memoranda
1500–Present Day

In the old days, when he and Cass were collaborators, Max-Ernest would have called Cass immediately. He might even have given the emergency signal. He wouldn't have read a single page without her.

But what to do now? Should he read the pages on his own? Rip them up without reading them at all?

As he struggled with his feelings, the alarm on his watch started beeping: he was late to go to his father's. For the first time ever.

He shoved the pages into his pocket, flew down the stairs, and ran across the street. By the time he got to his father's half-house, he'd reached a decision.

Or half of one, anyway.

CHAPTER NINETEEN

No Secrets in
This House

You know all about Cass's morning ritual. But she had a night-time ritual as well.

I'm afraid she might not have liked me telling you about *this* ritual – because it didn't necessarily match the tough image she liked to project. It was not part of her survivalist training; it was more, well, daughterly.

Every night, when Cass was ready for bed, her mother would knock on the door (she always knocked before entering; it was a rule) and then she would peek inside Cass's room.

"Please, can I tuck you in tonight?" her mother would ask. "Just one more time. I won't be able to sleep otherwise."

Cass would groan. "You're such a baby! Do you have to?" And then she would let her mother tuck her in, anyway. They both knew that Cass liked to be tucked in as much as her mother liked tucking her in, but it was more fun to think of Cass as the grown-up and her mother as the child.

At least, that had been their ritual until Cass was grounded. For the last few nights, Cass had gone to bed on her own.

Tonight, though, having painstakingly reconstructed her sock-monster, but not yet having fully reconstructed her courage, she knocked on her mother's door.

"Mom, will you, um, tuck me in?"

Her mother smiled as if she'd been paid the best compliment of her life. "Of course, sweetie," she said. "You know how much I've been missing that."

Later, as Cass's mother was giving her a last smothering goodnight kiss, the phone rang. Once.

"Must have been a wrong number," said Cass's mother, standing to go.

Cass nodded, not thinking anything about it.

Then the phone rang again. Twice. The signal!

For a second, Cass's eyes flared with excitement. Which she squashed just as quickly.

"What?" her mother asked from the doorway. "Do you know who that was?"

"No, it's nothing!"

"Cass...?"

"Probably just a wrong number, like you said."

"Cass, you're not a grown-up yet. You don't get secret calls from people I don't know."

"Fine. It was Max-Ernest. It means I'm supposed to call him, but I don't feel like it. I'll just talk to him tomorrow. There, are you satisfied?"

Her mother nodded. "Thank you. You know I don't like having secrets in this house."

Cass (snorting): "Whatever."

Mom: "Was that a snort?"

(Oops. Now she had blown it.)

Cass: "What?"

Mom: "Whatever snort what?"

Cass: "What are you talking about?"

Mom: "Don't whatever snort me."

Cass: "I didn't."

Mom: "You didn't what? Just say whatever you were going to say!"

Cass: "You don't want me to say it. You don't want to talk about it."

Mom: "Now you really better say it…"

Cass: "Fine – *whatever, you won't even tell me who my dad is!*"

There it was.

In a movie, that would be a big moment. There would be a crescendo of the score, or on television, a cutaway to an advertisement for diapers, or motor oil, or hammocks. However, in a plain old commercial-free conversation, an awkward sentence like that has to be followed by another awkward sentence.

Her mother stared at her in surprise. "Cass, where did that come from? You…you haven't asked about… that in years."

"Never mind," said Cass, regretting her words immediately. "Sorry. I shouldn't have brought it up. It's not my business…"

"Of course, it's your business," said her mother, walking back to Cass's bedside. "I just...wasn't expecting the question, that's all. Well, I was expecting it sometime, just not..." She trailed off.

There was silence for a moment, mother and daughter each waiting for the other to speak. Cass couldn't remember ever experiencing a more uncomfortable moment with her mother. Sure, they'd had screaming fights, even thrown things – a remote control, an oboe, a lasagne – but somehow this was worse.

"Anyway," said Cass, desperately wanting the moment to be over, "whoever he is, he's not really my father. I mean, he didn't raise me. So it doesn't really matter."

Her mother looked at her searchingly. "Are you sure, Cass? Is that really how you feel?"

Cass nodded vigorously. She knew that later she would kick herself for not pushing her mother to say more, but right now, for some reason – for a hundred reasons – it was the last thing she wanted.

"Good," said her mother, giving Cass a quick hug. "You and me – we're what matters, right?"

She left the room – but not without shouting "Love you!" one more time.

*   *   *

At exactly midnight, Cass found Max-Ernest waiting for her in the Barbie Graveyard. Hands in his pockets, he was bouncing up and down to ward off the chill.

Before she could say anything, he started talking in a long chain of words, connecting one thought to the next without stopping – almost like his old self. His breath made puffs in the air as he spoke.

"...I didn't read any of it because I didn't think it would be fair to read it without you, and...anyway, I wasn't sure whether I should read it at all. Maybe I should just give it to you, right? I mean, if I'm not your collaborator any more – I mean, am I? – and does that mean I'm not part of the Terces Society, either? But the package came to me, and it was addressed to 'Max-Ernest the Magnificent'! How 'bout that? And I've got a new trick. Actually, a couple. Well, one that I can do pretty well right now. But anyway, my name was on the note, too. So maybe I should read it. You know, if you want..."

It was a good three minutes before Cass could get a word in. Finally, she had to grab him by the shoulders.

"Max-Ernest, listen to me. Of course, you should read it. And of course, you're still my collaborator. And of course, you're still in the Terces Society. You're just being crazy, all because Yo-Yoji could tell those notes for us, which is totally ridiculous – anyway, I hardly even know him! And I have a million things to tell you."

Max-Ernest looked at her in silence for a moment, taking this in. "Okay, what?"

She told him about the break-in at her grandfathers' store and the broken-up sock-monster on her bed.

"That wasn't a million things. That was two."

"Max-Ernest...!"

"Okay, well, I guess you, I mean, *we* better find the homunculus fast, before they come back! Maybe it will tell us how in here." He held up the coiled pages of the Sound Prism file. "I mean, if the homunculus even exists. Which I still doubt—"

"You think it'll say why the Sound Prism belongs to me, you know, like Pietro said?"

Max-Ernest's eyes widened. "I dunno – let's see."

Together, they sat down on the ground and leaned back against the remains of the old doghouse. As Max-Ernest held the flashlight for her, Cass began to read aloud from the file.

Although they were shivering, they didn't seem to notice the cold. Sometimes just having a friend to keep you company can make a freezing night seem, well, a little less freezing.

CHAPTER EIGHTEEN

The File

Considering the documents in the Sound Prism file spanned five hundred years, there weren't very many of them.

The oldest was a wrinkled scrap of parchment covered with elaborate calligraphic script:

15 August 1817

For Sir Gilbert, on his Thirteenth Birthday — the day the Boy becomes the Man!

This musical ball known as the Sound Prism belonged to your late father. And before that to his father. And before that to his. I hope you cherish this family heirloom, but beware, the ball is not for play—

Beyond that, the parchment was too smudged to be legible.

Cass put it aside, wondering what it would be like to know not only who your father was, but your father's father's father.

The next letter was much more recent. As Max-Ernest shined the flashlight on it, Cass gasped. "Look at this one – it's from Grandpa Larry! How weird…"

"Not that weird. Remember, Mr. Wallace said he was their accountant, right?"

"Yeah, but still…"

Sept. 14, XXXX

Dear Mr. Wallace,

I confess I was surprised when you asked me to examine this "Sound Prism" of yours. Such a whimsical object – and you such a serious man!

I can't tell much without being allowed to touch it. (Just what are you afraid of?) But I believe it to be carved from alabaster and about 600 years old. Most of the workmanship looks Austrian – but the silver band is more typically English. A later addition?

With what tools the interior was carved I cannot guess. In its own small way, the Sound Prism is an engineering feat to rival the Roman aqueducts.

And that's all I have to report. Except for a strange coincidence… Imagine my shock yesterday when a lady walked in asking if I'd ever encountered a stone "Sound Ball".

And what a lady! So beautiful! But very cold. I asked if she would sell any of her exquisite gold jewellery, and she just laughed.

Naturally, I didn't tell her anything about you.

See you at tax time. As usual, our accounts are a mess!

Cheers,

Larry

"Wow, so my grandfather has seen the Sound Prism," said Cass, putting down the letter. "I wonder if we should ask him about it..."

"So do you think they know...?"

"About the Terces Society?" Cass shook her head. "It didn't sound like it..." Cass hesitated, then shrugged off the thought. "It's impossible!"

An old yellowed manuscript took up the rest of the pages. When they saw the title, they both breathed in sharply with excitement.

Max-Ernest still holding the flashlight, Cass sat back and started reading with the same kind of pleasurable anticipation you have when you're about to read, oh, say, the sequel to a favourite book.

The Legend of Cabbage Face
A Gothic Tale

NOTE: THIS STORY IS BASED ON ORAL TALES AND INTERVIEWS WITH OLDER TERCES SOCIETY MEMBERS, NOW SADLY DECEASED. I BELIEVE IT TO BE TRUE IN ESSENCE IF NOT ENTIRELY IN FACT. LIKE ALL SOCIETY LORE, IT SHOULD BE REGARDED AS A SACRED TRUST, AND NEVER SHARED WITH OUTSIDERS.

SIGNED, Xxxxxxx Xx Xxxx, 1898

Part the First

Four hundred years ago, in the city of Basel, in the country now known as Switzerland, there lived a great doctor.

At a very young age, this doctor rose to the height of his profession, treating grateful patients from all over the country and teaching many adoring students at the university.

And yet he was unhappy. He felt stifled by life in Europe and by the closed-minded state of the doctors around him.

Medicine in those days was not so far from magic, but he aspired to work in ways that even then were considered obscure and dangerous. Unbeknownst to his peers, the doctor was a devotee of that occult practice that is sometimes called the Secret Science, or alchemy.

And so, not much more than twenty years old, he closed his medical practice and left home on a quest to discover all the secrets of the East. He travelled far and wide – consulting the astrologers of Arabia, the metallurgists of Egypt, and the libraries of Constantinople – until he could justly claim that he knew more of the alchemical arts than any other man alive.

And yet he was not satisfied.

For it was not just the common goal of alchemy he was after, the turning of lead into gold, but something far more elusive: power over life itself.

When at last, after years and years of searching, he returned home, he immediately embarked upon another journey: a journey of the mind.

For as many years as he'd travelled abroad, he now remained home, locked in his basement laboratory, never emerging except to collect ever stranger and more exotic ingredients for his experiments. Powders ground from dried bugs. Roots of thousand-year-old trees. Liquids distilled from the blood of animals unknown outside the most remote jungles. Curious, quivering packages his housekeeper dared not peek inside.

At first, his housekeeper had asked about his work, but she soon learned not to question him. When he was younger, the doctor had loved nothing more than to discuss the mysteries of medicine. He had been kind and generous. Now, he was cruel and withdrawn.

He was interested only in himself. And yet he was no longer himself.

Finally, the time was nigh. The alchemist was about to complete his greatest task.

The raging furnace cast a scarlet glow over the cold, dungeon-like laboratory.

But it was a deeper, more internal – more *infernal* – fire that was reflected in the eyes of the man pacing to and fro across the stone floor.

A fire of ambition so great it had become madness.

Of greed so insatiable it had become a monster.

Never pausing, he checked pots and beakers and decanters, he gauged temperatures, he mixed liquids and poured powders – his impatience growing more feverish with every passing moment.

A door creaked open and a dusty shaft of light suddenly illuminated the laboratory.

"Shut the door, Fräulein! Now!" hissed the alchemist.

The door slammed shut, but not before the light landed on a large copper tub in the corner of the room. Dark, oozing sludge bubbled inside.

"What have I told you about interrupting me while I'm working? Are you stupid or merely obstinate?"

The woman addressed in this friendly fashion, his housekeeper, stood with her back to the now closed door, holding her hand to her nose.

"I'm terribly sorry, Herr Doctor," she said nervously. "But the stench – the neighbours are complaining…"

"Does it smell? I hadn't noticed," replied the alchemist coldly.

"It's suffocating! I fear for your health, Doctor."

The alchemist cackled, as if this were a great joke. "Oh, have no fear in that regard. I've never felt better, Fräulein. Never better."

"But all that…that horse dung…fermenting for

months! Even horses couldn't bear it. Please allow me to clean it up. What you could possibly want with—"

"Enough! Forget the neighbours. Soon they will worship and fear me and will dare not talk any longer."

"But you used to have their love – why now do you want their fear?"

"Silence, Fräulein! No more questions. Attend to your housekeeping."

"Very good, Doctor," said the housekeeper, clearly unsatisfied.

As she turned to go, a muffled cry echoed in the stone room. "Was that – it sounded like an animal," she said, peering into the darkness. "Or perhaps a—"

"Perhaps the smell is rather close in here," said the alchemist. "It seems to be affecting your imagination. Now get out!"

The housekeeper opened the door again and this time the beam of light fell on the alchemist.

"One more thing, Fräulein – I am no mere doctor any longer," he said, his face floating like some terrible apparition among the swirling particles of dust. "For I have learned secrets long buried under pyramids. Powers known only to the kings of ancient Egypt. From now on, you will address me as *Pharaoh*. No...*Lord Pharaoh*."

"Yes, Lord Pharaoh," said the housekeeper, hurrying out.

When the door closed behind the housekeeper, the newly crowned Lord Pharaoh hovered over the tub in the corner of the room. A large flask was half submerged in the sludge, its glass top glinting in the light of the fire.

Whimpering, gurgling sounds were emitted from the flask.

"Yes, my beautiful, my ugly little creature, your time has come," said the alchemist, pulling the dripping flask out of the tub and holding it high above his head.

"Oh, miracle of nature. Nay, miracle of man. Nay, miracle of my own hands!" he proclaimed. "The world will behold you with awe – and to me they will bow!"

The flask had a long, narrow neck and a large, rounded bottom. In the dim light, not much of its contents could be seen – except a tiny foot curled up under a little leg and an unexpectedly large nose pressed against the glass.

When Cass read the last line, Max-Ernest let out a little gasp.

Cass looked at him. "Scared?"

"Just keep reading...!" Max-Ernest peered over Cass's shoulder to see what came next.

"Can't I take a breath?" said Cass. "Besides, I thought you didn't believe in the homunculus, anyway."

"Yeah, but it's still a good story."

"Even though you don't think it's true? Then how come you always say you only like non-fiction?" Cass grinned. She was enjoying this.

"Just read already!"

"Here, you read – I'll hold the flashlight."

Part the Second

Ten years later...

The shimmering ball spun in the air, making a strange and wonderful sort of music. It seemed to incorporate all the sounds and voices of nature and yet to come from another world altogether.

Watching and listening from the opposite end of the King's throne room was a creature no less fantastical but far more earthly.

Normally, this creature – although called many names he had no name to call his own – hated crowds. They always stared and pointed and threw things. But he found if he concentrated on the wondrous, spinning instrument – if instrument indeed it was – then he could almost ignore the faces of the courtiers lined up on either side of him.

He felt a tug on his iron collar, followed by the sharp crack of a whip on his shoulder. His master was urging him forward.

"Your Majesty, Lord Pharaoh and his Homunculus!" a royal guard announced with a flourish.

The Homunculus – for he was the creature so described – shuffled forward, his shoulder still smarting with pain.

"Lord Pharaoh, is it?" asked the heavyset monarch sitting on the throne.* "And who granted you that title?"

"I beg your forgiveness, Sire. A village magician's folly – that is all," said Lord Pharaoh, bowing with uncharacteristic and clearly unfelt obsequiousness.

---

*IF THE TIME PERIOD NOTED BY THE AUTHOR OF THIS STORY IS CORRECT, THEN THE MONARCH MENTIONED HERE WOULD BE HENRY VIII OF ENGLAND – A KING FAMOUS FOR, AMONG OTHER THINGS, HAVING SIX WIVES, TWO OF WHOM HE BEHEADED.

The King nodded impatiently. "So this is the miraculous creation we have been hearing about, is it? The Bavarian marvel. He doesn't look like much – just another carnival dwarf."

Lord Pharaoh kicked the Homunculus from behind – whether to prove the King's point or to push him forward was unclear.

"If you please, Your Majesty, it is not so much how he looks, as how he was made…"

"Is it true he was made from dung?" asked the bejewelled Queen sitting by the King's side.

"Not from dung, Your Highness. In dung," Lord Pharaoh corrected. "He was incubated in a fertile mud that I confess was not entirely savoury."

"Disgusting! He's a monster!" said a pale woman standing nearby, the Queen's Lady-in-Waiting. "And so…small!"

"So what then is the recipe for this dung-dwarf?" asked the King, silencing the Lady-in-Waiting with a look. "They say you have discovered the secret of the Philosopher's Stone."

"Ah, a thousand pardons, but I cannot reveal that, Your Majesty. It may be that I am privy to secrets once known only to the Ancients. But such power, if it fell into the wrong hands—"

"Are you so sure your hands are the right ones?" asked the King sternly.

At this, his master's face turned red, the Homunculus observed. He knew he would pay for it later, but he couldn't help being pleased by the sight of his master's embarrassment.

"You jest, Your Majesty," said Lord Pharaoh, smiling to conceal his fury.

"I never jest – that is his job," said the King. He pointed to a small, wiry man who was now holding in his hand the strange musical ball that had so fascinated the Homunculus.

"Yes, His Majesty is not the Jester – for that is I," said the man, shaking the bells that dangled from his hat as if to demonstrate. "No more is His Majesty the *Ma-jester* – for that is my mother!"

He threw his ball into the air, punctuating his joke with a few notes of music. Then he burst out laughing, as if he tickled himself so much he couldn't help it.

"And what else of your creature – does he not speak?" asked the King, ignoring the Jester.

"No, sire," answered Lord Pharaoh curtly.

This was a sore subject for the alchemist. The Homunculus knew he would get extra lashings later just because the King had mentioned it.

Lord Pharaoh knew – or strongly suspected – that in fact his creation could speak. Once, when the Homunculus thought his master was away, he'd made the mistake of practising his speech at a slightly louder level than his usual whisper. His large, fleshy tongue made enunciation difficult, and he'd just managed to say the words "I am Cab—" when the door to his dungeon room flew open and his master entered.

Excited by the prospect of the fame and riches a talking Homunculus would bring, Lord Pharaoh demanded that he repeat the words. But the Homunculus never uttered another syllable again – even when he was alone. So little did he want to please his master, he was willing to endure years of beatings to avoid doing what his master wished.

The Jester studied the creature's reactions as his master spoke about him.

"Truly? Your carnival sensation – hath he not sensation?" asked the Jester. "He hath the nose of an elephant and the ears likewise. As for his eyes, we cannot help but see that he can see. His great tongue – does it only taste and never talk...?"

"Silence, Jester! We do not like the look of you, *Lord Pharaoh*," said the King, pronouncing the name with disdain. "But we think perhaps we are safer with you in our court than without. You will be our guest for as long as you wish to stay in our Kingdom."

"Thank you, Your Majesty," said Lord Pharaoh, bowing with as much humility as he could muster.

A royal guard stepped forward to escort them out.

"Where sleeps the Homunculus – with the servants?" asked the guard.

"With the livestock," said Lord Pharaoh, fixing the Homunculus with a hard, angry stare. "He is dumb like an animal so he will lie like an animal."

"Methinks he lies not like an animal, but like a rascal. And he be not dumb but would not speak," said the Jester with a twinkle in his eye. "If my thought be shrewd, he is no more fool than I!"

"But you are a fool, Fool!" said the King, laughing. "And you are hard on the poor creature."

"Not half so hard as his master. I inflict only puns; he inflicts punishments," said the Jester.

"Mind your own business, you meddlesome idiot!" hissed Lord Pharaoh, his mask of politeness slipping.

"But fooling is my business," said the Jester, tossing his ball into the air.

The Homunculus stared at the ball as it started once more to sing.

Max-Ernest turned the pages over. "I can't read if you don't shine the light on it..."

"Sorry, I just wanted to see the Sound Prism again," said Cass, unwrapping the object she had just dug out of the ground. It glowed in the darkness. "It's definitely the ball in the story. It has to be." She looked at Max-Ernest, waiting for him to contradict her.

"What? I agree. It's the ball in the story..."

Cass nodded in satisfaction and shone the flashlight on the manuscript again.

"But that doesn't mean the rest of the story is true."

"Why do you have to take the fun out of everything? It's like when you're reading a book, and you're really into it, and then at the end the writer says it was all a dream...I hate that!"

"I didn't say it was a dream."

Cass sighed. "Never mind. Just read." She flipped the manuscript back over for him and pointed to where they were on the page.

Part the Third

He might not get much sleep, but, at least, the Homunculus reflected, it wouldn't be a cold night.

The pigpen was nothing if not warm. The pigs were packed so tight they could barely turn around. Steam rose with every snort and kick and bowel movement.

Alas, warm did not mean comfortable. These pigs were not cuddly creatures. Instead, they had mottled bristly coats caked in mud and faeces, and they had hard hoofs and hungry mouths and long, fight-sharpened tusks.

In short, they were hogs. Swine.

The Homunculus cowered in the corner of the pen, waiting for the hogs to realize he wasn't one of them, and that he had quite possibly been left for them to eat. And yet he bore them no resentment. He felt an affectionate kinship with these beasts – and not only because their snouts resembled a bit his own. They too were helpless captives, condemned to feed on scraps, never satisfied, forever hungry.

Ah, hunger.

Hunger was his first memory, his only memory.

Before the red glow of the furnace there was hunger. Before the cold stone walls of his dungeon room there was hunger. Before the painful blows of his master there was hunger. Before the jeering crowds there was hunger. This gnawing pit inside him. This never-healing wound.

His master never fed him more than the bare minimum necessary to keep him alive – and sometimes not even that much. Often, he had to feed on the cockroaches that found their way into his room. If he was very, very lucky, and the housekeeper took pity on him, he might get a bone to gnaw on now and then. Bones were his favourite food. He sucked out the rich, buttery marrow as if his life depended on his extracting every last drop.

If only he could have some bone marrow now!

He looked at the hogs around him, weighing the odds: if he struck first, would he eat or would he be eaten?

Lost in his bloody reverie, he didn't notice the tune playing in the barnyard outside the pigpen until it was quite close. But his attention finally shifted to the ethereal music – so utterly unlike his muddy, grunting surroundings that it seemed to come from some other plane of existence altogether.

"Where art thou, my little 'Munculus?"

The Homunculus saw the Jester's face peering into the pen before the Jester saw him. Instinctively, he recoiled. No one had ever sought him out before except to throw rocks at him or worse.

"Ah, there you are – if not a pearl among swine, then certainly the Earl!" proclaimed the Jester with a laugh. "Here – I have brought you dinner. From the table of the King, no less!"

He tossed a turkey leg into the pen. The Homunculus caught it with his large hand – and immediately devoured it, bone and all.

"What? Nary a thank you?" teased the Jester. "Are you but a hog, after all?"

The Homunculus did not answer, but he looked up from his drumstick long enough to lock eyes with the Jester.

"Speak, Dung-boy! Prove thou art not pork but person!"

Addressed so directly, the Homunculus trembled uncontrollably. He did not how to react.

"Fear not your master. He is nowhere near. We are alone among animals. And unless they also speak, your secret is safe," said the Jester more gently.

"Come now, are we not alike, you and I?"

The Jester removed his hat, revealing for the

first time his ears – they were unusually large and pointy.

"Can you talk? If you can, I wouldst talk with you."

The Homunculus could not have said why he answered the Jester, when for years he had refused to speak. He was so unfamiliar with kindness that he did not recognize it; and yet he responded like a kitten to its first bowl of milk.

"I c-can," he whispered.

"What's that? I didn't hear you."

"I can," said the Homunculus more loudly. "I can speak."

"Well done!" said the Jester, smiling.

Hearing his first words of praise, the Homunculus's chest swelled with a feeling others might have known as pride. And something strange happened, something that had never happened before no matter how hungry he'd been or how hard his master had beaten him – he cried.

"Oh, talking is not so bad as that," said the Jester. "True, most people say only silly things when they speak. But it's easier to ignore them if you're saying silly things yourself."

The Homunculus stared, uncomprehending.

The Jester laughed. "So he can talk but he knows

not a joke. What use is that? But perhaps I can teach you to laugh. Fancy that – a Jester for a teacher! That makes for a joke already!"

Unfortunately, the Homunculus's unexpected speech had roused the hogs, and they were now closing in on him with hungry suspicion.

"Here, beat them back with this," said the Jester, throwing an oaken staff into the pen. "We must act fast if you are to escape. Methinks the hogs are easier to outrun than the King's hounds."

As soon as the Homunculus had extracted himself from the pigpen, the Jester stopped him with a raised hand. "Wait, my friend. What are you called? I cannot rescue a man if I know not his name!"

"But I…have no name," stammered the Homunculus.

"No name? Impossible. They must call you something."

"Only mean things. Awful things. Except sometimes…" The Homunculus hesitated.

"Yes?"

"Sometimes, the housekeeper, when my master is not around, she…she calls me her little Cabbage Face." The Homunculus covered his face with his large hand; years of taunting had made him immune to most embarrassments, but this was something else altogether.

"Cabbage Face, eh?" The Jester laughed. "It suits you perfectly!"

The Jester tossed his ball thoughtfully.

"Your master made you a monster. Your name will make you a man."

"So Cabbage Face is the homunculus's name!" Cass exclaimed.

"How 'bout that? I can't believe we didn't think of it," said Max-Ernest. "Or did we? Now, I can't remember…"

"Do you think that's true – that your name makes you who you are?"

"No. That's silly. Like, if your name is Dakota, you don't suddenly turn into a state. I have two names and I'm not two people."

Yes, but he often acted like he was two people, Cass wanted to say. Instead, she asked, "Why don't you think Lord Pharaoh gave the homunculus a name? You know, like Frankenstein or something."

"Actually, Frankenstein wasn't Frankenstein's name. He was just a monster – Frankenstein was the man who made him. You know, Dr. Frankenstein.

So that would be like calling the homunculus Lord Pharaoh. Which would be kind of funny considering the way he treated him. I mean in the story, not that he really—"

"Yeah, I get it!" said Cass. "Let me read the last part..."

Part Conclusive

It is said that a Homunculus must serve his maker – for that is the nature of a Homunculus.

But it is also said that if the maker takes advantage of his servant, and treats him too much like a slave, then the Homunculus will take vengeance on his maker and run away – for that, too, is the nature of a Homunculus.

The Homunculus called Cabbage Face ran far, far away from his master, Lord Pharaoh. Never resting, he crossed oceans and deserts, mountain ranges and city slums. Until the day Lord Pharaoh caught up with him and the Homunculus at last confronted the man who should have been to him a father, but instead was a mortal enemy.

When the Homunculus had vanquished his master, the Homunculus buried his remains far from the eyes of those who knew him. So that never again would another person – whether for greed or glory or science – repeat the mistakes his master had made, the Homunculus buried with him the means of the Homunculus's own making: the alchemist's secret notes and diaries, his recipes and ingredients, and the leftovers of his awful experiments.

And then the Homunculus laid himself down across the grave of Lord Pharaoh. Henceforward, he would protect the grave from the world – and, more importantly, the world from the grave.

Yet, in all those years, and for ever after, the Homunculus never forgot the Fool who freed him. Before he ran, he made to this funny man a solemn vow: that when the Ball called, he would come.

And he always did. He always has.

The End

Cass put down the last page in wonder.

"So do you think the Sound Prism really has the power to call the homunculus?" she asked.

"Well, it would be sort of crazy if it did. And kind of scary. But it looks like Mr. Wallace thinks it's all made up—"

He shone the flashlight on the back of the last page, where there was a handwritten note:

The Legend of Cabbage Face, indeed!

It is well known that the author of this story, my predecessor's predecessor's predecessor, fancied himself a great writer and novelist. Here, I fear, he let his literary ambitions – and his imagination – get away from him.

The fact that the Jester appears really to be a jester proves this "legend" to be just that. A hat with bells? Ridiculous! If we know anything, we know that our noble founder was a man of science, not a fool!

And a talking homunculus? Sentimental claptrap! If such a creature ever existed, he must have been a monster, incapable of thought or feeling.

Still, we know that the Masters of the Midnight Sun search even now for Lord Pharaoh's grave. So perhaps there is a grain of truth here, after all.

Deserves further study. – W. W. W. III

"Mr. Wallace is a sourpuss!" said Cass when she'd finished reading.

"Come on, be honest – you don't really believe

that some alchemist made a little guy out of horse...
poop...five hundred years ago, do you?"

"*In* poop. Not *out of* poop."

"And he's still alive? And he even talks?"

"I don't know. All I know is we promised to find
him, whether he talks or not. Are you going to help
or aren't you?"

Cass looked at him expectantly. She needed Max-
Ernest in fighting shape. Or whatever the Max-Ernest
version of fighting shape was. She couldn't afford to
have such a waffling, moody partner.

Max-Ernest nodded and extended his arm.

This was serious business, and they both knew it.
Whoever or whatever the homunculus was or wasn't,
the fact remained that Dr. L and Ms. Mauvais were
looking for him – and that alone made their job
extremely important.

And extremely dangerous.

They shook hands, both beginning at last to feel
the chill.

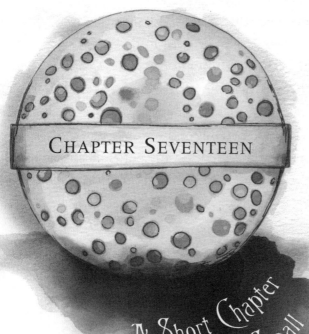

CHAPTER SEVENTEEN

A Short Chapter About a Small Matter

fter Max-Ernest had gone, Cass stood for a moment in the Barbie Graveyard contemplating what they'd read.

How odd that the Jester had pointy ears... She wondered if Max-Ernest had noticed.

A breeze rustled through the yard, stirring the autumn leaves. And a small piece of paper fluttered in the air, landing at Cass's foot.

It must have slipped out of the wand, thought Cass.

She shone her flashlight on the paper as she picked it up off the ground. It was a rather formal-looking document:

STATE BOARD OF HEALTH
DIVISION OF VITAL STATISTICS
Certificate of Live Birth

I'm sorry I can't tell you the name of the girl listed on the birth certificate. Or who her parents were. Or what city she was born in. But it hardly matters; Cass didn't recognize the names herself.

And yet something about the birth certificate bothered her – what?

Of course – the birth date! It was the same as

her own. What a strange coincidence. Almost like discovering a long-lost twin sister.

So why had the birth certificate been in the Sound Prism file?

A dreadful realization struck her: the Terces Society had made a mistake. They thought she was this other girl.

It was the other girl, not Cass, who was supposed to have the Sound Prism. It was the other girl, not Cass, who was supposed to hunt the homunculus.

Cass knew she ought to tell Pietro right away.

But what if he took the mission away from her? She couldn't bear the thought.

What good would that do, anyway?

Obviously, he didn't know where the other girl was or he would have given the Sound Prism to her.

On the other hand, if Cass found the homunculus, the Terces Society would be so grateful, it wouldn't matter who she was.

Staving off her pangs of conscience, Cass slipped the birth certificate into her pocket and walked back into the house.

CHAPTER SIXTEEN

Garbage Face

66 "T ommy! Tommy!"

The cries of Tommy's older brother ring in our ears – blocking out the song of the Sound Prism.

We are at the lake again. But on the other side.

Here we spy a little boy, maybe two or three years old. Tommy – we assume it's Tommy – is about twenty metres from the tent, just out of view of the older boys. He appears totally carefree, laughing and playing among the wet rocks. He runs this way and that, skirting the edge of the lake, oblivious to the possibility of falling onto something sharp or drowning in the icy water.

Thankfully, he turns away and starts running in another direction altogether. What's drawing his attention – something in the air maybe? A dragonfly? At any rate, he heads away from the lake and – oh no! – straight into the woods.

He disappears into a tunnel of brush so small it looks as though it was made for him. Most people wouldn't be able to follow him into the tunnel...

But we have no trouble. We don't even have to duck.

Soon the undergrowth opens up and young Tommy finds himself in a forest glade. A beam of sunlight peeks through the clouds and lights up the trees. Delighted, he spreads his arms and spins around and around until he falls dizzy in a heap on the ground.

In the background, the older boys' voices are heard again, but fainter than before. "Tom-my! Tom-my!" they cry. "Where are you? Come back!"

Tommy giggles and staggers to his feet. They're playing his favourite game – hide-and-seek! But where to hide? He looks around. There are almost too many options. Big rocks. Giant ferns. Fallen logs.

A tall fir tree has been hollowed out by fire, leaving a small charred cave at the base of the tree – perfect.

He runs stumblingly towards the tree. In his haste, he doesn't notice us darting past him.

Nor does he notice the sound his footsteps are making. It is the sound of crunching bones. The whole glade is littered with them.

By the time Tommy reaches the tree, we are inside, looking up at him. We let out a low, guttural grrrrrrrowl.

"Kitty...?" he asks. "Doggy...? Doggy go ruff-ruff!"

His pudgy hand reaches into the hole, and—

Cass woke up gnawing on her own hand, her pillow covered with slobber.

She shuddered in horror. What had happened to the little boy?

Cass jumped out of bed, trying to shake off her dream. When had she started believing her dreams were real, anyway? Probably, there was no boy and never had been. According to Max-Ernest, there might not even be a homunculus.

And even if there were a homunculus, according to that birth certificate, she was the wrong girl to be dreaming about him.

In any case, she had a job to do.

They'd decided the next step was to come up with a list of likely locations for the homunculus. After all, he hadn't come when she'd played the song of the Sound Prism the first time. Maybe they needed to be closer to the homunculus for him to hear.

Suddenly, Cass stiffened: on her Wall of Horrors, directly in front of her, was her dream. Well, the lake in her dream. In black and white. And blurry. But unmistakable nonetheless. There were the same jagged mountains in the background. And the same graveyard on the side of the lake.

BEAR OR BIGFOOT?
Three-Year-Old Boy Survives Mountain Encounter

She'd cut the article out of the newspaper a month or so ago, realizing that she was unsure how to respond to a bear attack (was it true you were supposed to play dead?), and she'd been disappointed that the article provided no instructions.

With an uncomfortable prickling sensation in the back of her neck, she reread the article now:

WHISPER LAKE – On Monday, forest service officials reported a mountain miracle.

For the last few weeks, a very hungry bear has been haunting Whisper Lake, a popular campsite for backpackers. According to a local ranger, the bear steals food and garbage from all the campers who stay at the lake – no matter how well it's hidden.

"Eats everyone's dinner – the sneak! Getting ready to hibernate for winter, I guess. A long winter," said the ranger.

Locals had taken to calling him Bigfoot – because of his big appetite. And because, until this past weekend, nobody had seen the elusive ursine in person – only his tracks.

But then three-year-old Thomas Xxxxxx went missing at Whisper Lake.

When his older brother told their parents that

Thomas was lost, the family immediately sought help. For three hours, rangers searched, to no avail. They all feared the worst.

"Then Tommy came stumbling back into the campsite – laughing like nothing was wrong," said his brother.

Tommy said he'd been playing in the woods with a little monster. Rangers are certain the monster was in fact the bear because of the name Tommy had for him, "Garbage Face"...

Garbage Face!?

It couldn't be a coincidence. It was too close to Cabbage Face.

The question in Cass's mind was: which came first?

Did she dream about Whisper Lake only because she'd read the article? In which case the bear was just a bear.

Or were her dreams telling her something, showing her something, something...she didn't know what the word was...else?

A dream was the fulfilment of a wish, Max-Ernest had said.

Her dream was so horrifying that it was hard to imagine that it fulfilled anything other than her worst fears. On the other hand, she *had* wished to locate the homunculus – could her dream have located him for her?

There was only one way to find out.

CHAPTER FIFTEEN

Pop Quiz

You *have five minutes to complete the following quiz. No flipping back through what you've read. Write your answers on a separate piece of paper, using HB pencils only, please.*

A homunculus is:

a. my little brother

b. a large glob pulled out of your nose

c. a wrestling hold

A sea anemone eats with its:

a. mouth

b. tentacles

c. I can't say in polite company

The Sound Prism is:

a. a special mental trick for locking out the sound of your parents yelling at you

b. an album by the seventies rock band Pink Floyd

c. an idea that makes no sense

Sigmund Freud said:

a. A dream is the fulfilment of a wish.

b. Beans, beans, the magical fruit, the more you eat, the more you toot.

c. I know you are, but what am I?

Feedback is:

a. vomit

b. a really horrible sound

c. when I tell Pseudonymous Bosch his book stinks

What is the Secret?

a. the secret of immortality

b. never take your eyes off your opponent

c. a lot of butter

What happens next in this book?

a. how should I know? You're the writer!

b. if I told you, I'd have to kill you

c. nothing good

Okay. Time's up. Pencils down.

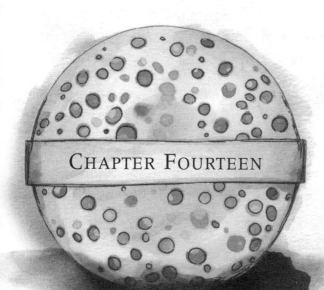

CHAPTER FOURTEEN

Quaking
or Trembling

One of the first rules of parenting – or so I hear – is that you should always be consistent with your child. If you tell your daughter she's grounded for a month, well, then ground her for a month. Otherwise, she'll lose respect for you and she'll run wild like a heathen.

Cass's mother, I'm sure, was fully aware of this rule. She probably had every intention of keeping her word in regard to Cass's freedom or lack thereof. But you know what they say about good intentions.

By the time Cass asked her mother if she could go camping with her grandfathers, her mother was itching for Cass to get out of the house just as much as Cass was. That's the only explanation I can think of for why Cass's mother didn't instantly refuse Cass's request.

Cass: "It'll still be like I'm grounded – I mean, they're practically my guardians."

Mom: "You won't have any fun, right?"

Cass: "Promise! No fun at all!"

Mom: "And you won't have any desserts while you're gone?"

Cass: "None!"

Mom: "You won't even put any chocolate chips in your trail mix?"

Cass: "None!"

Mom: "Not even any peanut-butter chips?"

Cass: "None! I'll put raisins in. And you knowhow much I hate them. It'll be the worst punishment ever!"

Mom: "And you'll do everything Larry and Wayne tell you?"

Cass: "Everything!"

Mom: "Except when it's crazy or dangerous or they're just getting sidetracked because there's something they want for their store?"

Cass: "Except then!"

Mom: "Even though that's pretty much all the time?"

Cass: "Even though."

Mom: "And you won't run off without telling anyone – on this trip or ever again?"

Cass: "I won't. I promise."

Mom: "Okay, then. You can go. But don't tell anyone I let you!"

Cass: "Thanks, Mom. You're the best. By the way, you have to watch Sebastian while we're gone. That's the only way I could get Larry and Wayne to go – bye!"

Mom: "Cass, come back here right now! I am not changing some blind dog's diaper – and I thought you said *they* asked *you* to go!"

Cass: "Sorry, can't hear you!"

* * *

Even on a good day, the firehouse was so crammed it was hard to move around. Now that it was a staging ground for a backpacking trip, it looked like a refugee camp after a hurricane.

Max-Ernest lugged in all his camping equipment – including two brand-new backpacks, one red, one blue – only to find himself stuck right inside the door; there was just too much stuff for him to move further.

Yo-Yoji was already there, standing by Cass's side. He looked at Max-Ernest like Max-Ernest was insane.

"Dude, why do you have *two* backpacks?"

Wait. Halt. Freeze.

Let me guess: you're wondering what Yo-Yoji was doing at the firehouse. Was he actually invited to go backpacking with them, you want to know.

I don't blame you – I'd be surprised, too.

Here's what happened:

The three kids had met again in detention the day after Cass decided they had to go to Whisper Lake.

While Max-Ernest furiously redid his maths homework (even though it was correct the first time), Cass peppered Yo-Yoji with questions about backpacking:

"What kind of mosquito repellent do you use?"

"What kind of water purifier do you like the best?"

"Have you ever been caught in a storm?"

Yo-Yoji was happy to answer. However, if Cass and Max-Ernest were going backpacking, he said, he was going with them. Indeed, he downright insisted.

"I know you guys are going on some kind of cool secret adventure, and I don't care if I'm invited or not – this time you're not leaving me like at the tide pools, yo!"

Of course, Cass denied that they were going on a secret adventure, but instead of trying to dissuade him, she turned to Max-Ernest:

"What do you think – should we let him? I mean, he's gone backpacking before and we haven't. What if we get separated from my grandfathers? I have my compass and maps and everything, but it's different to have somebody with experience."

I don't know how Max-Ernest would have reacted if Cass had said straight out that she wanted Yo-Yoji to come on their trip, but by appealing to his logic, she'd put him in a corner.

All Max-Ernest could say was: "That makes sense."

"Cool," said Yo-Yoji. "Everybody else in this school

sucks. They're all boring Amber clones. You guys are the only interesting ones."

Cass's ears had reddened – or at least pinked – hearing this praise.

Max-Ernest had remained absolutely expressionless, as if he'd decided he was done with emotion altogether.

Now, back to the fire station:

As they assembled for the backpacking trip, Cass was on tenterhooks, anxious to see how well – or not – the two boys would get along. I think that's why she intervened so quickly when Yo-Yoji asked about Max-Ernest's two backpacks.

"He has to do everything in twos 'cause of his parents – it's kind of complicated," she said, stepping between them. "But seriously, Max-Ernest, why don't you just leave one? Your parents won't even know."

"Yeah, but *I'll* know. And if I pick one and not the other, it's like—" Max-Ernest shuddered. "Anyway, they both have wheels."

"Those aren't even the right kind for backpacking," said Yo-Yoji. "This is what you're supposed to have—" He picked up his backpack and handed it to Max-Ernest, who handed it right back without allowing himself to show any interest.

"See how light it is," Yo-Yoji continued. "My parents are really strict about packing. I'm not allowed to carry anything heavy. Like toothpaste. Or changes of underwear."

"That's gross," said Cass.

Yo-Yoji laughed. "I was just kidding – partly. We're allowed underwear. But my parents are pretty serious. Everything we eat has to be freeze-dried."

"Well, don't tell your parents, but we're going to be eating a little better than that," said Grandpa Larry, who was tying a big pot to an old army backpack. "Even if it means sweating on the way up."

There are any number of Whisper Lakes in the world. Perhaps not as many as there are Emerald Lakes or Mirror Lakes, but plenty nevertheless. Look on any given map and you have a good chance of finding one.

That is why I feel no compunction about naming the lake to which our young heroes now headed. Furthermore, I do not hesitate to tell you that their destination was high, high up in the mountains; after all, a multitude of lakes exist at high elevations.

What I will *not* tell you is where the trailhead was. Only that it was in the foothills of a famously rugged mountain range, separated from a small dirt parking lot by a deep gorge.

As soon as Grandpa Wayne's truck pulled into the parking lot, Cass, Max-Ernest and Yo-Yoji hopped out.*

"You better go now, if you have to," said Cass to Max-Ernest. She pointed to the decrepit outhouses by the side of the lot. "'Cause once we're in the mountains, you have to dig a hole and bury it. And you have to make sure you're far away from any lakes or rivers, otherwise you contaminate the water. Right?" she asked Yo-Yoji, eager to show she knew what she was doing – even if she'd never been backpacking before.

He nodded. "Yeah, pretty much."

Alarmed, Max-Ernest eyed the outhouses. Their doors were half open, flies buzzing in and out.

"We're just going for two nights, right?" he asked, clearly wondering whether he could hold it in the whole time.

After they'd all braved the port-o-potties – even

---

*GRANDPA WAYNE HAD AN OLD PICKUP TRUCK THAT WAS HIS PRIDE AND JOY BUT THAT WAS ALWAYS IN A STATE OF HALF-REPAINTED SEMI-DISREPAIR. CASS'S MOTHER, WHO CONSIDERED THE TRUCK AN "ACCIDENT WAITING TO HAPPEN", STRICTLY FORBADE CASS FROM RIDING IN THE FLATBED IN THE BACK – WHICH, ACCORDING TO CASS'S MOTHER, WAS NOT ONLY DANGEROUS BUT ILLEGAL. I HATE TO GIVE CASS AWAY, BUT THINK ABOUT IT – IT WOULD HAVE BEEN HARD TO FIT THREE KIDS IN FRONT WITH TWO ADULTS, EVEN ON A BENCH SEAT.

Max-Ernest, who'd sounded from the outside oddly like he was reciting multiplication tables while he went to the bathroom – they hoisted their backpacks on their backs.

"Here goes nothing!" said Grandpa Wayne.

"Just breathe in that fresh mountain air," said Grandpa Larry. "It's like fuel – it'll take us all the way to the top!"

A wooden footbridge spanned the gorge, leading to the trail. Next to the bridge, a message board stood under a wooden overhang. Flyers warned against bears as well as various other high-country hazards. "No campfires?!" said Larry. "How're we going to make s'mores?"

"We better not," said Cass. "You want to start a forest fire? Plus, campfires pollute. Do you know that in Yosemite it gets smoggy from all the campfires?"

"We've been making fires in Yosemite since before you were born, young lady," said Grandpa Larry.

"I hope you're not going to be one of *those* kind of campers," said Grandpa Wayne. "Or I'm turning around right now."

Yo-Yoji laughed. Cass marched forward with her nose in the air.

But as she crossed the bridge, she slowed, looking down at the tops of ferns and a small waterfall that might have been a mighty force in the springtime but right now didn't roar so much as purr, lulling the innocent passer-by.

Did the water flow all the way from Whisper Lake? Cass wondered. What would they find at the end of this hike? Friend or enemy? Man or monster? Or would they only find a mockery of her dreams?

Cass reached behind her and felt the bottom corner of her backpack: yes, the Sound Prism was still there. Why did she feel as though it might disappear at any second?

After a short climb out of the gorge, the trail rose gently for the first kilometre or so, wending its way through a forest of pale-trunked trees that flickered in and out of the shadows like an old black-and-white filmstrip; the silver-dollar-sized leaves rustling as if other, much larger beings were walking among the trees.

"Quaking aspen," said Grandpa Larry.

"Also known as trembling aspen," said Grandpa Wayne.

Soon, the hikers emerged from the aspens to find themselves walking across a golden meadow surrounded by pine trees. Although it was autumn, a few wild flowers remained, and dandelion spores floated lazily in the sunshine.

"See, the mountains aren't only about survival," said Grandpa Larry to Cass.

Cass rolled her eyes, but there was no denying the beauty in front of them.

By the time they'd crossed the meadow, their shoes were muddy and the mood of the hike had changed; they stared up at a steep, wide, and totally bare mountainside. The trail zigzagged across it.

Switchbacks.

A word sure to strike terror in the heart of any hiker.

As they traversed back and forth, inching up the mountain, Grandpa Larry tried to entertain them with stories about previous travels. Stories with which Grandpa Wayne invariably had some minor quibble.

Like: "Oh, come on, Larry, you know you were never in the Peace Corps!"

Or: "But you couldn't have hiked the *entire* Andes range – it stretches all the way to the bottom of South America!"

Or: "Funny, the way I remember it, *I* was the one who fixed the Land Rover *and* diverted the lions!"

But eventually, even Cass's grandfathers fell silent.

Max-Ernest, who was pulling one of his backpacks behind him even as he carried the other on his back, looked like he was having the hardest time. "So, if you're such a backpacking expert, how much longer do you think it is to the top?" he asked Yo-Yoji between big sucks of air.

"I dunno, I've never been here before."

"Well, how much further then?"

Yoji looked up the mountain. "Like five hundred metres?"

"So how long should that take us?"

"I dunno – twenty minutes?"

Max-Ernest kept checking his watch.

"Okay, it's twenty minutes, and we're not at the top," he announced twenty minutes later.

"No kidding. I guess I was wrong."

"Well, how long do you think now?"

"I don't know. It's hard to tell 'cause of all the false peaks. Ten minutes maybe."

"It's ten minutes," announced Max-Ernest ten minutes later, to Yo-Yoji's extreme annoyance. "I thought you were the backpacking exp—"

"Hey, Max-Ernest – you want my pedometer?" Cass interrupted before he could finish his sentence.

Max-Ernest shrugged unpleasantly but he took the device out of her hand.

"You put it on your shoe and it says how far you've gone."

"I know," said Max-Ernest, attaching the pedometer

to his shoelaces. He pushed ahead, dragging his second backpack behind him.

Cass watched anxiously. Should she say something more? She decided to leave him alone. Besides, she was breathing so hard, she couldn't really talk.

As it turned out, it took another thirty minutes – and another "one point two nine kilometres", according to Max-Ernest, who'd checked the pedometer at every step – to get to the top of the switchbacks.

It took three more hours – and "four point one kilometres" – to get to Whisper Lake.

They reached the graveyard first. It was to the right of the trail sloping up behind the remains of a stone gate. Slabs of broken rock – once tombstones – dotted the hillside. A few crumbling statues stood under the spindly pine trees.

"Who'd get buried all the way up here?" Grandpa Wayne asked. "Miners?"

Grandpa Larry shook his head. "This cemetery is hundreds of years old – there was no mining community here then. Very curious. We'll have to come back tomorrow—"

Cass stopped by the gate as her grandfathers and Yo-Yoji forged ahead. Max-Ernest lingered with her.

"Is this it?"

She nodded, picking up a handful of pine needles,

as if to confirm that they were real. "It's just like in my dream. We must be in the right place."

She waited for Max-Ernest's rebuttal, but he just shivered, evidently as spooked as she was. Nobody had been buried in the graveyard for a very long time. But the sense of death still lived.

"C'mon," said Cass.

Yo-Yoji was looking at them curiously from down the trail, and she didn't want to arouse his suspicions.

When the hikers first caught sight of the lake through the trees, the sun was setting, the lake a sparkling gold. But as they walked closer, the sun disappeared, and the lake turned lead grey and ominous – as if the gold had been some kind of alchemy at work and now they were seeing the lake's true colours.

Across the lake, mountains climbed steeply, treeless and bare save for a few luminous patches of snow. At the top: the jagged, toothlike peaks Cass remembered from her nightmares.

They chose a campsite that backed up against a small cliff with roots dangling out of it.

"How about over here by this tree stump?" Cass asked.

Yo-Yoji shook his head. "Too many rocks. Look at

that one, right in the middle—" He pointed to a piece of granite sticking up out of the ground. In his other hand, he held his parents' bright yellow backpacking tent – still rolled up.

"Max-Ernest, what do you think?" Cass asked.

"Whatever you guys think." He continued looking at the boulder-strewn lake shore about ten metres below.

"Well, I think this is perfect because we can say whatever we want without them hearing us." Cass nodded towards the opposite end of the campsite where her grandfathers were erecting their tent – a patchy contraption in fading camouflage fabric that billowed dust whenever they touched it.

"Okay, but don't blame me if you can't sleep 'cause there's a rock in your back," said Yo-Yoji.

After they put up their tent and pulled their sleeping bags out of their stuff sacks to air, Grandpa Larry handed Cass a length of rope and a pillowcase, and he asked the kids to collect all the food they wouldn't be eating for dinner.

"We have to tie the other end of the rope to a rock, so we can throw it over a tree branch and pull it up," Cass explained to Max-Ernest, checking for Yo-Yoji's reaction.

He nodded. "Like a piñata."

"You guys do it – I'm not very good at throwing," said Max-Ernest, stepping out of the way, still refusing to let himself participate, or even smile.

As Cass and Yo-Yoji took turns trying to toss the rope over a tree limb, a ranger reined his horse next to their campsite and saluted them. "Make sure you get that bag good and high. I suppose you heard some bear's really been having at it lately."

Cass's grandfathers joined them, and the ranger asked to see their wilderness permit – which, I'm surprised and delighted to report, Larry and Wayne were able to supply.

"Alrighty, then, be safe, y'all! It's a bit nippy because it's late in the season – but on the bright side you've got the place to yourselves... Hey, before I go, anyone know why they call it Whisper Lake?" The ranger smiled at the kids. "If you've ever been fishing early in the morning, then you can probably guess. It's because of the way sounds – even the softest little whispers – carry across the water. Most lakes it only happens at dawn – but happens here in the evenings, too. So be careful what you say, if you don't want anyone to hear your secrets!"*

---

*I WILL EXPLAIN THIS PHENOMENON IN THE APPENDIX FOR THE SCIENTIFICALLY CURIOUS (OR FOR ANYONE WHO HAS FINISHED THE BOOK AND DOESN'T HAVE ANYTHING BETTER TO THINK ABOUT).

He waved and gave his horse a kick.

Yo-Yoji looked at Cass and Max-Ernest. "Well…?"

"Well, what?" asked Cass.

"Are you going to tell me what we're doing here, or you still keeping everything secret?"

"We're just going camping – that's all," said Max-Ernest.

"Yeah, right. I thought we were friends…"

"We are," said Cass.

"But not enough to tell me…"

Visibly disappointed, Yo-Yoji headed down to the lake shore and started skipping rocks.

Cass and Max-Ernest watched, not moving.

"I feel bad – I wish we could tell him," said Cass.

"Well, we can't!"

As the ripple rings spread across the water, the plunking of the rocks echoed in the twilight.

CHAPTER THIRTEEN*

Summoning
a Ghost

*IN MY LAST BOOK, I CROSSED OUT CHAPTER THIRTEEN TO WARD
OFF BAD LUCK. IT DIDN'T WORK. SO THIS TIME LET'S KEEP THE
CHAPTER IN — AND SEE WHAT HAPPENS.

Yo-Yoji had a mummy-style sleeping bag with a pull cord that closed up the top. He liked to burrow inside and pull the cord as tight as possible, leaving only a tiny circle of light to spy out of.

Tonight, though, he found himself tossing and turning because he was too hot; he loosened the cord and unzipped the side of the bag to let a little air in.

Half asleep, he stuck his head out and looked around the tent. It was hard to see in the dim light but – was it possible the other sleeping bags were empty?

"Cass? Max-Ernest?" he whispered.

Getting nervous, he patted their sleeping bags.

Where were they?

He forced himself to sit up and think.

He knew there was something they weren't telling him, and whatever it was, he suspected that it might be dangerous.

Had something happened? Could they have been kidnapped? Or worse?

Then he remembered that they'd insisted that he sleep in the back of the tent so they could both be nearer the entrance.

Max-Ernest: "I have claustrophobia!" Cass: "I pee ten times a night!"

He'd accepted their arguments at the time, but

now he realized the real reason they wanted him in the back: they'd been planning to sneak out while he was sleeping.

The moon had not yet risen, but the stars were bright enough to see by, and Cass and Max-Ernest had no trouble finding the boulder they'd picked out earlier in the evening. It was the size of a truck and had the advantage of being visible from all sides of the lake.

When they climbed to the top, they found themselves on a natural platform, roomy enough for two kids – and, if all went according to plan, one homunculus – to stand comfortably.

Down below, they would see their campsite, and beyond the campsite the graveyard, shrouded in darkness.

To the other side of their campsite was the lake, ink black save for the occasional twinkle of a reflected star. The lake was ringed by pine trees, the front row in a natural outdoor amphitheatre. Above the trees, the silvery mountains rose on all sides. It was as if Cass and Max-Ernest were onstage in front of an audience of giants.

Cass pulled the Sound Prism out of her jacket

pocket. "I feel like we're trying to summon a ghost," she said.

"They usually do that with crystal balls, not sound balls," Max-Ernest pointed out. "Not that I believe in them – I mean, in ghosts. Crystal balls are real, obviously. They just don't necessarily—"

"Yeah, I get it. You ready?"

He was.

"Okay, here goes nothing."

Cass stood on the edge of the boulder and tossed the Sound Prism into the air. But she was so nervous that she let go too early; it was like trying to serve a tennis ball, right when the PE teacher is watching you.

The Sound Prism emitted only a short whistle before she had to lurch forward and catch it.

Taking a breath, she tried again, this time releasing the ball directly upwards. It climbed higher than it ever had before, playing its haunting tune under the night sky.

When the ball crested, it seemed for a moment to hover, singing, before falling back into Cass's hand.

Cass tossed again – even higher this time. And the music grew more forceful, echoing across the lake, from mountain to mountain, until it sounded like an entire celestial chorus was singing in harmony.

They listened in wonder.

"If he's here, he'll definitely hear that – he won't even need to see us," said Max-Ernest. "He'll find us by echolocation – you know, like bats."

"I just hope my grandfathers don't hear us first," said Cass.

She peered down at the campsite: no movement – so far.

The last echoes of the Sound Prism died away.

Then:

"Shh – what's that?" whispered Cass.

There was a scrabbling sound, as if something were trying to climb up the boulder. They waited, tense—

Until Yo-Yoji pulled himself up onto the boulder and joined them.

"Wow!" he said, catching his breath. "That Cabbage Face song sounded so trippy – and kinda beautiful!"

They exhaled – relieved and at the same time chagrined to see him.

"So let me guess – this is a secret meeting."

Silence. Cass and Max-Ernest looked at each other.

"C'mon, dudes. I hiked all the way up here, same as you. And now you're not gonna let me in on the fun part?!"

"Well..." Cass hesitated. "You know how before you were joking about a secret society?"

"Cass, we can't! What about the oath?!"

"Well, we never took it, did we? Besides, I'm sure Pietro would understand if it was the only way we could catch the homunculus."

Max-Ernest held his head in his hands. It was too late now.

Yo-Yoji looked from Cass to Max-Ernest and back. "What's a *homunculus*?"

Cass calmly explained to Yo-Yoji that they were looking for a five-hundred-year-old creature made in a bottle.

"Ha, good one! You should write some songs for my band."

"No, I'm serious," said Cass.

Yo-Yoji stared. "Whoa. You're even crazier than I thought."

Max-Ernest, previously the naysayer, defended their sanity:

"Just because nobody knows about something, doesn't mean it can't happen. If you'd seen the Midnight Sun – well, some of them are almost that old!"

"If you say so…" Yo-Yoji clearly didn't believe them, but he seemed ready to be proved wrong. Or up for a thrill, anyway. "So, then, what happens now?"

"We wait," said Cass.

As she spoke, a sudden breeze whipped across the lake.

For a second, all their senses were on alert.

But nothing happened. Nobody arrived.

Except a chipmunk, who scurried under their feet and then dived under the boulder.

After that, a profound silence fell over the lake.

If you've ever spent the night camping in the mountains or out in the desert, you know this kind of silence.

A silence so total it makes you think you've never experienced silence before.

A silence that makes certain kinds of people feel like they have to talk in order to fill it.

People like Max-Ernest.

After about three or four or five (or was it only two?) unbearable minutes of quiet, he pointed at the sky. "Look at all the stars – I don't think I've ever seen so many. There's Venus – not that it's a star, it's a planet. And the Milky Way – which is a galaxy, so it's a bunch of stars. And the Big Dipper – which is a constellation. And the Little Dipper. And Orion's Belt. And..." He trailed off, overwhelmed by the sheer scope of the exercise.

"Hey," he picked up after a moment, "did you ever think about the fact that you're just a speck on a planet that's just a speck in a galaxy that's just a speck in a universe that's probably just a speck in the fingernail of some giant alien being that's too big to even imagine? How 'bout that?"

"Can't we just concentrate on the little alien being we're waiting for?" Cass asked.

"You know, technically, he's not an alien, he's – yeah, okay, fine."

And they waited.

And waited.

Jumping every time the wind picked up or one or the other of them made the slightest movement.

An hour passed.

"Okay, that was fun and all. But maybe it's time to face it, your little homunkey isn't coming," said Yo-Yoji.

"Or else he came and he got scared. Because there are so many of us," said Max-Ernest, eyeing Yo-Yoji meaningfully.

"That's a good point," said Cass. "You guys go into the tent. I'll stay out here and keep waiting."

"All right," said Max-Ernest, already looking for the best way down. "Maybe that's a good—"

"No, it's not!" said Yo-Yoji. "We can't leave her out here alone."

"Why – okay, you're right." Max-Ernest turned

back, shooting an annoyed glance at Yo-Yoji. "We can't leave you, Cass. It's not safe. Anything could happen."

"You mean like a homunculus could come?"

"Exactly."

"Isn't that why we're here?"

"Yeah, but they're some real-life scary creatures out here, too," said Yo-Yoji. "Remember the bear?"

They waited another twenty minutes or so. Their teeth started to chatter.

"C'mon, let's go," said Cass.

Something inside her had just given up.

What had made her think they'd find the homunculus at Whisper Lake, anyway? Her dream, that was all. A dream she'd probably had only because she'd read the article on her wall.

The bear was just a bear, after all.

Bleak with disappointment, she took a last look around, then followed the others off the boulder...

Unaware that every sound they made was being heard all across the lake.

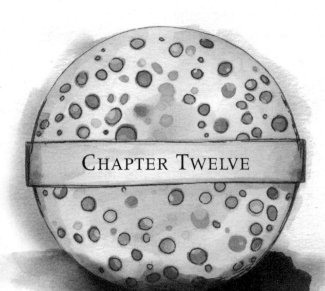

CHAPTER TWELVE

Man, Bear
or Monster?

Cass awoke to find the interior of their tent filled with a soft yellow glow.

Was it daylight already?

She propped her head up and looked around. Yo-Yoji and Max-Ernest were both fast asleep in their sleeping bags.

Max-Ernest still wore his watch: *three a.m.*

Craning her neck, Cass peered out through the tiny space left at the top of the tent's zipper.

A full moon hung above the mountains. It shone like a searchlight across the lake.

Snap!

Cass's ears tingled. Her hairs stood on end.

Snap! Snap!

Twigs breaking – that was the sound.

Was it...? Could it be...?

Afraid to move, Cass crouched on top of her sleeping bag.

She knew she was being silly; she should go look outside. This was why she had come. To meet the homunculus – if it really was he.

And if it wasn't – well, what was there to be afraid of?

Unless it was the bear.

Probably, Larry or Wayne had got up to go pee. It was one of them stepping on the twigs – it had to be.

But it would be comforting to know for certain.

Snap! Snap! Snap!

Crack!

Now she could hear actual footsteps. On top of the twigs. And they were coming closer.

It didn't sound like a bear. Not that she'd ever heard a bear's footsteps before.

It didn't sound like a grandfather, either.

Cass looked over at Max-Ernest and Yo-Yoji, ready to shake them awake. But they were already sitting up. Eyes wide with fear.

They didn't have a plan, Cass realized in a flash. All this time, all this effort had gone into getting to this moment – and they hadn't planned on what to do next.

After reading "The Legend of Cabbage Face", Cass had simply assumed the homunculus would be friendly. But what if Mr. Wallace was right and the legend was wrong? What were they supposed to do then?

Fight the homunculus? They had no weapons.

Trap him? They had no chains. No net.

Follow him? But why? To where?

None of them moved a muscle. They didn't dare. They only waited.

Then, suddenly, silhouetted against the side of the tent:

Hands – huge hands. And ears – huge ears.

And, for a second, in profile:

A nose – a really huge nose.

It was not a bear. It was not a grandfather.

It was, without doubt, a monster – a huge monster.

Why, Cass wondered fleetingly, did the dictionary say a homunculus was small?

For a moment, he just stood there, his shadow rippling on the yellow tent fabric – as if he were contemplating whether it would be best to rip the tent open or to devour the tent whole.

Silently, Cass pointed to the tent entrance. "Should I open it?" she mouthed.

Her friends nodded – and gave her the courage she needed.

While they watched, she unzipped the tent and stepped out into the moonlight.

Cass got one look at the startled creature standing on top of the tree stump next to the tent before he—

Toppled to the ground with a thud.

"Ow! How dare you scare me like that!" he complained in the surliest and most gravelly voice Cass had ever heard.

Grumbling to himself, the homunculus got back up on his feet. He looked up at Cass with disdain as he brushed dirt and pine needles off his toddler-sized trousers. "Don't tell me it was *you* who called me!"

The image on the side of the tent hadn't been entirely misleading: in fact, his hands *were* big, if not huge; likewise his eyes, ears, nose and mouth. It was his legs and arms that were teeny, as well as his torso (although his tummy protruded more than a little).

Cass stared down at him. She couldn't believe he was only—

"Sixty centimetres tall. In answer to your very rude question. Oh, don't pretend – I can see it in your eyes. Almost sixty centimetres. More like fifty-eight centimetres. Or fifty-six. Well, fifty-four centimetres. And a half. Don't forget the half!"

Cass nodded, still staring.

The resemblance to her sock-monster was striking, but no more so than his outfit. In a crazy mishmash of centuries, he wore a ruffled shirt under a velvet waistcoat in the style of a Renaissance painting; his cap looked like something a newspaper boy might have worn a hundred years ago; meanwhile, his shoes, a young child's sneakers, couldn't have been more than a few years old at the most.

A large skeleton key hung around his neck, giving him an unexpected dignity.

"Well, was it you?" the homunculus demanded.

Cass nodded again.

"You mean *you* have the Sound Prism? Oh, say it isn't so!" He clasped his enormous hand to his much smaller forehead.

"I...uh..."

"Cat got your tongue?"

"Are you...?" Cass stammered.

"Spit it out!"

"...Cabbage...Face?"

"Who told you that?" He pointed a fat accusatory finger up at her. "And that's *Mr.* Cabbage Face to you!"

"Sorry. It's just...we got the name from the Sound Prism."

As she spoke, Max-Ernest and Yo-Yoji had slipped out of the tent.

"These are...my friends...Max-Ernest...Yo-Yoji... This is, um, Mr. Cabbage Face... Oh, and I'm Cassandra!"

They stared down at the homunculus with undisguised amazement. He stared back with an expression of scornful scepticism – insofar as he could manage from his low vantage point.

"Oh, it's you guys! I thought you were the bear!"

The kids froze. It was Grandpa Larry. Sticking his head out of his tent.

"What are you doing up? It's three in the morning!"

"Um, I had to go to the bathroom – then they did, too!" Desperately, Cass motioned for the homunculus to hide behind her. Which he did with a shrug and a scowl.

"Well, go back to bed. It's cold out here – and I don't want anyone getting sick!"

After Grandpa Larry zipped his tent back up, Cass turned to the homunculus.

"Sorry if I wasn't who you were expecting," she whispered. "I'm not sure whether the Sound Prism is really supposed to be mine or not. But I promise – we don't mean you any harm."

"We'll see about that. If it's really yours, then you should be able to tell me the Jester's name – not just mine."

"But how would I—?"

"Well, it's inside the Sound Prism, isn't it? If you're truly the heir of the Jester, then you'll be able to open it. If you can't, this is our last conversation. If you can, come find me tomorrow. Around lunchtime—"

"Where?" asked Max-Ernest.

"By the Hollow Tree. You'll find it—"

"But how will we—?"

But the homunculus was gone by the time Max-Ernest finished asking the question.

The three kids looked out into the darkness, lost in wonder: if the homunculus was real, if the homunculus was possible, then what wasn't?

CHAPTER ELEVEN

A Trail of Bones

"**S**tolen! And nobody heard a peep!" exclaimed Grandpa Larry.

The kids had emerged from their tent to find the sun shining and Cass's grandfathers standing over an empty pillowcase and the remains of their food supply. They were both shaking their heads.

"How the heck did he get it down?" asked Grandpa Wayne, sounding more impressed than angry. "He must be the first bear with opposable thumbs!"

"And so picky, too!" marvelled Grandpa Larry. "He took our Zinfandel and the Camembert. But look – he left the cup-o-noodles and the instant oatmeal…"

"A gourmet bear – that's a first!" said Grandpa Wayne. "Maybe he has a future in the circus."

"An eating bear? I don't think it has the same ring as a dancing bear. Now maybe if he could cook…"

The kids looked at each other. They were all thinking the same thing: *that bear was no bear at all*.

"Anybody want to go fishing after we make the oatmeal?" asked Grandpa Wayne. "I figure we better catch lunch while the trout are still biting."

"With that thing?" asked Cass, pointing to the taped-together fishing rod leaning against the tree next to Wayne.

"So what – you think the fish are going to notice?"

The kids laughed.

"If it's okay, we'll just hang out here," said Cass. "Then maybe go on a little hike a little later."

"Well, don't go too far. We don't want to get in trouble with your mom," said Larry.

As soon as her grandfathers left to go fishing, Cass, Max-Ernest and Yo-Yoji crawled back into their tent.

"Come on," said Cass. "If we don't figure out the name of the Jester before lunch, the homunculus will never come with us!" She pulled the Sound Prism out of her sleeping bag and held it up.

"So how do we open it?" asked Yo-Yoji.

They'd spent about an hour the night before trying to answer this very question. Until they'd all fallen back asleep.

Cass touched her finger to the silver band that circled the Sound Prism. "Are you *sure* these don't mean anything? They're just lines?"

"No, I'm not sure – how could I be?" asked Max-Ernest. "But if the Decoder didn't pick up anything I don't see how we could."

"Can I see it?" Yo-Yoji took the ball from Cass and turned it around in his hand.

"Careful," said Max-Ernest. "It's very old and very valuable."

"Hey, look—" Yo-Yoji succeeded in loosening the band. It spun around—

"I told you – now you broke it!"

"Dude, first of all, why are you hating on me all the time?"

"Wha-what do you mean?" Max-Ernest sputtered. "I'm not—"

"Yeah, sure you aren't! Second of all, I'm pretty sure it's supposed to spin like this."

"What? Like a combination lock or something? Let me see," said Max-Ernest, obviously very sceptical. He reached for the Sound Prism.

"No, let *me*," said Cass, reaching at the same time.

As they collided, the Sound Prism dropped out of Yo-Yoji's hand. It fell onto a bump in the middle of the tent – and it split evenly in two.

"It hit the rock!" Yo-Yoji picked up a half in each hand, peering inside one after the other. "Well, the good news is we got it open. There wasn't a trick – it was just stuck."

"What's the bad news?" asked Cass.

"Look – there's no name inside, just a poem."

Engraved in the alabaster, the poem spiralled around the inside of one half of the Sound Prism. The tiny letters looked like the inscription on the inside of a ring.

"Here, you read it," Yo-Yoji said, handing the two halves to Cass. "I'm kind of dyslexic."

Max-Ernest looked at Yo-Yoji, as if about to say something.

But then Cass started to read aloud:

My brother is A, the god of the sun:
he gave me his wand; I gave him my lyre.
My father is Z, god of all and one:
I gave him my word; I'm no more a liar.
No more am I a thief, just god of thieves;
See, what need I to lie or cheat or steal?
I have no tricks in my cape and up my sleeves;
I have wings on my helmet and my heels.
I put wit on thy tongue and in thy head,
and when I touch thine eyes thou know'st it's time
to cross the River Styx and join the dead.
And the last thing thou hear'st will be my rhyme.
For in the end it is all just a game;
that's all thou need'st to know to know my name.

"Aaargh, it's so annoying – we don't have time for this!" said Cass, putting down the two halves of the Sound Prism. "What does it mean? What's the name?"

Yo-Yoji shook his head. "I'm not really good with

this kind of poem – the kind I write don't rhyme. Plus, it's, like, in Shakespearean."

"I think it's kind of like a riddle – you can tell by the way it ends," said Max-Ernest. "Can I see it? I mean, if I'm allowed."

"Ha-ha." Cass rolled her eyes and handed him the two halves of the Sound Prism.

Max-Ernest looked inside...

"Well, the river Styx is from Greek mythology, right? It's the river on the way to Hades..."

"Yeah, maybe...I mean, okay," said Cass.

"Think about it – that means if it was a secret code, Greek mythology would be the key. So A is Apollo and Z is Zeus..."

"Nice!" said Yo-Yoji, looking at Max-Ernest with new respect. "You're pretty good at that stuff, huh, bro?"

"I guess. Hey, Yo-Yoji..." Max-Ernest hesitated. "Well, one of my doctors thought I was dyslexic, so I know lots of exercises you're supposed to do. I could show you. If you want."

"I don't usually like exercises very much, but, um, sure, if you think they're good..." Yo-Yoji wasn't all that much better at emotions than Max-Ernest, but he had an idea what Max-Ernest was trying to say.

Cass smiled to herself. She knew better than to ruin the moment by saying anything.

* * *

Cass's grandfathers didn't seem at all surprised by the kids' sudden interest in fly-fishing, or in their even more sudden interest in Greek mythology. Grandpa Larry loved mythology as much or more than Grandpa Wayne loved fishing, and he considered it perfectly natural that his granddaughter would ask him who the Greek god of thieves was.

"Ah, well, there's a story that goes along with that," Larry said, as Wayne cast out over the lake with his makeshift fishing rod. "You see, before he was really the god of anything, and he was just a mischievous little boy god, he stole a herd of cows from his big brother, Apollo. Apollo went ballistic and in order to appease Apollo, Zeus made him return the herd. Problem was – two cows were missing. Their hides had been turned into strings and strung over a tortoiseshell, making the first lyre. Luckily, Apollo loved music so much that he forgave his little brother, and even gave him his magic wand in return for the lyre. And that's how this little boy became not only the god of thieves, but the god of magic as well."

"That's a great story," said Cass impatiently, "but what was the god's name?"

* * *

Finding the homunculus's trail wasn't very difficult; they identified it by all the bones and scraps and candy wrappers that the homunculus had left in his wake.

Following the trail was another matter. In order to avoid all the low-hanging branches, they had to crawl most of the way.

"Ouch! These scratches aren't good for my eczema," Max-Ernest complained as he pushed branches out of his face. "And I know my allergies are going to get really bad—"

"Forget your allergies," said Cass. "If we don't have the name right, we're going to have a lot worse problems."

They knew they were getting there when the bones on the ground started appearing closer together: mostly little leg and thigh bones but there was the occasional whole carcass (bird? squirrel?!) and two or three bones from larger animals that the kids preferred not to identify.

Finally, about five hundred metres from their campsite, they reached a clearing in the woods. Here the bones were so dense they created a carpet. It was a gruesome but – with the dappled sunlight and canopy of trees above – a not unbeautiful sight.

On the other side of the clearing, surrounded by a circle of rocks, a campfire blazed. A pillar of smoke curled upwards. The smell of grilling meat filled the air.

"Look at that," said Max-Ernest. "What if the ranger sees?!"

"Forget the ranger – what if there's a forest fire?" said Cass.

"I dunno, smells pretty excellent to me," said Yo-Yoji.

Behind the fire stood a tall fir tree with a burned-out base; they all jumped, startled, when the homunculus stepped out of it.

"It better smell good – I've been cooking all morning. And don't worry about the ranger – I know his schedule. He's on the other side of the mountain right now."

Cass decided not to lecture him about fire safety.

Instead, she took a brave step towards the homunculus and asked, "So, um, Mr. Cabbage Face, was the Jester's name *Hermes*?"

"Shhh!"

"But you said…"

"Sure, sure, but names have power. In case you didn't notice, mine made me rise from a grave."

"Sorry, I didn't think about that," said Cass, pale.

"So do you want your three wishes, Cassandra?"

"I get three wishes…?"

"Of course not! Why does everybody always think I'm some kind of genie?" The homunculus made a loud hacking sound that might have been a laugh. His brown, broken teeth made his mouth look like a jack-o'-lantern.

"You know, I would have found you eventually – if you'd just called me a few more times," said the homunculus, studying Cass. "Pretty resourceful, tracking me here in the mountains."

"She's a survivalist," said Max-Ernest proudly.

Cass looked down, suddenly embarrassed.

"Ah, well, that explains it! Come now, we can talk business later. Let's eat."

The homunculus made them all sit around the fire. Nearby, he'd laid out piles and piles of food on a bed of pine needles.

"Hey, that's our food – you stole it!" said Max-Ernest, recognizing the Camembert.

"Don't get your knickers in a twist – it's not all yours. Some of it's from other campsites. Besides," continued the homunculus blithely, "that Camembert needs at least a week before it's going to be ripe. And this Zinfandel has no nose at all. How can you drink such mediocre wine? Now, if you like, I have a wonderful Châteauneuf-du-Pape courtesy of some hikers from Montreal." He held up a fancy bottle of wine. "Those fellows had taste!"

Yo-Yoji stopped him before he could start pouring.

"Um, do you have anything else? We don't really like wine."

The homunculus looked appalled. "You don't drink wine?! Don't tell me you're beer drinkers! I didn't take you for such ruffians."

They shook their heads.

"We don't drink beer, either," said Max-Ernest.

"Ah, so then it's liquor for you," said the homunculus, relieved. "I agree, quite right – why monkey around with the soft stuff? So what can I get you – vodka? Gin? I have a very nice single malt scotch."

They shook their heads.

"Tequila with a squeeze of lime? Not the classiest, true, but what the heck – we're camping, right?"

They shook their heads.

"A drop of cognac?"

They shook their heads.

"Why are you insulting my hospitality like this?" The homunculus looked at them, distressed.

"We're *kids*. We drink soda and stuff," said Max-Ernest.

"You know what's in soda? Sugar and food colouring. And diet soda? Worse. I refuse to let you destroy your bodies with soda!" The homunculus drew himself up in a huff.

Cass was about to point out that it was a little

hypocritical for him to forbid soda when, judging by all the wrappers they'd seen, he ate plenty of candy, but then she thought better of it.

They compromised with lake water (purified with tablets Cass had in her backpack). And then they proceeded to feast on all the stolen goods. Or rather, the homunculus did. The others didn't have much of an appetite.

All they could do was stare at the long grey hairs that sprouted from his nose and his ears – and try to avoid smelling his breath.

"I'm sorry there's so little," said the homunculus, his mouth full of cheese.

He held a charred sausage in one hand and a barbecued drumstick in the other. He might have looked like a munchkin, but he ate like a *T. rex*. "I have to make do with what's around. My life isn't what it used to be. Gone are the days of dining with King Henry the Eighth…"

"You ate with Henry the Eighth?" asked Max-Ernest.

"In a manner of speaking. I ate with his hogs."

"So that story we read was true? About you escaping from the hogs with the Jester?" Cass asked eagerly.

"Well, I don't know what you read – I'm sure people write all kinds of things about me. That happens when you're a celebrity. But yes—"

The kids watched in fascination as he sucked the marrow out of a chicken bone with lightning speed, then tossed the bone onto a pile behind him.

"And the Jester – was he really a jester?" asked Cass.

"Of course – why wouldn't he be? Not the funniest maybe – although he thought he was. You know what they say about not laughing at your own jokes? Well, he never learned it."

"I knew it," said Cass. "And what about Lord Pharaoh?"

The homunculus scowled. "What about him?"

"Well, the story said that you...met each other years after you ran away. What happened?"

"I ate him," said the homunculus, biting into his sausage.

The kids couldn't hide their looks of horror.

He smiled, sausage juice running down his chin. "Oh, don't worry – I cooked him first. I'm not a barbarian. Sadly for me, he was not a young man any more, so he wasn't very tender. But even old flesh isn't bad, if you know how to prepare it properly. The key is to brown the meat first to seal in the juices."

The kids all shifted nervously on their pine-needle seats.

"What's the big deal? Meat is meat! You know

what they say – tastes like chicken, right? Although, honestly, more like pork..."

"I don't care how it tastes, I couldn't ever eat a person." Cass shoved her pile of food away as if it were the person in question.

"I thought you were a survivalist! You'll never last in the wild if you're so squeamish," said the homunculus. "Personally, I would consider it an honour to be eaten – assuming I was already dead, of course."

"*Can* you die?" asked Yo-Yoji.

The homunculus eyed him suspiciously. "Why do you want to know?"

"Uh, no reason," said Yo-Yoji quickly. "Except these guys said you were five hundred years old—"

"You forgot to say, and looking pretty good on it!"

Cass pulled the Sound Prism out of her sweatshirt pocket. "So, Mr. Cabbage Face, am I supposed to give this to you? It's sort of yours, I guess."

"No, it's yours. But please – would you play the song? It's been a while since I heard it up close. Matter of fact, no one's called me on the Sound Prism for a couple hundred years. Last one was a boy named Gilbert. Excuse me, *Sir* Gilbert. What a spoiled brat!"

Cass obligingly tossed the ball into the air. It played the same song it always played – but it was different with Cabbage Face himself there.

Listening, the homunculus looked at the ground, lost in time.

Was that a tear in his eye? It was hard to be sure.

She had to ask: "So, then, am I the...rightful heir?"

"Of course you are," said the homunculus. "I could tell the Sound Prism was yours the second I laid eyes on you."

"You could? How?" asked Cass in amazement.

"Those pointy ears of yours. Just like the Jester's. Anybody could see from a mile away..."

Cass felt her ears reddening at the homunculus's words. "The Jester? I'm descended from the Jester?"

She couldn't believe it: somebody else had walked the earth with her big, pointy, target-of-joke-y ears.

She tried to remember everything she'd read about the Jester and the way he'd saved the homunculus from his horrible master. He may have been named after the god of thieves, but the Jester – Hermes – was a hero, and somehow, in some way, he was hers.

Who, then, was the girl named on the birth certificate? Cass wondered suddenly. She was about to ask the homunculus when she realized his information would be hundreds of years out of date. The answer would have to wait.

Max-Ernest pointed to the Sound Prism. "You

know, the Midnight Sun are looking for that. They already stole it once."

"Ah." The homunculus's face darkened. "So they're still at it, are they?"

"You didn't know? There's a hundred of them at least – plus Ms. Mauvais and Dr. L. They're the worst!" said Max-Ernest.

"Well, I don't get out much these days. Just to get a bite every now and then..."

Cass touched her ears to make sure they'd cooled. "The reason they want the Sound Prism is that they're looking for you."

"Not for me. For the grave."

"Grave?" repeated Yo-Yoji.

"Lord Pharaoh's grave. Where do you think I've been all these years? Guarding it. Just in case."

"Why do they want to find it? Would it be really bad if they did?" asked Yo-Yoji.

"Oh, I don't know – is the end of the world bad? The destruction of everything you hold dear?"

"Why, what's inside it?" Yo-Yoji persisted.

"Waste. Lord Pharaoh's waste. The excrement of evil."

"You mean his" – Max-Ernest reddened – "poop?"

"No – although, believe me, his bowel movements were bad enough! When I was little I had to clean out his chamber pots." The homunculus shook off the memory. "No, I mean the remains of his alchemical work. I buried it all with him – but as hard as I tried, I couldn't destroy it. Its power never dies. It only festers."

"So, it's kind of like nuclear waste?" asked Cass. "Like radiation?"

"I don't know about that – but if you say so."

"You have to come with us. We'll take you to Pietro. He'll know what to do. He's the leader of the Terces Society."

"The Terces Society?" The homunculus laughed.

"Sure. Why not? They'll protect you," said Cass defensively.

"What can they do? Bunch of...*librarians*!" He pronounced the word as if it were a terrible insult. "Just keeping records – how does that help anybody?"

There was silence for a moment. The kids found it hard to defend the Terces Society; after all, they didn't really know very much about it.

Then Cass did what any good survivalist would do. She improvised.

"Well, there are also a few chefs," said Cass, emphasizing the last word.

"Chefs?" echoed the homunculus.

Yo-Yoji jumped in. "Yeah, you should see the meals! They're like full-on banquets. More food than you could ever eat..."

"I doubt that," scoffed the homunculus. But they could tell they'd sparked his interest.

"Well, more food than *we* could eat," said Max-Ernest, catching on. "But it would be just the right amount for you. All the meat you could want – and they always sear it. Everything's totally juicy and delicious! Well, not everything. Only the things that have natural juices, I mean, but there are a lot of them! How 'bout that?"

"Yeah, they make crown roast every day, best you've ever had," said Cass. She wasn't sure what crown roast was, but it sounded like something that somebody who ate with a king's hogs might like.

"Hmm..." The homunculus hesitated. "Maybe it's not such a bad idea to check in with the Terces Society, after all. Everybody I knew died two hundred years ago. Maybe the new crop isn't so useless. If they know how to cook a good crown roast, that obviously speaks well of their character."

"Great!" said Cass. "You won't regret it."

"Wait – how are we going to take him back without your grandfathers seeing?" whispered Yo-Yoji.

"Um, we'll figure it out by tomorrow..." Cass scanned their surroundings, as if the answer might be hidden among the bones on the ground.

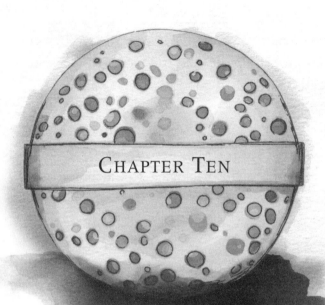

CHAPTER TEN

A Heavy Load

Walking down a mountain, I'm sure you'll agree, is almost always more fun than hiking up.

For Max-Ernest, however, the descent from Whisper Lake was far more difficult than the ascent to Whisper Lake – because now his second backpack was full.

Thankfully, as Max-Ernest had pointed out earlier, the backpack had wheels, so he could drag it. The problem was: whenever the descent became very steep, the weight of the backpack would push him forward down the mountain. Twice, he'd fallen on his face – although so far he'd suffered nothing worse than a scrape and a bruise.

The third time he fell it looked especially painful.

"Ouch!" / "Aaargh!"

"Are you okay?" asked Grandpa Larry as Max-Ernest picked himself up off the ground. "That sounded pretty bad."

"Yeah, I'm all right," said Max-Ernest, but simultaneously he also seemed to be crying out, "Ummph! Ugghh!"

"You sure? You sound like you're a hundred years old all of a sudden…"

"He's just got a little cough or something," said Cass, coming between them.

Max-Ernest forced a smile as the moaning

continued. "Yeah, that's it. Really, I'm fine!"

Grandpa Larry eyed Max-Ernest suspiciously. "All right, but if you're in any pain at all, we have a first-aid kit. I don't want to get in trouble with your parents when we get home. I always catch enough from Cass's mom, right, Cass?"

"Right," said Cass. Surreptitiously, she gave a little kick to the backpack and the moaning stopped.

"What's in there?" asked Grandpa Wayne, catching up with them. "Looks kind of heavy."

"Oh, just some trash," Yo-Yoji interjected from a couple of metres ahead. "You know what they say – take only pictures, leave only footprints!"

At the trash comment, a growl of protest issued from the backpack. The kids stifled laughs.

Grandpa Larry smiled, unhearing. "Ah. Such good citizens of nature!"

"We should just be glad Max-Ernest thought of bringing an extra backpack," said Yo-Yoji. "Definitely came in handy."

He flashed an apologetic grin at Max-Ernest before continuing to lead them down the trail.

"I'm hungry!"

After hiking, riding in the back of Wayne's truck

felt comparatively luxurious. They lay back against their backpacks, feet up, out of view of the highway patrol.

But they had another issue to contend with:

"I'm hungry!"

A hungry homunculus, in case you've never encountered one, is irritable and combative, if not downright dangerous.

Even, maybe especially, when he's stuck in a backpack.

The kids wouldn't let him out; they were afraid Cass's grandfathers would be able to see him through the rear window of the truck's cab. But they opened the backpack enough so he could eat.

In the first five minutes of the drive, the homunculus called Mr. Cabbage Face (but now known privately to the kids as Mr. Stuff Your Face) ripped through a bag of beef jerky, the remains of Cass's trail mix, and an old apple that had been sitting at the bottom of Yo-Yoji's backpack from his last trip.

When he kept complaining that he was hungry, Max-Ernest offered him a pack of gum. The homunculus swallowed every piece in rapid succession.

"You know they say gum stays in your ribs for ever," said Max-Ernest.

"Yeah, well, they say a lot of things, don't they?

And not many of them apply to somebody who's five hundred years old and made in a bottle! Now what else have you got to eat?"

"Nothing!" said Cass, who was growing tired of his constant harping.

"Oh yeah? You've got ten fingers and ten toes, don't you? Not to mention those ears. A little chewy on top maybe, but those lobes look tender..."

Everyone assumed he was joking – but they all balled their fingers and curled their toes just in case. And Cass lowered her hat protectively.

"Yeah, you hide those little toesies!" the homunculus harrumphed. "See if that stops me from chewing through your boots."

"Where does he put it all?" the kids asked each other more than once. "And where does it go?"

The answer to that last question became clear soon enough; the homunculus asked for rest stops almost as often as he asked for food.

In order to explain the constant need for bathroom breaks, Cass told her grandfathers that Max-Ernest had "stomach problems". If Larry and Wayne thought it was strange that Max-Ernest always took a backpack into the bathroom, they didn't say anything. After all, they'd seen how afraid he was of the port-a-potties.

"It's kind of like having to take care of Sebastian,"

whispered Cass to Max-Ernest, when the truck pulled back onto the highway after a particularly long break.

"Who's that?" asked Yo-Yoji.

"Her grandfathers' dog," said Max-Ernest.

The homunculus stuck his head out of the backpack. "Oh yeah? What kind? I love dog!"

"He's a basset hound."

"Huh. Not bad. Short legs. You cook them like hot wings—"

"He's old and he wears a diaper and I'm sure he tastes really really bad," said Cass. "So don't get any ideas!"

"Great – not only don't you have any more food for me, I'm not even allowed to *think* about eating! You're a laugh and a half!"

Cursing, the homunculus stuck his head back inside the backpack.

Cass geared herself up for the one other item of business that had to take place before they got home:

"So, Yo-Yoji, I hope you don't mind, but I don't really think it's a good idea for you to come to the Magic Museum."

"What – now that we're back, you're gonna act like I didn't go with you guys?" Yo-Yoji kicked the side of the truck in frustration.

"We might get in trouble..."

"Don't worry – I'm great with the grown-ups. Besides, you *have* to tell them about me – I know about the Secret."

Cass looked at Max-Ernest. He shrugged: Yo-Yoji had a point.

Behind him, purple mountains receded in the haze.

CHAPTER NINE

Meanwhile

*MEANWHILE? DID I REALLY JUST WRITE *MEANWHILE*? *MEANWHILE*
IS TO WRITING WHAT *UM* IS TO SPEAKING. A SPACE-FILLER. A SIGN
THAT SOMEONE DOESN'T KNOW WHAT TO SAY OR HOW TO SAY IT.
(CONT.)

The Midnight Sun schooner had dropped anchor again – this time at a harbour more befitting the luxurious ship than that rotten old dock at which we last saw it.

On all sides there were impressive, massive yachts – the floating mansions of the rich and powerful.

And on the deck of the *Midnight Sun* there was one very impressed – but not very massive – girl.

Amber, I'm afraid to say, looked rather diminished by her new surroundings. At school, where everyone knew her as the nicest and third prettiest, Amber loomed large in the eyes of her peers and even of her teachers. Out here on the water, stripped of her credentials, she seemed a mere wisp of a thing; she practically cowered in the presence of her twin heroes, the Skelton Sisters, as she met them in person for the first time.

Of course, the invitation had been a fabulous honour. The secret text messages she'd been receiving ever

---

MEANWHILE BELONGS WITH PHRASES LIKE *ON THE OTHER HAND* – PHRASES THAT A GOOD WRITER SHOULD NEVER USE. ON THE OTHER HAND, THERE'S SOMETHING ABOUT *MEANWHILE* THAT I RATHER LIKE – ESPECIALLY WHEN IT'S FOLLOWED BY AN ELLIPSIS, LIKE THIS: *MEANWHILE*... CAN YOU HEAR THAT SENSE OF MENACE? THAT SENSE OF, UH-OH, JUST WHEN YOU THOUGHT IT WAS SAFE TO GO BACK IN THE WATER...

since she got her pink Skelton Sisters twin♥hearts™ cellphone had been thrilling enough. But this time Romi (or was it Montana? she hadn't dared ask) had called her *personally*!

Amber immediately made her parents rush her to the ship, which she boarded wearing all of her latest Skelton Sisters twin♥hearts™ fashions and in a state of excitement I can only compare to – well, I don't know what to compare it to. (Perhaps the excitement you feel meeting the author of a book, he suggested modestly.)

But which sister was which?

Even Amber, who'd watched every single Skelton Sisters twin♥hearts™ DVD ever filmed, and who'd listened to every Skelton Sisters twin♥hearts™ CD ever recorded, and who'd read every issue of every Skelton Sisters twin♥hearts™ magazine ever released, even Amber had trouble telling Romi and Montana apart.

As soon as they'd welcomed Amber onto the boat, and assured her parents that she would be safe alone with them for an hour ("We'll treat her like she's our own sister!"), one of the sisters – the pinker one; I *think* it was Montana – held out (more like dangled) a gift for their young visitor in her gloved hand.

"Wow, thanks! He's soooo cute!"

Shaking with nervousness, Amber took the little creature from Montana (or was it Romi?). It looked, Amber couldn't help noticing, just like Cass's sock-monster – except that it was pink and sparkly and it came on a little jewelled leash you could wear around your wrist. (And I'll bet it wasn't hand-stitched by a survivalist, but rather manufactured by child labour in Sri Lanka.)

It also had a large tag bearing the words:

sock❤roach®
a twin❤hearts™ inc. original
by romi and montana

"They come in twelve colours – plus rainbow," said Montana (or was it Romi?). "If you do everything we tell you, we'll give you one of each – before they're even in stores!"

"Really? That would be so awesome!" said Amber, strapping the **sock❤roach**® to her wrist.

Not to be outdone, Romi (or was it Montana?) took a heart-shaped cupcake out of a pink box. "Here, eat this – it's from our new chain of **twin❤hearts**™ bakeries!" she said, tracing the heart and trademark signs in the air with her finger.

Montana (or was it Romi?) gasped. "No! Don't give that to her – she's too fat!"

Amber looked down at her stomach in alarm – nobody had ever called her fat before.

"Oh, that's just baby fat," said Romi (or was it Montana?). She sniffed the cupcake, inhaling with a look of rapture. Then put it under Amber's nose. "Doesn't it smell good? Here – eat!"

"No, don't!" said Montana (or was it Romi?), pulling Romi's (or was it Montana's?) arm away from Amber. "She'll turn into a pig!"

"Don't be silly – eat!" said Romi (or was it Montana?), thrusting the cupcake back under Amber's nose.

"No!" Montana (or was it Romi?) tugged on Amber's arm to keep her away from her sister. "Just think *oink! I'm turning into a pig!* That's what I do whenever I'm about to eat something. It's, like, my anti-eating mantra."

"C'mon, one little cupcake never hurt anybody – eat!" Romi (or was it Montana?) tugged on Amber's other arm, to bring her closer to the cupcake.

"Oink!" Montana (or was it Romi?) tugged the other arm again.

"Eat!" Romi (or was it Montana?) tugged back.

"Oink!" Tug.

"Eat!" Tug.

"Oink, I mean, oww…stop!" said Amber, whose face, pink with pain, was beginning to look decidedly piggish.

But the sisters, caught up in their battle, ignored her cry.

"Oink!" Tug.

"Eat!" Tug.

"Oink!" This time, instead of tugging, Montana (or was it Romi?) grabbed the cupcake – but not in time to keep Romi (or was it Montana?) from shoving it into Amber's helpless mouth.

As the relieved Amber chewed, the two skeletal sisters fell silent and stared at her like starving wolves eyeing a plump chicken. Nobody watching would have been surprised to see them pounce and sink their teeth into her neck.

"It's really good – don't you guys want some?" asked Amber, her mouth full.

"NO!" they both yelled in unison.

"Are you *kidding*?!" asked Romi (or was it Montana?).

"We don't *eat*!" said Montana (or was it Romi?), as if the very idea were preposterous.

"We just like to watch," said Romi (or was it Montana?).

"Here, do you want another?" asked Montana (or

was it Romi?), picking another cupcake out of the box. Her eyes glazed, she seemed to have forgotten all about her fears of Amber getting fat.

"Girls – control yourselves! Have you forgotten why we're here?"

Ms. Mauvais had emerged onto the deck from the cabin below. No longer in her nautical outfit, she was resplendent in gold and she lit up her surroundings as if she were a kind of human beacon.

"You must be Amber," she said, training her icy blue eyes on the dazzled girl. "I'm Ms. Mauvais. I've heard so much about you."

As if possessed, Amber dropped to her knees and bowed.

"Really, darling – that's not necessary." Ms. Mauvais gestured dismissively with her golden-gloved hand.

"Are you…a queen?" Amber asked, trembling.

"Ha! No, not…at the moment." Ms. Mauvais made a chilly, tinkling sound that might have been a laugh. "But you are very shrewd – something tells me you'll go far."

She stepped forward and stroked Amber's bowed head as if she were rewarding a little lapdog. "I have a very special job for you, Amber… How would you like to go to a concert?"

CHAPTER EIGHT

A Polite Way
of Saying Weird

From the beginning, there'd been a flaw in Cass's plan: how to get to the Magic Museum once they were home? Their parents would never allow them to go so soon after returning.

Luckily, Cass's mother had decided to visit her sister while Cass was away (mainly, Cass thought, so her mother would have an excuse to leave Sebastian in a kennel for the weekend) and the house was empty when Cass's grandfathers dropped off the young campers.

Cass's mother wouldn't be home for a couple of hours. Time enough to get to the museum and back – hopefully. Max-Ernest and Yo-Yoji could call their parents when they got back to Cass's house, pretending they'd only just arrived from the mountains.

"Bye!" / "Thanks!" / "Later!"

They waved goodbye and waited to hear Grandpa Wayne's truck disappear down the road. Then they let themselves out of the house, leaving all the backpacks except one – the one that wobbled back and forth all on its own.

"City buses don't have seat belts, either," Max-Ernest noted when they mounted the bus. "Why do you think that is?"

"Funny, I feel totally strapped in, even without a seat belt," said a muffled voice. "You know, just because somebody spends most of his life underground doesn't mean he likes being stuffed inside a backpack for hours and hours!"

"Shh," said Cass. "It's just a little while longer."

"Hey, look at her," whispered Yo-Yoji, pointing to a rather heavyset (which is a polite way of saying *fat*) and hirsute (which is a polite way of saying *bearded*) woman sitting on the bus.

"Don't point – it's rude," said Cass.

But all three kids had trouble resisting looking at the Bearded Lady. And in fact, whenever one of them accidentally caught her eye, she winked as if she were used to being looked at – and didn't mind at all.

When they got onto the second bus, our friends had to try even harder not to stare.

Up front behind the driver sat two little people (which is a polite way of saying *midgets*), one male, one female, wearing a tuxedo and a ball gown, respectively.

Behind them sat a man who looked perfectly normal, except that his shirtsleeves hung rather loosely (which is a polite of way of saying *he had no arms*). When the Bearded Lady walked onto the bus, the Armless Man smiled and waved at her with his bare foot – which she then shook exactly as you would shake a hand.

Eerily (or was it just coincidentally?), when Cass and Max-Ernest and Yo-Yoji all transferred to the next bus, so, too, did this motley group of bus riders.

"Are they following us?" whispered Max-Ernest nervously.

"I dunno, just act…normal," whispered Cass.

Yo-Yoji laughed. "That'll be the day."

On this, the third and last bus, they joined several other unique (which is a polite way of saying *peculiar*) passengers, including three colourfully costumed comedians (which is a polite way of saying *clowns*) and one strong (which is a polite way of saying *bald, moustachioed and wearing a leopard-skin leotard*) man.

"It's like the circus is coming to town – aren't they supposed to be on a train or something?" whispered Max-Ernest, thinking of the pictures they'd seen on the wall of the Magic Museum.

"Where do you think they're going?" asked Yo-Yoji.

They didn't have to wait long for an answer.

As soon as they got off the bus, they found themselves in the middle of a noisy crowd of carnies (which is an impolite of way of referring to *carnival workers and circus performers*) moving en masse in the direction of the Magic Museum.

Over the entrance to the museum hung a bright striped banner:

THE OLE TIME TRAVELLING CIRCUS REUNION

Welcome, Freaky Friends and Kooky Comrades!

"Hey! Can you guys go a little easier on me?" asked the homunculus from inside the backpack as it bounced down the stairs that led to the museum's front door. "And why don't I smell the crown roast? Are you sure this is the right place?"

"We're not inside yet," said Cass. "Just be quiet until we let you out—"

The crowd had gathered in the big room that housed the collection of automata – which, it must be said, looked comparatively harmless next to some of the museum's new inhabitants.

At the far end of the room stood a very old (which, in this case, is a polite way of saying *doddering*) man in a top hat and a red coat holding a large ring and a bullwhip – a Lion Tamer? Beside him was a silver-studded (which is a polite way of saying *pierced all over*) and fully illustrated (which is a polite way of saying *tattooed up to his eyeballs*) man juggling bowling pins.

Behind them, Pietro – now wearing a necktie rather than his woodworker's apron – sat on a riser, smiling at the sight of so many old friends. Mr. Wallace sat next to him, a pained expression on his face.

The Lion Tamer spoke, quavering, into a cone-shaped megaphone.

"Hello, dear friends! Our esteemed colleague, Pietro, has brought us here…because…because…" His voice cracked as he struggled to remember. "Because he wants us all to…to do a reunion show, that's it!" He scratched the side of his head. "Odd to call it that, though, considering we just performed last night…"

"You mean, fifty years ago last night!" the Illustrated Man corrected, tossing the bowling pins into the crowd. The Strong Man caught them and started juggling without missing a beat.

The Illustrated Man grabbed the megaphone: "C'mon – let's show the world what the Circus was like before it was just another way to sell hotel rooms in Las Vegas!"

The carnies all cheered. "Right on!" "Hooray for the Ballyhoo!" "Vegas sucks!" "Long live the Circus!"

"We are freaks and geeks, and we're not going away

quietly!" shouted the Illustrated Man. "We are nuts and we are proud of it!"

More cheers. "Yay, Freaks!" "Go, Nuts!" "Down with normal people!"

Our young heroes watched from the middle of the crowd, sandwiched between a chess-playing automaton and a heavily whiskered clown in a hobo outfit. They were trying to move towards the *Gateway to the Invisible*, but it was too tight.

"No grub in this joint, huh?" asked the clown loudly. "What are they thinking? A guy's gotta eat!"

"Um, uh..." Cass panicked.

The three kids looked as one at Max-Ernest's backpack. But the homunculus didn't appear to be listening.

"Excuse me, do you folks mind coming with me?" Lily beckoned from the side of the room.

Cass braced herself as they squirmed through the crowd: this was the moment she'd been dreading.

"Hi, Lily," said Cass when they reached her. "This is our friend – he's been, um, helping us." She nervously indicated Yo-Yoji.

Lily nodded. "Hello, Yoji. It's been a long time.

While Cass and Max-Ernest gaped in astonishment, Yo-Yoji bowed as deeply as he could in the packed room. "Master Wei."

"You've been practising, I trust?"

Yo-Yoji shook his head sheepishly. "Just, uh, the guitar."

Lily looked at him with clear disapproval. "You know what my father always said—"

"Practice makes permanent, I know. I'm sorry."

Surprised, relieved, and deeply confused, Cass and Max-Ernest glanced back and forth from each other to the boy they thought they knew.

"Yoji was one of my most talented students. It only seemed natural to ask him to help in our cause," Lily explained a few minutes later. "I hope he has been more responsible in keeping up his Terces duties than his violin."

They were all standing in the sawdust of the basement workshop, safe for the moment from the crowd upstairs. It was the same group as last time – with the addition of Yo-Yoji and the subtraction of Owen, who was away on secret Terces business.

"Well, we found the homunculus, didn't we?" said Yo-Yoji, unable to resist defending himself.

Pietro smiled at the kids. "You have all done better than I dared to hope. If only all my projects went so well." He gestured to the old tree-growing vase, totally disassembled on the table in front of him.

Cass's ears flushed with pride. The news about Yo-Yoji was disconcerting – very – but Pietro's words were exactly what she'd been longing for.

"I didn't believe it was possible, but we met him – he's real! How 'bout that?" said Max-Ernest excitedly.

"So where are you keeping the homunculus now?" Lily asked them.

"He's here. We brought him with us," said Cass.

The adults looked at the kids in alarm.

"I don't understand – where is he?" asked Mr. Wallace, looking around anxiously as if the homunculus might be locked up in one of the trick cabinets. "A creature like that – he's dangerous. A thing of evil. Do you have him tied up?"

"He's not like that," said Cass. "He's really kind of nice once you get to know him."

"Except for the fact that he's a cannibal," said Max-Ernest.

"But not in a bad way," said Cass. "Here – meet him yourself—"

Cass nudged Max-Ernest and he bent down to unzip his backpack, only to find—

"Um, Mr. Cabbage Face?"

The backpack was already open.

The homunculus was gone.

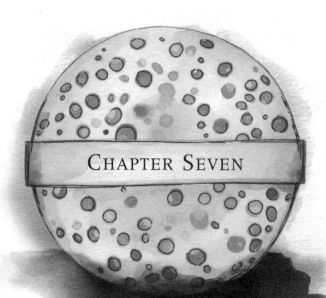

CHAPTER SEVEN

A Spy in
the Bushes

T hey tried the museum's kitchen first. And saw at once that the homunculus had been there – but left in disgust.

The kitchen looked like it hadn't seen a meal in years; it was being used to store office supplies. The closest thing to food was a package of microwave popcorn that the homunculus had opened – then scattered without popping, as if to say "thanks, but no thanks!"

Next, they tried the reunion party upstairs.

Cass crawled under people's legs, hoping to find a trail of corn kernels if not bones, but no such luck.

Max-Ernest thought he saw the homunculus slip into the *Gateway to the Invisible*, only to see one of the midgets step out a second later.

"Not too hard for him to disappear in this crowd," commented Yo-Yoji, looking out at the sea of carnies – half of whom looked as weird as the homunculus.

"Well, you'd know better than we would," Cass snorted.

"Not really. I only met those guys once before. I know about as much as you do."

Cass looked sceptical.

"Seriously, I didn't even know anything about the homunculus before you told me."

"Yeah, because you already *had* a job," Cass said stonily. "Us."

"The only reason I didn't tell you guys was that they said not to!"

"Whatever. It's not important."

"What's important is that we just lost a sixty-centimetre-tall, five-hundred-year-old man-eater, and we have no idea where he is!" said Max-Ernest, who had been having trouble following the logic – let alone the underlying feeling – behind the conversation.

Giving up, they headed back downstairs.

"Could the Midnight Sun have got to him?" asked Lily as they reconvened in the workshop. "If Dr. L or Ms. Mauvais had been here, wouldn't we have seen them? Perhaps an operative of theirs…?"

"I think he was just hungry," muttered Cass.

The kids felt miserable. They were all thinking the same thing: that the homunculus had left because they'd lied about the food at the museum.

Cass kept kicking herself for telling him that he would get crown roast. Why hadn't she thought about what would happen when they got there? Had she expected Pietro to conjure a roast out of thin air?

Pietro never said an unkind word. But that made it worse.

Had he expressed any anger, our young heroes might have defended themselves. After all, they'd brought the homunculus all the way into the museum. Into the workshop, even. How were they supposed to know he'd escape from right under their noses?

But instead of berating them, Pietro tried to hide how worried he was. He even showed Max-Ernest a quick card trick before they went home.*

They were being treated like children and they knew it. There was no discussion of the Oath of Terces. No talk of future missions.

Mr. Wallace never said, "I told you so," but you didn't have to be a mind-reader to know what he was thinking.

"What about the Sound Prism – shouldn't they leave it with us? I think it would be safer," he said.

"But it's hers – she's the heir," Lily reminded him.

They debated as if Cass herself were not present until finally Pietro decided it was best that she keep the Sound Prism. "We don't know much about this

---

*IT INVOLVED SHUFFLING VERY SLOPPILY, ONLY TO REVEAL THE CARDS NEATLY ARRANGED AT THE END. NORMALLY, A FUN TRICK. (PERHAPS I'LL TEACH IT TO YOU SOMEDAY.) BUT TO BE HONEST, IT FELL A LITTLE FLAT THIS TIME.

object. Perhaps the Sound Prism, it would not like to be in someone else's hands."

But before they left he made the kids promise not to look for the homunculus.

"It's too risky," he said. "That much we now know."

For nights afterwards, Cass slept with the Sound Prism under her pillow – right next to her resurrected sock-monster. She was afraid even to keep the Sound Prism buried outside.

Needless to say, she didn't sleep very well.

The Sound Prism whispered to her in her dreams, seeming to give voices to people and animals and inanimate objects indiscriminately. All taunting her for failing the Terces Society. For failing Pietro. Every barking dog was laughing at her. Every honking car was jeering at her.

And you call yourself a survivalist! they said. *You can't even keep a homunculus in a backpack.*

Cass was convinced that the Sound Prism wanted her to call the homunculus again. Or at least that the Sound Prism would make her go crazy if she *didn't* call him. But she resisted. If she couldn't save the world, at least she could prove to Pietro that she could keep her word.

One night, she woke up from an especially restless sleep. A rustling sound was coming from under her pillow.

At first, she didn't think much of it; she was getting used to odd, unidentified noises. But when she put the Sound Prism to her ear she became certain that the noise it was picking up was coming from the backyard.

An animal perhaps? A cat? No, something larger… the homunculus? Was it Mr. Cabbage Face himself looking for her?

She tiptoed downstairs and out into the backyard in her pyjama bottoms and favourite Tree People sleeping T.

Although she held the Sound Prism in front of her, she didn't hear any more rustling, or much of anything at all. For a second, she thought she heard some kind of drumming, then she realized it was her own heartbeat being broadcast back to her by the Sound Prism.

Slowly, Cass made a circuit around the yard, peering into the darkness.

"Mr. Cabbage Face?"

She waited for a few minutes, hugging her arms against the cold. But there was no response.

And yet, she was certain someone or something had been out there.

Naturally, she thought of Ms. Mauvais and Dr. L – but wouldn't they already have crept inside to look for the Sound Prism or to kidnap her or to do whatever horrible thing they were going to do?

Perhaps the homunculus had come, but then changed his mind, or thought he had the wrong house?

There was one way to know for sure: if she called him on the Sound Prism, he would have to come.

True, Cass had promised not to look for him, but this was clearly a different situation. And she would try only a small, short toss – a small, short call. Audible only if he were close by.

Cass looked back at her house to make sure no lights had gone on, and that her mother was still sleeping. Then she stood in the middle of the yard and tossed the Sound Prism into the air...

The ball rose a little higher than she'd intended but not so high that the tune would carry all the way around the world. It had been a long time since she'd heard it, and the eerie song was strangely comforting.

Almost immediately, she heard the rustling sound. All of her senses on alert, she scanned her surroundings for a sign of the homunculus. Surely, he would show himself now? Or was he still too angry with her?

She saw a glimmer of light in the bushes behind the Barbie Graveyard...

"Mr. Cabbage Face?" she whispered again.

By the time she reached the spot, whatever or whoever it was was gone.

As a cold, unhappy Cass walked back upstairs to her room, a smug, smiling Amber walked quickly down the street away from Cass's house.

She held her sparkling pink cellphone aloft like a trophy. And with good reason. On her phone was the freshly recorded song of the Sound Prism.

Ms. Mauvais would be very happy.

CHAPTER SIX

A Knock-Knock Joke,
A Bathroom Window
and a Puke-Worthy
Proposal

Max-Ernest released the two straws from his mouth and put down his two juice boxes. It had been less than two weeks since the disaster at the museum, but he appeared to be in high spirits.

"How about this one…?" He looked at his lunch companions to make sure he had their attention.

"Knock, knock…"

"Who's there?" asked Yo-Yoji gamely.

"I am."

"Um, 'I am' who?"

"No, that was the answer."

"Just 'I am'?"

Max-Ernest nodded. "I read that a joke is when you expect one thing, then something else happens. Well, in a knock-knock joke you always think there's going to be a joke after you say 'Who's there?' And I thought, what if there wasn't a joke – would that be like a joke on a joke?"

"I don't know," said Yo-Yoji, laughing. "That's either the stupidest joke I've ever heard or the deepest."

"I was thinking I could try it in my Comagedy Act in the talent show – that's what I'm calling my magic-comedy routine. How 'bout that?"

Yo-Yoji grinned. "You're gonna kill, man!"

"*Kill?*" Max-Ernest looked alarmed.

"It means you're gonna rock the talent show. It's a good thing."

Cass rolled her eyes. She knew she should be happy about the growing friendship (or was it only a temporary peace?) between Max-Ernest and Yo-Yoji; instead, she found it irksome.

She'd never come right out and said what she was afraid of: that Yo-Yoji had never really liked them – her – and had only befriended them because it was his job. But as far as she was concerned, Yo-Yoji was still on probation – and would be for a while.

As Yo-Yoji and Max-Ernest continued to discuss plans for the talent show, Amber and Veronica walked towards their table, glancing quickly at Yo-Yoji, giggling, then looking away.

Cass's mouth dropped: something truly disturbing was dangling from Amber's wrist.

"Is that your sock-monster?" asked Max-Ernest, aghast.

"No, it's a copy – I think," said Cass, furious and more than a bit freaked out.

"But how...?"

Cass couldn't help it – she had to know. "Hey, Amber," she asked, trembling slightly, "where did you get that?"

"Oh, do you like it?" asked Amber, sugary as ever,

stopping at their table. "I'm not supposed to say where it's from, but it does say Twin Hearts on it, and that's the Skelton Sisters – oops!" She put her hand to her mouth. "I almost gave the secret away…! Anyway, I was just telling Veronica, I have six tickets to their concert tomorrow night – which is totally sold out, by the way. They're going to let me onstage – can you believe it? Do you guys want to go? Not that I can take everybody. I already have a waiting list of thirty people – but I could put you guys on it. I'm going to decide who gets to go later tonight, based on a bunch of things. I can't say what 'cause I don't want anyone to cheat." She seemed to be addressing all of them but she was looking at Yo-Yoji.

"Actually, I kind of think they suck," he replied. "So…no thanks."

"Well, excuse me for being nice," said Amber, stung.

"I told you he was a jerk," said Veronica.

"Let's go," said Amber. Cass watched them walk away, each tossing her hair like a girl in a shampoo commercial. Why had she ever had a hard time saying no to Amber? Cass wondered.

And more importantly:

"Hey, you guys – why do you think the Skelton Sisters are letting her onstage? Don't you think that's weird? And they gave her all those tickets…"

"Probably her daddy bribed them," said Yo-Yoji. "Is she rich?"

"I dunno. I don't think that's it," said Cass. In the distance, she could see Amber and Veronica disappearing into the girls' bathroom. "I'll be right back."

She stood up, pulling her sweatshirt hood over her head. Checking to see nobody was watching, she took the Sound Prism out of her backpack and hid it under her hood behind her big right ear.

The window in the girls' bathroom was small and located high up in the wall; normally, you wouldn't be able to hear a conversation taking place inside the bathroom if you were outside. But with the Sound Prism, Cass could hear Amber and Veronica talking as clearly as if she were standing next to them...

"No way, dude!" said Yo-Yoji to Cass after she returned. "Forget it! I would rather eat puke!"

"I agree – this is the worst idea you've ever had in your life," said Max-Ernest, putting down his two matching hummus sandwiches. "Are you sure you're not having a psychotic episode?"

What, you ask, could prompt such extreme reactions?

Simple: Cass's proposal that they all go to the Skelton Sisters concert the following night.

"We have to," she insisted, pulling off her sweatshirt hood and restowing the Sound Prism in her backpack. "Amber's like part of the Midnight Sun now. Well, maybe she's not really *in it* in it yet, but she was on the boat – and Ms. Mauvais gave her a job! She wouldn't tell Veronica what it was, but she said that was why she got the tickets and everything. And I have a feeling something bad's going to happen. I know nobody ever believes my predictions, but trust me on this!"

"But it's going to be the suckiest concert in history," said Yo-Yoji. "I think I'll get ill if I have to hear their music."

"Yeah, or they'll just kill us for real – I don't mean, like, kill in a good way, I mean, like, kill kill," Max-Ernest added, flustered. "Besides, even if we wanted to go, she said the concert was sold out. We wouldn't be able to buy tickets. And besides that, our parents would never let us go. And besides that, it's just totally deranged! I think you may need a doctor."

Cass listened calmly, not telling them what she was secretly hoping: that the concert would somehow provide a way for them to prove themselves to the Terces Society once more.

"Well, I know how to get tickets – that's not a problem," she said.

"How?" asked Yo-Yoji.

"You."

"What do you mean?"

"Ask for them."

"Wait – you mean, Amber…? Like, I have to ask *her*?"

Cass nodded. "She likes you."

"Oh, man! Is this, like, a joke or something?" Yo-Yoji practically gagged as the full horror of it all sank in. "Now, I'm really going to be sick. Seriously, I think I'm tasting barf!"

"You don't have a choice." Cass lowered her voice. "It's your duty as a society member."

Yo-Yoji laughed. "I don't remember getting orders to go to a concert."

"Okay, then – do it because we're friends. I mean, if we are."

She looked at him challengingly. This was a test, and they both knew it.

Just as Cass had anticipated, Yo-Yoji had no trouble convincing Amber to give him three tickets.

How did he do it?

I like Yo-Yoji too much to humiliate him by quoting him in full. Occasionally, we all have to eat humble pie.

CHAPTER FIVE

The Concert

As far as Cass could tell, she hadn't been grounded since she'd been back from the mountains.

She was never officially *un*grounded, but she and her mother seemed to have come to some kind of unspoken agreement to drop the pretence of punishment.

But a concert – an unchaperoned concert – was another matter altogether. Cass had to draw on all her creativity to convince her mother to let her go.

First, she tried the obvious: "Yo-Yoji's and Max-Ernest's parents are all letting them...!"

"Do I look like Max-Ernest's mom? You're lucky I let you go anywhere these days!"

Then Cass tried playing the girl card:

"Is it because I'm a girl you don't want me to? 'Cause that's really sexist! I can't believe you would be such a male chauvinist!"

"Don't even go there, Cassandra – I was fighting sexism before you were a blink in my eye!"

Finally, she hit on it:

"Plus, Yo-Yoji's turning thirteen tomorrow, so it's, like, his bar mitzvah. But he's Japanese so he's not really having one. And the *only* thing he wanted to do was go to the Skelton Sisters concert with me and Max-Ernest. I can't disappoint him. He *loves* the Skelton Sisters!"

A lie? Yes. But, I hope you agree, a whitish one. After all, she didn't know for certain that it *wasn't* his birthday.

As for Max-Ernest's parents, they were delighted that he wanted to go to a concert. For years, he'd never gone anywhere; now he was practically a world traveller.

"Maybe you aren't agoraphobic any more!" said his mother.

"Could be you kicked that old agoraphobia!" said his father.*

In fact, they were so delighted that they fought over the chance to take the three kids to the stadium where the Skelton Sisters were performing.

The entrance to the stadium was so crowded the kids almost wished they had a grown-up with them to help them push through.

When they finally managed to reach the front of the line, an usher looked at their tickets suspiciously. "Row A, huh? Funny, you guys don't look like big

---

*As far as I know, Max-Ernest never actually had agoraphobia (which is usually defined as a fear of crowds and open spaces). But over the years Max-Ernest had been diagnosed with so many conditions that his parents were in the habit of assuming he had each and every condition there was.

shots. You got famous parents or something?"

"Uh, yeah," said Yo-Yoji.

"Really famous," Cass added.

"I'll bet. Some of us have to work for a living! You're in the Lounge, down there—" He gestured in the direction of the stage.

They thanked him and headed off before he could question them further.

The Lounge wasn't really a lounge any more than their seats were really seats; it was a roped-off area right beneath the stage, furnished with tables and chairs and rugs and couches – even though it was outdoors.

Inside the ropes, our three friends could see music-industry types in shiny black clothing – and a few very lucky kids – talking and mingling as if they were at a big party and not a concert.

Waitresses wearing pink **twin♥hearts**™ T-shirts circulated, handing out free **twin♥hearts**™ cupcakes and bags of Skelton Sisters stuff.

A burly bouncer in a silver jumpsuit spoke our heroes' names into a headset, then lifted the red velvet rope and let them in past the sign that said **VIP Lounge**.

"What's *vip* mean?" asked Max-Ernest.

"It's not vip, dummy – it's V-I-P. Very Important Person," said Amber, standing nearby with Veronica, a brand-new **sock♥roach**® dangling from each of their wrists. "But I guess you wouldn't know that, would you, Max-Ernest? No offence."

While Max-Ernest's friends glared at Amber, Veronica giggled as if Amber had just said something very witty.

Amber turned to Yo-Yoji: "I thought you said you were bringing your bandmates from Japan."

"They couldn't get here in time." Yo-Yoji shrugged innocently.

"Well, anyway, I'm so glad you're here, Cass," said Amber. "You know we really couldn't have done it without you!"

Before Cass could ask who "we" were and what they couldn't have done without her (make a **sock♥roach**®, maybe?), Amber continued, "You should really try a cupcake – they're amazing!" And then she sailed off with Veronica to the other side of the Lounge.

Suddenly, the crowd erupted.

Everyone was yelling and cheering and whistling. Girls as young as five and six screamed at the top of their lungs. Even their parents hooted a bit. So many glow sticks waved in the air, it looked like a plague of phosphorescent locusts had descended on the stadium.

Our friends looked up at the stage to see what had provoked such a ruckus: a giant heart made of hundreds of bright pink light bulbs had just lit up. The Skelton Sisters, in matching silver miniskirts, stood on top, waving to the crowd. The Lounge was so close to the stage that the light was blinding.

"I think my retinas are burning!" yelled Max-Ernest.

Outside the Lounge, the frenzied Skelton Sisters fans pressed against the velvet rope; more bouncers in silver jumpsuits lined up like soldiers to keep them out.

As their band started to play a pounding beat, the Skelton Sisters somersaulted off the heart into the waiting hands of yet two more silver-clad young men.

"I think my eardrums are bursting!" yelled Max-Ernest, eyeing the giant speakers only a few metres away.

"Hi, everybody! Having fun?" Romi (or was it Montana?) shouted at the crowd.

"To kick off the night, we've got a special treat for you! Our brand-new single – never performed before!" said Montana (or was it Romi?).

"Oh no..." said Cass to no one in particular.

"What's wrong?" asked Yo-Yoji.

"I can't believe it – it's like I'm having a nightmare."

A dozen dancers in big fuzzy sock♥roach® costumes had appeared onstage – Cass's sock-monsters brought to larger than life in a dozen fluorescent colours.

"And to introduce the song, we'd like to bring onstage a special guest – Amber, winner of our You've Got the Music in You contest!" said Romi (or was it Montana?).

Amber, looking smugger than ever, was lifted onto the stage by one of the bouncers.

"You're on, girlfriend!" said Montana (or was it Romi?), handing Amber a microphone.

"Hi. This is such an amaaaaazing honour! Romi and Montana's new song is called 'C'mon, C'mon!' It's a special message for a special somebody," said Amber as confidently as if she spoke to crowds of hundreds every night. "And I think it's their best song ever!"

Then she turned back to Romi and Montana: "Go, girls!"

As the Skelton Sisters started to sing, the giant sock♥roaches® waved their multicoloured arms and danced in circles around them.

"Yo, seriously, this music sucks worse than anything I've ever heard in my life," Yo-Yoji grumbled to his friends. "I can't stay. It's a crime. Like helping somebody commit murder or something. Let's bail."

"He's right," said Max-Ernest. "I think this music is going to cause permanent brain damage."

"No, wait. Listen—"

"Why – you don't actually like this song, do you?" Yo-Yoji asked, incredulous. "How can you stand it? And they ripped off your sock-monster!"

"Just listen for a second," Cass said. "Doesn't it remind you of something?"

Her friends concentrated. Mostly, it sounded like any other bad, bubblegum pop song. But when they listened closely they heard a familiar tune underneath – not nearly as eerie or beautiful as they remembered it, but unmistakable, nevertheless.

"It's the song of the Sound Prism!" said Max-Ernest.

With growing horror, the kids listened to what the Skelton Sisters were singing:

C'mon! Come here now!
C'mon, cuz our time is here now!

C'mon! Can you hear it?
C'mon! Don't fear it –
Just listen to the sound now,
And come on round now...
Cuz we're calling,
We're calling...YOU!

Yo-Yoji looked at the others: "It's almost like they're talking to…"

"…the homunculus," Cass finished for him. "It's a trap – to get him to come here."

Max-Ernest was the first to jump into action. If you call nervously tapping your feet and wiping your brow action. "We have to stop the song – before he hears it!"

"Yeah, but how?" asked Cass.

"Like this!" said Yo-Yoji.

And, like that, he leaped onto the stage.

"Hey, Amber," he shouted. "You still want me to be in a band with you? Give me that mic—" Before Amber realized what was happening, he grabbed her mic away from her.

Without thinking, Cass and Max-Ernest scrambled onto the stage after Yo-Yoji.

"Hey, we know them!" shrieked the startled Romi (or was it Montana), pointing at Cass and Max-Ernest.

"Yeah, they're…them!" shrieked the startled Montana (or was it Romi?).

What was weird was that as they spoke, the song continued just as if they were still singing.

C'mon! Come here now!
C'mon, cuz our time is here now!

"I've got a better song, it's called, 'You Suck, You Lip-Synching Fakers!'" shouted Yo-Yoji into the mic so that the entire crowd could hear. "The Skelton Sisters suck! The Skelton Sisters suck!"

Cass and Max-Ernest picked up the chant. "They suck! They suck!"

"Get them!" yelled Romi (or was it Montana?).

The twelve sock♥roaches® stopped dancing and started to close in on Cass and Max-Ernest.

"Hey, Cass – look out there!" Max-Ernest pointed into the crowd.

A spotlight shone on the centre aisle where a certain fifty-four-and-a-half-centimetre-tall creature was visible, walking towards the stage. He looked like another sock♥roach® – just smaller.

The audience cheered him on, straining their necks to look at this short but wonderful addition to the show.

"Noooo! Mr. Cabbage Face!" Cass screamed. "Go away! It's a trap!!!"

But she had no microphone and her voice was drowned out by the music and the cheers of the crowd.

Cass's screams had distracted their assailants long enough for Max-Ernest to slip out from the circle. Quickly, Cass pulled the Sound Prism out of her sweatshirt. Before she was grabbed by the nearest sock♥roach®, she rolled it in Max-Ernest's direction and...

Fumbling, he caught it.

Yo-Yoji joined him and they jumped offstage—

Just as the grumpy homunculus was climbing up.

"You better have a good explanation for this," he said to Cass, not yet realizing that her arms were pinned behind her back. "I don't dance – let's just get that clear."

"I'm sorry, I didn't, I mean, I couldn't—" said Cass tearfully.

By the time the homunculus had any clue what she meant, two dancers had grabbed him from behind. And now he, too, was locked in the fuzzy but firm grip of a bright orange sock♥roach®.

"Unhand me, you oversize baby toy!" he snarled. "I've had bigger than you for lunch!"

Max-Ernest and Yo-Yoji watched helplessly from the crowd as their twelve-year-old friend and the five-hundred-year-old homunculus were dragged backstage. There were too many of the enemy to even contemplate a fight.

The sock♥roaches® dropped Cass and the homunculus to the floor in front of Ms. Mauvais like dogs presenting fresh kill to their master.

"Welcome to the green room. Make yourselves at home."

Ms. Mauvais gestured grandly around the dingy backstage waiting room as if she were welcoming them to a palace, her gauzy gold gown rippling with every movement.

Palms sweating, pulse racing, Cass looked around for a way out; there was only one door, and there were no windows.

As if deliberately mocking her, Dr. L relaxed, feet up, on a long couch. A near life-size photo of a tropical beach was pasted to the wall behind him.

"Can I offer you something to eat from craft services?" Ms. Mauvais asked, indicating a long table piled high with all kinds of food.

The homunculus eyed a big standing rib roast with bones sticking up in a circle, making a crown. Meat juices puddled on the plate underneath.

"Yeah, I'll take...some of that." He pointed at the roast, his eyes glistening.

"The crown roast? It does look...bloody, doesn't it? You can have the whole thing – *if* you tell us where Lord Pharaoh's grave is."

So *that's* a crown roast, thought Cass. You'd really have to be a cannibal to find one of those appetizing!

With enormous effort, the homunculus tore his

eyes away from the roast. "Never," he said, practically trembling with hunger. "I'd rather starve."

"Oh, what a noble little creature you are," said Ms. Mauvais.

"Hardly," sneered the homunculus. "But compared to you..."

"We have other means of convincing a person – or whatever you call yourself," said Dr. L from the couch. He studied the homunculus with a scientific eye.

"Go ahead and try," said the homunculus. "No torture can compare to what I endured from Lord Pharaoh when I was young. And death doesn't scare me – at my age, it would be a relief! You should try it yourselves!"

"I'd really rather not," said Ms. Mauvais. "In fact, you could say *not* dying is my life's work."

"We're patient. And resourceful," said Dr. L. "Let's see – what means of persuasion do we have on hand?"

As his glance fell on Cass, the homunculus visibly stiffened.

"I think you just found it," said Ms. Mauvais.

Dr. L smiled grimly. "I think I did."

★   ★   ★

Don't worry, nobody laid a hand on Cass – other than the electric blue sock♥roach® who was still gripping her arm. But Dr. L's description of what he would do to her if the homunculus didn't tell them where to find the grave site was so horrifying I shudder just to think about it.

And you know me – I'm as cold-hearted as they come.

Imagine how Mr. Cabbage Face reacted.

I know the homunculus comes off as a gruff and surly sort of fellow. But remember his history: he'd been so ridiculed and abused as a child he couldn't bear to see another child treated harshly.

Then there's this: Cass was the heir of the Jester. When he looked at her ears (if not her face) he saw his old friend. His only friend. The one he would have sacrificed all for.

"All right," he said, struggling with himself. "I'll tell you. Just don't touch the girl!"

Perhaps it would have been wiser to leave Cass to whatever tortures the Midnight Sun might have had in store – if their finding Lord Pharaoh's grave was really going to be as disastrous as the homunculus predicted. But I confess I sympathize with him and like him better for his choice.

Dr. L nodded, as if the homunculus were merely

confirming something he'd known already.

And Ms. Mauvais's frozen face cracked just slightly into something like a smile.

"Good. Now, give me that key," she said.

His large hand shaking, the homunculus removed the skeleton key from around his neck.

For the first time since he'd hung it there centuries ago.

A moment later, hidden in the crowd, Yo-Yoji and Max-Ernest watched Cass and the homunculus being escorted out the gate, surrounded by a cluster of silver-clad bouncers.

"We have to follow them!" said Max-Ernest.

"Well, come on then," said Yo-Yoji.

The two boys made it out of the stadium just in time to see Cass and the homunculus pushed into a waiting limousine. Ms. Mauvais and Dr. L climbed in after them and a bouncer slammed the door shut.

As the gleaming vehicle took off into the night, Yo-Yoji and Max-Ernest ran after it. But it was no use – they'd never catch up.

They stood, panting, under the harsh lights of the huge parking lot.

"What do we do now?" asked Max-Ernest, miserable.

"I dunno. We don't even know where they're going."

"Wait – I just remembered!" Max-Ernest pulled the Sound Prism out of his jacket pocket.

He motioned Yo-Yoji to his side then turned the Sound Prism around in his hand. Beyond the sounds of the concert behind them, they heard cars honking, a baby crying...

Then, faintly, in snippets, the sound of Cass speaking in the distance.

"I can't believe...told...WHISPER LAKE! And now... to the GRAVEYARD!"

Walking around in circles as if he were trying to get a better cellphone signal, Max-Ernest managed to focus on the voices in the limo.

"Shush, girl!" they could hear Ms. Mauvais say. Cass spoke in an oddly clear voice, emphasizing certain words: *"It's too bad they won't know to FIND PIETRO and tell him to MEET US THERE."*

"It's almost like she's trying to tell us to find him," said Yo-Yoji.

Max-Ernest shook his head in amazement. "Only Cass could boss us around – even when she's a kilometre away!"

"Yeah, well, she's got a good teammate."

"You mean you?"

"No, you, dude."

"Oh." Max-Ernest grinned, surprised. "So are you ready to go save Cass?"

"Definitely."

Without having to confer out loud, they both started running in the direction of the nearest bus stop.

CHAPTER FOUR

Ending

No, not that kind. Although that would be bad enough.

I mean, the ending of *life*.

Which, come to think of it, is why I hate the ending of a book so much. Because it's a kind of death.

There are two kinds of people in the world: those who like graveyards and those who don't.

When I was younger, I loved graveyards. They weren't spooky so much as mysterious. Each tombstone another story to uncover. Another life to learn about.

Now that I'm older – I won't say how old – I *hate* graveyards. The only life – or rather death – I see in the tombstones is my own.

Believe me, if I didn't have to end this book in a graveyard I wouldn't. (Okay, so I lied – it is that kind of ending. Or the beginning of the ending.)

Come to think of it, who says I have to end the book in a graveyard?

Just because that's where Dr. L and Ms. Mauvais headed with Cass and the homunculus, just because that's where a big climactic confrontation and dramatic resolution to the story I've been telling took place, who says I have to write about it?

Contrary to what some may believe, this is still my book – isn't it?

If I want to, I could take things in a radically new direction.

Like this:

Just when Cass thought they were all headed for the graveyard, the limousine got caught in the tractor beam of an alien spaceship that sucked the limousine up into its belly. As luck would have it, the aliens were on a mission to find a survivalist to lead their disaster-prone planet...

Or this:

Just when Cass thought they were all headed for the graveyard, Ms. Mauvais and Dr. L both suddenly fell into anaphylactic shock, thanks to a pill the homunculus dropped in their champagne...

Or even this:

Just when Cass thought they were all headed for the graveyard, she blinked and woke up. She, Cassandra – a survivalist? She laughed. What a funny thing for a ballet dancer to dream about...

No? None of those versions ring true? I'm betraying you, my reader, by taking off in these wild directions?

Well, I tried.

Your criticism is harsh but fair.

I'll tell you what – you know how much I like deals – I will write the graveyard scene, if, and only if, you hold my hand through it.

You be the strong and courageous one, and I'll provide the commentary. If you're the kind of person who happily runs through graveyards laughing at death, so much the better.

Now: how to start our ending?

Normally, when a writer doesn't know how to start, he might begin with a description of place. But I did that already – you read all about the graveyard and Whisper Lake in the camping chapters.

I have an idea: why don't we show how the place has changed since we last saw it? How much time has passed. That sort of thing.

To make our job easier (and maybe a little less scary), let's pretend we're making a movie and imagine that Whisper Lake and the surrounding mountains are being filmed from high above in a helicopter – that's called an aerial shot.

What we see from up here in the sky is that the entire mountain range has been blanketed in snow, and Whisper Lake has been frozen over. In fact, it is snowing now, very softly, giving our movie the look of slow motion.

Little specks of colour move against the white background – people, we see they are, as the camera pushes in. They make tracks through the snow, all converging on the same point above the lake.

We watch as one by one these silent hikers salute each other. Strange – for a second, it looks as though they have no hands...

Oh – I know why! It's because they're all wearing white gloves that don't show up against the snow...

From her earthbound vantage point, tied to a tree some twenty metres above the grave of Lord Pharaoh, Cass made the same observation.

Gloves.

She knew what they meant. She'd seen these same sinister people on a similar occasion at the Midnight Sun Spa. They were the acolytes of the Midnight Sun – and if they were gathering like this it could only be because something truly terrible was about to occur.

What was once Lord Pharaoh's grave was now a large gaping hole, surrounded by frozen clods of mud.

A team of silver-clad men – bouncers from the concert – stood in the hole removing dirt and rubble so expertly and methodically that I have to believe they had dug up many graves before.

Around them, the Masters of the Midnight Sun – several still in sock♥roach® costumes – stood in a wide circle, chanting something deep and resonant like a yoga master's *Om*, yet somehow much darker and more foreboding.

Impervious to the cold, Ms. Mauvais stood on the edge of the grave, her gauzy gold gown blowing in the wind. Snowflakes swirled around her.

Like a high priestess, she spoke to her congregation: "A great man was buried here. No, a great *being*. Even a god. For he had the power to create life itself! Who knows what miracles Lord Pharaoh would have achieved had not his own creation turned against him? This miserable, ungrateful little creature here—"

She gave a dismissive kick to the homunculus who was lying in the snow beneath her, his hands and feet bound together with rope. "But now we will continue Lord Pharaoh's work, and we will be gods ourselves!"

With excited cries, the gravediggers hoisted a large and cumbersome coffin out of the grave, and laid it on the snow.

An oozing, festering crust covered the entire casket save for a gleaming golden lock. The coffin seemed almost to be alive.

"Behold – in this coffin lies the Secret we have so long sought!"

"The Secret...the Secret...the Secret..." chanted the crowd.

"Doctor...?" Ms. Mauvais looked expectantly at Dr. L.

He nodded and stepped forward, skeleton key in hand. The coffin's golden lock beckoned.

"You don't want to open that!" warned a gruff voice from the ground.

"You mean *you* don't want us to open it," scoffed Ms. Mauvais.

"Me? It's nothing to me," the homunculus responded. "This isn't my time. This isn't my place. I'm not one of you."

"Are not Lord Pharaoh's papers in there with him?" asked Dr. L.

"Among other things, yes."

"And is not the Secret written there?"

"I don't know anything about that," said the homunculus, as if the Secret were the least of his concerns. "But I'm telling you, if you let out what's in that coffin – then everything and everyone you see around you will die. And it won't *smell* very good, either! I speak only out of concern for the girl, you understand—" He gestured awkwardly towards Cass, without looking at her. "And because I think the trees deserve to live."

"Perhaps we should listen to him," said Dr. L, turning to Ms. Mauvais. "His words have the ring of truth."

"Are you mad?!" yelled Ms. Mauvais, sounding quite mad herself.

By now, snow had started to pile on top of Cass's head and shoulders and feet; she looked as if she were one of the statues in the graveyard.

Cass had long ago memorized the symptoms of frostbite: discolouration of skin, tingling or burning feeling, numbness. But she'd never before experienced them.

Unfortunately, her extensive research on the subject did her no good now. How did it help to know that if her frostbite was left untreated her skin would gradually darken until it became black and began to loosen from her flesh? That her nerves would be damaged beyond repair? That she would probably fall prey to gangrene?

She liked to think she would be brave enough to face amputation if it were ever required, but there was little chance that even such a drastic treatment would be available here; Dr. L was much more likely to chop off her head than her leg.

How, why, had she let herself become their prisoner? It was like the boat all over again – with one big difference. On the boat, Max-Ernest had been imprisoned with her. Now, here in the mountains, she was alone.

Cold and alone.

She looked out into the empty, snowy world around her. The Midnight Sun had scared even the birds away. Where was Max-Ernest now?

I should never have given him the Sound Prism, she thought. It was my only tool, my only power. Why did I trust him with it? What made me think he'd be able to get here to save me?

Wasn't a survivalist supposed to save herself? And here she was, waiting helpless, tied to a tree like Snow White!

And now, she thought, I'm going to die.

Tears trickled down Cass's cheeks only to collect in an ugly icy crusty combination with the frozen snot beneath her nose.

As Ms. Mauvais and Dr. L fought over whether or not to open the coffin, the homunculus was dragged through the snow and dropped next to Cass.

He looked up at her, a small sad smile on his face.

"The Jester would have been proud of you," he said.

"Why? Look at me! I'm crying."

"Oh, I don't think he would have cared about that. He saw me cry once and told me it made me human. Only a miserable pathetic human wretch would shed tears like that, he said."

Cass laughed through her tears.

"Sorry about the crown roast," she said after a moment. "I shouldn't have lied."

The homunculus snorted. "The Jester wasn't exactly famous for his truthfulness, either."

"Well, thanks for not holding it against me." Cass sniffled, unable to wipe her nose. "You know, I used to dream about you. I even dreamed this – sort of." She nodded in the direction of the open grave. "Max-Ernest says that a dream is the fulfilment of a wish. I couldn't figure out what my dreams were wishing for – they seemed so scary. But I think I know now."

"I thought I told you – I don't grant wishes," the homunculus joked, wriggling closer.

"But you did – that's the point." Cass was so cold it was almost impossible to speak, but she had to get it out.

"I think my wish had to do with wanting to know who my father is. Even though I never totally admitted it. Because I didn't want to have to miss him or whatever. Or maybe just because I didn't want to hurt my mom's feelings. It's kind of hard to explain... but what you told me about the Jester, and his pointy ears and everything, it's the only clue I've ever had. I mean, I know he couldn't be my father – then I'd be as old as you, but he could be my father's father's father's father's father – or something like that. Right?"

The homunculus nodded. "Something like that."

"Anyway, I think that's why I dreamed about you. Although it still doesn't make any sense, considering I never met you before..."

"Very little in this world makes sense," said the homunculus with uncharacteristic solemnity.

They fell silent as the wind picked up.

Then, suddenly, Cass:

"Hey, what's that?"

"What's what?"

Cass cocked her head, listening. "Sounds like – horses?"

"I can't hear anything," said the homunculus. "Then again, I don't have your ears."

"What do you mean, *my* ears?"

"It's your gift, isn't it? The Jester could hear all kinds of things. Too much, if you ask me. Even without the Sound Prism."

As Cass contemplated this, they heard Dr. L's voice ring out – so loud it echoed across Whisper Lake.

"Hello, my fellow Masters of the Midnight Sun – this is your leader, Luciano, Dr. L, speaking. There has been a change of plan. This is not Lord Pharaoh's grave. It contains no Secret."

Still standing by the coffin, Ms. Mauvais looked at Dr. L in outrage. "What are you doing?"

He whirled around, distressed. "But that wasn't me! Pay no attention!" he shouted at the Midnight Sun members.

"Everyone must leave – now!" boomed the voice of this other, louder Dr. L.

The Midnight Sun members mumbled and grumbled in confusion. Those who couldn't hear the real Dr. L beckoning them to stay began to disassemble.

"Who's speaking? Who stole my voice?" Dr. L shouted. "Pietro, is that you?"

But his voice was drowned by the sound of galloping horses. As everyone turned in the direction of the horses, the sock♥roach® nearest the grave ripped his head off—

"Owen?!"

He waved at Cass as he shed the rest of his lime green costume. "I'll come get you in a second!" he shouted in the seldom-used voice she'd come to recognize as his own.

Then he wrestled a yellow fellow sock❤roach® to the ground.

"Pietro, where are you?" cried Dr. L, still looking for his brother.

As if Dr. L had summoned him from the beyond, Pietro arrived out of the trees on horseback at the other side of the graveyard. In his hand was what looked from a distance like a large snowball.

"Everyone, go home!" he shouted into the snowball as if it were a megaphone.

Alongside Pietro, a lively and diverse (which is a polite way of saying *rambunctious* and *ragtag*) sort of cavalry rode into the graveyard. With cheers and cries of "Ballyhoo!" they attacked (which is a polite way of saying *created chaos among*) their gloved adversaries.

On one horse (which, in this case, is a polite way of saying *donkey*) sat the two little people seen earlier on the bus, still in their formal attire. As soon as they entered the graveyard, they jumped off and started running under the legs of the silver-clad bouncers, tripping them and occasionally biting their ankles.

The Bearded Lady also jumped off her horse (which in this case is a polite way of saying *elephant*) and started swinging her fists at unsuspecting Midnight Sun members.

The Strong Man, meanwhile, marched in on foot, supporting (which is a polite way of saying *wielding like human barbells*) two Chinese plate-spinners – and knocking over enemies on all sides.

Standing on top of a horse (which, in this case, is a polite way of saying *camel*), the Illustrated Man breathed fire from his mouth, lighting torches that he juggled then threw at fleeing sock♥roaches®.

In a cart behind him, the red-coated Lion Tamer waved his bullwhip and bowed this way and that as if before a cheering crowd (which is a polite way of saying he was *off his rocker*).

Alone among this brave-ish band, there was one who truly followed the Way of the Warrior: that was, of course, the one and only Warrior Wei. Lily wore full body armour over her black gi and had her horse's-head violin strapped to her back as if it were a sword (which in fact it was).

Like laser beams, her eyes locked on her old nemesis, Ms. Mauvais, who was standing slightly removed from the melee, a look of intense rage on her face.

Screaming a vengeful word I cannot repeat (not because it was obscene, but because it was utterly unrecognizable), Lily kicked her heels into the sides of her horse and charged—

Just before she could make contact, however, Ms. Mauvais signalled six of her gloved gravediggers with a flick of her gloved wrist, and they blocked Lily's way, pulling her off her horse.

By the time Lily kicked, chopped and swung her way through the line of silver-clad thugs, Ms. Mauvais had disappeared – but, undeterred, Lily plunged into battle with the rest of the Midnight Sun. Running behind the circus folk, looking winded but also exhilarated, were two much younger and comparatively uncolourful people: Max-Ernest and Yo-Yoji.

Pietro stalled his horse next to them.

"Thanks for this!" He tossed Max-Ernest the snowball which, of course, was actually the Sound Prism – and which Max-Ernest caught with two hands.

"Now, all we need is that—" said Max-Ernest. He pointed to the senile Lion Tamer, still standing on his horse, bowing to an imaginary crowd. "Hey, mister – can we borrow your whip?" he shouted.

Yo-Yoji looked at Max-Ernest in surprise: what the heck did he want a whip for?

Pietro urged his horse forward, then jumped off when he neared the grave. In the commotion, Lord Pharaoh's coffin had been left unguarded.

"Pietro?!"

It was his brother.

Suddenly, they were face-to-face. And almost nose-to-nose. They were so close – so quickly and unexpectedly – that they each stepped backwards as if frightened by a ghost.

Although Pietro's face had aged so much more than Dr. L's, their movements remained identical, and watching the two of them together was like watching one person standing in front of a mirror. (Or maybe like watching two people playing mirror in a drama class.)

"Nice trick with the voice," said Dr. L, recovering. "I don't remember that one."

"I guess I've learned one or two since the Bergamo Brothers last performed."

Dr. L smiled wanly. "You look...old, brother."

"And so I am. So we are. Luciano, come home with me. It is not too late. You are not this...thing." He gestured to Dr. L's handsome but lifeless face, his slick clothes, his telltale gloves. "I don't believe it. I won't believe it."

Dr. L blinked – for a moment he seemed almost to waver. To regret what he'd become. To agree to repent.

"You always thought you knew better than me, didn't you?" he asked with a sneer.

"I do know better," said Pietro.

They stared at each other – their old love for each other vying with their newfound hatred.

"Kill him!" Ms. Mauvais screamed, striding towards them.

Dr. L raised his gloved hand. He held the skeleton key like a weapon.

"Goodbye, *fratello mio*," Pietro said sadly. "Do you remember this one…?"

He reached down and grabbed a fistful of snow. "We used to use smoke—"

Before his brother had time to react, Pietro threw the powdery snow into his brother's eyes, creating a sparkly cloud. He remounted his horse and escaped into the fracas.

A moment later, Max-Ernest and Yo-Yoji climbed up onto the boulder overlooking the lake, the boulder on which they'd stood when Cass first called the homunculus a few long weeks ago.

Below in the graveyard, chaos reigned.

"Are you sure this is going to work?" asked Yo-Yoji. He held the lion-tamer's whip in his hand, and he flicked it nervously.

"Define *sure*," said Max-Ernest, holding the Sound Prism so tight his knuckles were white. "Am I absolutely positive? No. Am I reasonably certain?... Uh, no. Do I think there is a good chance of success? Depends what you mean by good. Do I think it will work? Um, I hope it will. Does part of me think the plan is insane? Uh, yeah. Is it the kind of thing I would usually do—?"

"Okay, I get the point!"

"Anyway, it's a fact that a whip creates a sonic boom – I've read about it. It's because when you crack it, it moves faster than the speed of sound."

Yo-Yoji eyed the whip in his hand, as if wondering how it could possibly move that fast.

"Plus," said Max-Ernest, standing a little taller, "it's the only way to save Cass. Well, the only way I can think of. Do you have a better idea?"

Yo-Yoji gave the whip an experimental crack. Max-Ernest jumped back, startled.

"Okay, you're the boss," said Yo-Yoji. He made a fist and looked meaningfully at Max-Ernest.

"Paper scissors rock?" asked his confused friend.

Yo-Yoji laughed. "No, like this—"

And he showed Max-Ernest how to bump fists.

It was strange for Cass, being on the sidelines of the battle waging in front of her in the graveyard. (Owen, it seems, was still too busy fighting sock♥roaches® to untie her.) In her fantasies at least, she was always the hero in these situations, not the damsel in distress.

Still, she was glad there were heroes around – even if they weren't her. She'd barely caught a glimpse of her two friends, but it had been enough.

True, the Midnight Sun had numbers on their side. Not to mention just about every other advantage you could think of. But just knowing Max-Ernest and Yo-Yoji were there – and that they'd called Pietro just as she'd planned – made her feel hopeful.

She wasn't alone, she realized. She had a friend. In fact, she had two. And more if you counted Pietro and Owen and Lily. She looked down at her feet: and the homunculus. How many friends could a person have? Perhaps there was no limit. She made a mental note to discuss the subject one day with Max-Ernest.

She thought again of the last time she'd been tied up – on the Midnight Sun boat. She hadn't yet tried to re-enact Max-Ernest's worm wriggle, because she'd been under constant guard. But now, she realized, nobody was looking at her.

Even the homunculus, still tied up in the snow beside her, was absorbed in the scene in front of him, as though it were a movie.

She tested the rope for slack; sure enough, they'd used too much rope again. Then she kicked her shoes off – the first step – and, wincing, stood in her socks in the snow. Now she'd get frostbite for sure.

Imagining a future life without toes, she shimmied herself out of the rope. Sooner than she expected, she was tying her shoes back on, and untying the surprised homunculus.

"Nice job, Jester junior."

"Any time."

As she spoke, her voice was lost in the—

BOOM!!!

It sounded like a crack of thunder – followed by the loudest rumbling Cass had ever heard, indeed, the loudest rumbling the homunculus had ever heard, and he'd been hearing rumbling for five hundred years (though mostly in his own stomach).

"Look – it's working!" said Yo-Yoji.

He and Max-Ernest watched as rocks started to

shake loose from the peaks above.

"Yeah, but they're not going in the right direction."

"Maybe we should trying aiming for that? That'll come right down on them," said Yo-Yoji, pointing to a tall mountain peak that seemed to rise directly out of the graveyard. The snow on the peak was piled so high it created a lip...

"You mean that cornice? I don't know how to aim for it exactly," said Max-Ernest, looking from the Sound Prism to the mountain peak. "I was just figuring if I created a big enough sonic boom, the whole thing would avalanche."

"Well, let's try again – but don't close your eyes this time."

"Okay – but it's hard not to; it's a reflex."

Bravely keeping his eyes open, Max-Ernest held the Sound Prism as far out in front of himself as he could.

With an unusual intensity of focus, Yo-Yoji flicked the whip backwards, then – crrrrracked it just a centimetre or so away from the Sound Prism.

BOOOOOOOOOOOOOOOOOOOOOM!!!!!!!

It was even louder this time. The mountains shook. A big crack zigzagged through the frozen surface of Whisper Lake.

Max-Ernest and Yo-Yoji stared in amazement, at first not noticing that the boulder they were standing on had dislodged from the mountainside and started to ROLLLLLLLLLLLLLLLLLLL—

Cass heard the boulder before she saw it.

She had only a hazy hunch that the sonic booms had been created by Max-Ernest and Yo-Yoji, and only the very haziest of hunches that the purpose of the booms was to bury Lord Pharaoh's coffin for good.

Nonetheless, she snapped into action as though the plan had been her own.

"C'mon," she said to the homunculus, pointing to the coffin as the boulder hurdled towards Lord Pharaoh's grave, gaining speed every second.

(Thankfully, Max-Ernest and Yo-Yoji had managed to jump off.)

While the Midnight Sun and Terces members alike scattered this way and that, running away from the boulder's path, Cass and the homunculus sprinted to the coffin.

Together, they pushed the coffin (it was still on wheels) back to the grave, and heaved it over the edge into the hole.

"Cass!" warned the homunculus.

The boulder had bounded off another rock, sailed through the air, and was now rolling directly at them like a giant bowling ball.

With superhuman effort, the little homunculus rammed into Cass, pushing her out of the way just in time. But as he did so, he lost his footing and –

"Mr. Cabbage Face!!!"

– fell backwards into the hole.

The boulder crashed on top of him.

Sealing the homunculus – and Lord Pharaoh's deadly coffin – in the grave for ever.

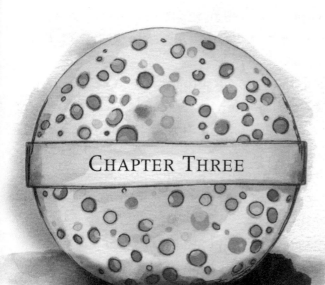

CHAPTER THREE

The Oath
of Terces

As the last remaining members of the Midnight Sun retreated into the snowy wilderness, a black helicopter rose out of the trees and flew off into the dawn sky – like a creature of the night fleeing the encroaching day.

Were we to have looked into the helicopter's cabin, we would likely have found Dr. L and Ms. Mauvais sitting in stony silence, or furiously plotting their revenge, or both.

Rather humiliating to be defeated by three children, a defunct circus, and a tiny man grown in horse dung – don't you think?

But let us stay on the ground this time, and watch the motley assortment of people known as the Terces Society gathering around Lord Pharaoh's grave – now marked by a giant boulder sunk halfway into the earth.

The scene looked something like it did when the Midnight Sun had gathered earlier. But the differences were telling.

And not only because the sun – the real sun – had started to rise.

For one thing, the Terces Society members smiled. Not in the greedy, sinister, conniving way in which the Masters of the Midnight Sun occasionally smiled, but in an easier, friendlier, if still mischievous and not altogether innocent way.

For another thing, their attention was not trained on the grave and the terrible Secret it might contain but on the three kids in their midst.

I don't know whether it was due to Terces Society custom, or rather, as I suspect, to Pietro's intuitive understanding of the kind of ceremony they wanted, but the three kids were kneeling almost as if they were being knighted, Pietro standing above them like a proud father.

Cass and Max-Ernest were taking the Oath of Terces at last. And with them their new friend and partner, Yo-Yoji.

As Pietro recited the words, they repeated them:

I HAVE A SECRET I CAN'T TELL NOR INK;
THOUGH IT HAS NO SCENT, IT DOES OFTEN STINK.
THOUGH IT MAKES NO SOUND, IT CAN MAKE YOU ROAR;
WHEN IT'S TASTELESS, I LIKE IT ALL THE MORE.
THOUGH IT HAS NO SHADE, IT LACKS NOT COLOUR;
THOUGH IT HAS NO SHAPE, NO CAUSE FOR DOLOUR.
IF YOU THINK YOU KNOW IT, YOU'RE INCORRECT,
AND FROM YOU THE SECRET I WILL PROTECT.
THE SECRET OF LIFE IS NOT STONE NOR CENTS,
FOR THE SECRET SENSE IS BUT A NONSENSE.

"I thought it was supposed to be an oath," said

Yo-Yoji, confused, as the three friends stood up. "That sounded more like another riddle."

"Well, I liked it," said Cass, her face still red from crying. "Are we allowed to know where it's from?" She wiped her nose and looked at the grown-ups standing behind them.

"The Jester, of course," said Mr. Wallace, pulling up the collar of his coat. "Everything he wrote is a bit of a puzzle."

Owen patted Mr. Wallace on the back. "And if you had it your way, we'd spend all our time sitting in some library solving them."

"Yeah, but what's weird is, the way it goes, if you think you know the Secret, you're wrong," said Max-Ernest. "So how're you supposed to figure it out then? It's almost like you're not supposed to solve the riddle. How 'bout that?"

"How 'bout that?" Pietro smiled at Max-Ernest. "I think you have come pretty close to solving it just now."

"Perhaps Cass is not the only one who has something in common with the Jester," said Lily with a laugh.*

---

*I KNOW – YOU'RE FRUSTRATED. ALL THOSE NOBLE TERCES MEMBERS MAY WAX PHILOSOPHICAL, BUT YOU WERE HOPING TO LEARN SOMETHING MORE ABOUT THE SECRET. IF IT'S ANY CONSOLATION, THINK ABOUT IT THIS WAY: WOULD YOU RATHER KNOW THE SECRET OR SAVE THE WORLD? IN A SENSE, THAT WAS THE CHOICE OUR THREE

Later, as they all started heading down the mountain, Cass stopped and turned back to look at the enormous ball of granite sticking out from the glistening snow. There was something very fitting, she thought, about such a little creature getting such a big tombstone.

"Goodbye, Mr. Cabbage Face," she said softly.

Her eyes beginning to tear again, she pulled that much smaller ball, the Sound Prism, out of her jacket pocket, and tossed it into the air one last time.

FRIENDS FACED — AND THE HOMUNCULUS HIMSELF FACED — WHEN THEY DECIDED TO BURY LORD PHARAOH'S COFFIN.

OF COURSE, I MYSELF MIGHT HAVE CHOSEN THE SECRET. BUT THAT IS WHY I'M A WRITER AND NOT A HERO.

CHAPTER TWO

The Foundling

I'm sure I don't have to tell you how hysterical Cass's mother became when Cass didn't come home after the Skelton Sisters concert. This time around she didn't bend and it would be months before Cass could step foot out of her house again without an accompanying adult.

You try telling your mother you'll be home by eleven p.m. – then get kidnapped by evil alchemists, save the world with the help of a broken-down circus, have *your* life saved by a five-hundred-year-old homunculus, swear an oath you'll keep this all secret from everyone *including* your mother, and then show up the following day with no explanation whatsoever.

Cass was no longer allowed even to take the school bus. She had to be driven back and forth to school by her mother or her grandfathers.

Or – as happened one day a few weeks after the incident at Whisper Lake – by her mother *and* her grandfathers.

That afternoon, Cass's mother was waiting on the kerb in front of Cass's school with Grandpa Larry and Grandpa Wayne; it was Grandpa Larry's birthday and they were all going to an antiques auction to celebrate.

As she stepped outside, Cass heard them

speaking – even though they were about half a block away:

"You know, it's our story, too – not just yours," Grandpa Larry was saying. "Maybe *we* should tell her if you won't."

"No, no. I will. Very soon. I promise," said Cass's mother. "I just need to find the right—"

"But there's never going to be a right time!" said Cass's grandfathers in unison.

Reflexively, Cass felt in her pocket for the Sound Prism. But she wasn't carrying it. She was hearing them with her own ears.

Could the homunculus have been right?

One thing was certain: whatever their powers, her ears were unique, and they were her inheritance from the Jester.

And something else: it was time.

Right now.

Right here in front of her school.

Before she could change her mind, Cass marched up to her startled mother and grandfathers, and took a big breath—

"I know why you didn't want to say who my father was."

Another breath.

"It's because you don't really know."

Breath.

"Because I was adopted, and you were afraid to tell me."

Breath.

"But it's okay, I still love you."

Breath.

"And you're still my mom."

Breath.

"So don't worry."

Big breath.

"But how...?" asked her mother, beginning to cry.

"Somebody sent me this – I can't really explain why."

Suddenly teary herself, Cass showed her mom the piece of paper that she'd found on the ground in the Barbie Graveyard. The birth certificate that had been in the Sound Prism file.

She couldn't pinpoint the exact moment when she'd realized that she was the girl whose name was on the birth certificate. It could have been when the homunculus told her she was the heir of the Jester. Or it might have been one of those sleepless nights after they'd lost the homunculus, when Cass thought she'd lost her chance to be part of the Terces Society as well.

But she'd been carrying the birth certificate around

with her ever since she'd found it – as if she'd known what it meant all along.

"Oh, Cass, I love you so much," said her mother, hugging her tight.

"Me, too," said Cass, hugging back.

"Us, too," said her beaming grandfathers, closing in for a group hug.

Cass was a foundling.

As Grandpa Larry and Grandpa Wayne would tell her later that evening, and many more times after that, one night twelve years before, Cass's mother happened to be having tea with them.

She was in tears – she had no husband or boyfriend in sight, and, she told them, she was afraid she would never have a child.

While Larry and Wayne tried to cheer her up, Sebastian started barking down below. A customer, they wondered, at this hour?

By the time they got downstairs, whoever had been there was gone. But a box had been left on their doorstep – just as so many other boxes had been left on their doorstep over the years. (Everyone knew Larry and Wayne could never bear to throw anything away.)

The box was taped up, just as if it contained old magazines or a mismatched set of plates, and it said nothing but the words "Handle With Care". A single hole had been poked through the cardboard to let air inside.

When they opened the box, they found a tiny baby wrapped in a blanket. There was no note, only a meticulously written label: "Baby girl. 7 lbs. 3 oz. Time of birth 6:35 p.m."

But Cass's mother hadn't needed to read a label to know the baby was hers.

Likewise, Cass hadn't needed to hear the story twelve years later to know who her mother was meant to be.

Then again, hearing a good story never hurts. Especially when it's about you.

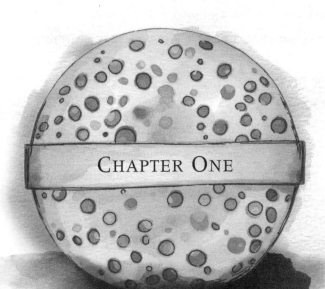

CHAPTER ONE

The Talents Show

Months later...

Cass was in the audience.

Let me repeat that. Because she was very emphatic about it.

Cass was in the audience.

As in – *not onstage*.

As in – she wouldn't be in a talent show if her life depended on it.

As in – yeah, sure, she, Cassandra, was a dedicated survivalist and she was ready to face all the disasters in the world, natural *or* supernatural, but she would never, as in *not ever*, face – her – peers – from – up – there!

Their school's annual talent show had recently been renamed *The Talents Show* because, as Mrs. Johnson had explained, people had many kinds of talents ("That's *talents* with an *s*, children – plural!") and no one talent was superior to any other.

The students, of course, knew better. They knew that some talents were *always* superior to others – the talents that happened, coincidentally, to belong to the most popular students – and to show their disdain for the talent show's new name, they mockingly called it the "Talents With an *S* Show".

Cass had been a little disappointed that Yo-Yoji was

refusing to perform in the talent show; if anybody had the power to shake up the school hierarchy with a little guitar playing he did. But her disappointment about Yo-Yoji *not* performing couldn't match the anxiety she felt about the fact that Max-Ernest *was* performing.

After a ten-year-old boy named Lucas delivered a surprisingly strong rendition of Tom Jones's swinging song "It's Not Unusual", Mrs. Johnson called Max-Ernest's name.

Twice.

When nobody appeared onstage, Cass, sitting discreetly near the back of the auditorium, was almost relieved. Maybe he was backing out after all.

"Max-Ernest, if you don't come out now, you're going to lose your turn!" Mrs. Johnson bellowed as only a principal can.

"But I can't get my hat to stay on!"

Suddenly, as if someone had pulled him out of the wings with a cane, Max-Ernest stumbled onto the stage, holding a top hat on his head with one hand, and holding a wand with the other. He wore a magician's cape that was about five sizes too big for him.

"Hi. I'm...I'm Max-Ernest," he stammered. "Most of you know me already because you go to school with me. But some of you are parents, so you don't

go to school – well, that's not exactly true, but...
Anyway, um, like I was saying, I'm Max-Ernest,
but today I am *Max-Ernest the Magnificent* and I'm
going to do a *magi-comedy* act – that's comedy, plus
magic—"

"Get on with it, Max-Ernest – and use the
microphone!" said Mrs. Johnson, not very gently.

Cass groaned: it was even worse than she'd
feared.

"Okay. Okay. I was just about to tell a joke. Here
it is – Knock, knock! Now somebody say – 'Who's
there?'"

"Who's there?" shouted a man in the corner.

"Who's there?" shouted a woman in the opposite
corner.

"I am! Get it?" Max-Ernest looked out at the
audience expectantly.

"Ha-ha! *I am* – I get it!" shouted the man.

"*I am* – that's really funny!" shouted the woman.

Cass didn't have to look to know who they were:
Max-Ernest's parents.

Nobody else laughed.

Just then, Yo-Yoji ran onto the stage from the wings,
his guitar around his neck. "Say *I am* again!"

"Um, *I am*," said Max-Ernest, surprised.

Yo-Yoji plucked his guitar, making that sound

you hear on television after somebody makes a joke: *wah wahhh*.

This time, everybody laughed.

Slunk down in her seat, Cass smiled gratefully. Thank you, Yo-Yoji.

"Okay, now for some magic," said Max-Ernest, gaining confidence. "I need somebody who's really beautiful and really really nice to volunteer. Amber?"

Everybody craned their necks to look at Amber, sitting in the front row. She looked at Max-Ernest, startled.

Next to her, Veronica applauded loudly. "Go, Amber!"

She stood up, feigning modesty. "Well, I don't know, but if he really wants me to..."

As Amber stepped onto the stage, swinging her hair, Max-Ernest gestured behind him where the *Gateway to the Invisible* stood in a spotlight, on loan from the Magic Museum.

"Look at this booth here – looks totally normal, right, Amber?"

"Right, Max-Ernest," she said, smiling at the audience to show she was taking this very seriously.

"But actually, it's the door to another dimension – the *Invisible*!" said Max-Ernest dramatically. Or almost dramatically. "Okay, now close the curtain behind me after I step inside—"

She did.

"Knock, knock," he said loudly from inside.

"Who's there?" replied Amber, playing along.

"Nobody!" declared Max-Ernest. "Now open the curtain."

As Amber opened the curtain, Yo-Yoji played some spooky, build-up-the-tension-type guitar chords.

The booth was empty.

The audience gasped. Then burst into applause.

Not bad, Cass thought. Maybe he won't be such a disaster after all.

"Now, close the curtain," said the voice of the missing Max-Ernest.

As soon as Amber had closed the curtain, Max-Ernest pulled it open again and stepped out.

He smiled. "How 'bout that?"

More applause. Victorious guitar chords.

"Now, how would *you* like to disappear, Amber?"

She smiled nervously. "Uh. Okay, I guess."

Max-Ernest held up his bandanna. "First, you have to put on this blindfold. Looking straight at the Invisible can be very scary and disorienting for somebody who's never experienced it before. Whatever you do, don't take the bandanna off!"

Obviously reluctant, but afraid to show it, Amber allowed him to tie the bandanna around her eyes and escort her into the booth.

But when the curtain closed behind her, the audience heard Amber cry in protest, "Hey – what's happening?! Help!"

"Relax, Amber – you are now invisible!"

While Yo-Yoji strummed his guitar repeatedly – almost like a drumbeat – Max-Ernest opened the curtain with a flourish. She was gone.

"How 'bout *that*?"

More victory music. More applause. Most of it from Cass, who couldn't stop smiling: if only Amber would disappear for ever!

"And now..." As Yo-Yoji strummed, Max-Ernest once again closed and reopened the curtain.

But this time the booth was still empty!

The audience tittered nervously. Yo-Yoji stopped playing and looked confusedly back and forth between the booth and Max-Ernest.

"Huh," said Max-Ernest, scratching his head. "I guess the magic was a little too strong..."

He closed and opened the curtain again. Still empty.

Everyone squirmed in their seats, uncertain what was happening.

"Sorry, Mrs. Johnson, this has never happened

before," said Max-Ernest, making a big show of his confusion. "I think we lost her."

Mrs. Johnson looked outraged. "Well, you better find her!"

Suddenly, the loudspeaker crackled. "TRY THE PARKING LOT!" boomed a spooky voice with a hint of an Italian accent.

It was a stampede. Led by Cass.

When they got outside, people pointed, giggling: Amber was stumbling around the parking lot, blindfolded, her hands out in front of her.

"Where am I?? Somebody help me!!!"

Of the whole school, only Mrs. Johnson was not amused. Everybody else cheered for Max-Ernest. Even Amber's friends.

How did he do it? they asked over and over, impressed and amazed.

Cass had an inkling of the answer when she saw Pietro walking quickly out of the parking lot. He waved at her, then disappeared into the distance.

Cass waved back, grinning from big pointy ear to big pointy ear.

Who said being a member of a dangerous secret society didn't have its benefits?

APPENDIX

APPENDIX

THE SECRET STORY SO FAR...

In case you come upon this book with no inkling of the terrible trials that have gone before, let me introduce you to the heroes – and the villains – who play a part in the fearful events within...

(Of course, as my story involves the dreaded and deadly dangerous Secret, all names have been changed to protect the identities of those concerned.)

Cass

Survivalist supreme. Cass's persistent investigations into the origins of a mysterious wooden box known as the Symphony of Smells (which appeared in her grandfathers' junk shop) led to her ending up in a very sticky situation as a prisoner of the Midnight Sun. Yet she escaped with the help of...

Max-Ernest

Cass's enthusiastic sidekick, and wannabe stand-up comedian. Saved Cass from a fiery death as they made their escape from the burning pyramid of the Midnight Sun Sensorium and Spa (after Cass's successful plan to rescue their classmate from having his brains sucked out through his nose went slightly awry). Following their gruesome adventure, he and Cass became proud members of the Terces Society.

Cass's mother

Extremely loving; occasionally overprotective. If she knew exactly what dire situations Cass had got herself into at the hands of the Midnight Sun, she'd ban Cass from leaving the house ever again. So it's just as well she was on a business trip in Hawaii at the time.

Grandpa Larry and Grandpa Wayne

Cass's grandfathers – well, actually not her real grandfathers, who aren't around any more, but her substitute grandfathers. They live in an old fire station with their blind basset hound, Sebastian, where they run a junk shop full of hidden treasures and let Cass use the firemen's pole when her mom's not looking.

Owen

The first member of the Terces Society Cass and Max-Ernest actually met. A master of disguise, he helped them escape from the burning Midnight Sun spa (although with his getaway driving style, they may have been safer where they were).

Ms. Mauvais and Dr. L

Founding Masters of the terrifying Midnight Sun, determined to hunt down the Secret and use it for their own unimaginable purposes. To be stopped at all costs. Ms. Mauvais may appear to be the most beautiful woman in the world, but gloves can hide more sins than you can imagine. And Dr. L (known in a previous life as Luciano Bergamo) will stop at nothing to fulfil her wishes – even betraying his own twin brother. The evil duo were last seen galloping off into the night after watching their carefully laid plans go up in flames. But they can never be far enough away for comfort...

Pietro Bergamo

Mysterious magician, suspected to be the head of the ancient Terces Society and, as such, sworn to protect the Secret against his mortal enemies – including his estranged brother, Dr. L. So reclusive that some doubt he even exists...

Mr. Cabbage Face's "Roast Villain" Recipe

Note: Before roasting, sear your villain at a high temperature. Mr. Cabbage Face says that is the key. "It seals in the juices."

1 villain, freshly slaughtered
10 cloves of garlic, minced
6 sprigs of rosemary
3 pinches of paprika
1 apple for stuffing in villain's mouth
Salt and pepper to taste
Baste liberally with butter

Serves four to six people – or one homunculus.

Sound Waves: How Whispers Travel Across Whisper Lake

Sound waves travel at faster speeds in warm temperatures than they do in cold temperatures.

Thus, in the early morning, when the air high above a lake is starting to warm but the air at ground level is still chilled by the cold water, the higher-up sound waves travel faster than the lower-down sound waves. This makes the higher-up sound waves curve over the lower-down waves, creating an arc of sound across the lake. Imagine a rainbow of sound with the colder sounds on the bottom and the warmer sounds on the top. The result is that you can hear sounds from across the lake that normally would disappear before they reached you.

If you don't understand, don't worry. Like magic tricks, the mysteries of nature are sometimes more exciting when they're left mysterious.

MAX-ERNEST THE MAGNIFICENT'S MAGIC CONE TRICK

With this magic cone, you can make silk handkerchiefs and other small objects like coins or trading cards vanish in thin air. Whether or not you make your own cone, please don't reveal the cone's secret to anyone.

What you'll need:
- 2 pieces of construction paper (they must be the same colour)
- Scissors
- Glue
- Glitter and/or other decorating supplies
- Silk handkerchief or other small flat item (bandanna
- not recommended)
- An audience to amaze and confound

Making the cone:

1. Take your two pieces of construction paper and align them one on top of the other. Make sure the paper is oriented horizontally with the shorter edges to either side and the longer edges above and below.

   Now grip both pieces of paper together at the bottom left corner and fold up so the corner touches the top like this:

2. Make a second fold like this:

3. Finally, make a third fold so that you end up with a cone like this:

4. Unfold the pages. Then cut a triangular piece out of the top sheet (only the top sheet!) like this:

5. Discard the biggest part of the top sheet. Then glue the triangular piece from the top sheet to the matching part of the bottom sheet. Glue only the long edges, leaving the short edge and the interior of the triangle open. You've now created a secret pocket in which you can hide a handkerchief or anything else that will fit.

6. Decorate the cone – very lightly – with glitter or whatever else you like for magical effect and to hide the glued edges.

Performing:

First, hold the unfolded paper open in front of you with the secret pocket facing the audience. Your right hand should be covering the opening of the pocket from above. The idea is to make it seem like you have a perfectly normal piece of paper in your hands.

Say something like: "Any magician can pull a handkerchief out of a hat, but only the best magicians can make a handkerchief vanish into thin air. Now watch and be astounded!"

Then fold the paper into a cone again. With the secret pocket now facing you, casually adjust the cone so the pocket is open wide enough to accept your handkerchief. (The opening should be hidden by the top of the other side of the cone.)

Push your handkerchief into the secret pocket (or drop in your coin or whatever else you want).

Now unfold the paper and hold it open for the audience, again being careful to keep the secret pocket closed between your fingers.

It will look like your handkerchief has disappeared!

Say: "Ta-dah!" or, as I prefer, "Voilà!"

Remember: you should always practise a magic trick in front of a mirror before trying the trick on an audience. And if you don't get it right the first time, try again.

Or just give up in frustration like I do.

WHO IS PSEUDONYMOUS BOSCH?
An Interview With Pseudonymous Bosch
by Pseudonymous Bosch

Bowing to the enormous pressure from readers to reveal more about myself, I have granted myself permission to interview...myself.

PB: Mr. Bosch, I'd like to begin by asking the big question – is Pseudonymous Bosch your real name?
PB: What do you think?

PB: Can you tell us your real name?
PB: You're very funny. You should do comedy.

PB: I've noticed that the initials, PB, appear several times in your book. But sometimes the initials are not yours; they are the magician Pietro Bergamo's. Is that your way of hinting you are the same person?
PB: No comment.

PB: Is it true you are the greatest writer of all time?
PB: Yes.

PB: In your opinion, you mean.
PB: (silence)

PB: It is well known that you are a lover of chocolate and also cheese. To what do you attribute these passions?

PB: Good taste.

PB: Why are you so scared of mayonnaise?

PB: I nearly drowned in a jar when I was a young child. Also, it's disgusting.

PB: What is your favourite animal?

PB: To eat?

PB: Mr. Bosch!!!

PB: Just kidding. What happened to your sense of humour? My favourite animal would have to be my pet rabbit. His name is Lorraine (long story there!), but we call him Quiche.

PB: Who are your heroes?

PB: Cass and Max-Ernest, of course.

PB: What dead person would you most like to have lunch with?

PB: I wouldn't want to have lunch with a dead person. Would you?

PB: We're not here to talk about me.
PB: Oh…right.

PB: Can you tell us your real name?
PB: #*##*@%*&%^*!!!!!

PB: Please.
PB: No!

PB: Why all this secrecy surrounding your identity?
PB: Fear.

PB: One of your readers has suggested that the true reason you won't reveal your name is that you are embarrassed by it.
PB: Um. I don't think…(cough) never mind.

PB: Some say you are really a woman.
PB: They also say I'm a highly intelligent chimpanzee.

PB: Did you say "highly intelligent"?
PB: Are you here to interview me or insult me?

PB: What is your real name?
PB: If you ask me that one more time I'm going to kill you!

PB: I'll be your best friend...

PB: (pause) Okay. But I'm only telling *you*.

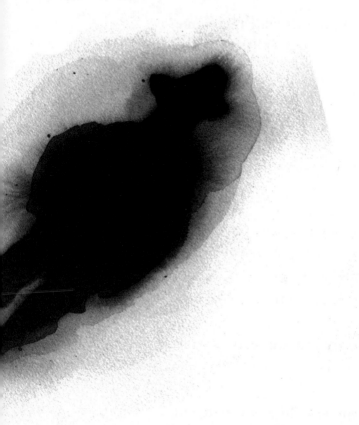

WWW.PSEUDONYMOUSBOSCH.COM

WHAT? THE SECRET SERIES ISN'T ENOUGH FOR YOU?
THEN LOOK OUT FOR MORE FROM THE PEN OF PB...

BAD MAGIC

OUT NOW

For Enieledam, Sacul and Illil
With special thanks to Xwp Ahsatan for
letting me steal her sock-monster

This edition first published in the UK in 2014 by Usborne Publishing Ltd.,
Usborne House, 83-85 Saffron Hill, London EC1N 8RT, England.
www.usborne.com
First published in the UK in 2009
Text copyright © Pseudonymous Bosch, 2008
Published by arrangement with Little, Brown and Company, Hachette
Book Group USA, 237 Park Avenue, New York, NY 10017
The right of Pseudonymous Bosch to be identified as the author of this
work has been asserted by him in accordance with the Copyright, Designs
and Patents Act, 1988.
Illustration copyright © Usborne Publishing Ltd., 2009
Illustrations by Abigail Brown.
The name Usborne and the devices ♈ ⊕ are Trade Marks of Usborne
Publishing Ltd.
A CIP catalogue record for this book is available from the British Library.
FMAMJJASOND/16 04063-1 ISBN 9781409583837
Printed in India.

CONGRATULATIONS ON SURVIVING THE SECOND STARTLING ADVENTURE OF THE TERCES SOCIETY.

The first book of revelations detailing THE SECRET is out there...somewhere. Do not stop until you find it! But remember...

THE NAME OF THIS BOOK IS SECRET

IBSN: 9781409583820

If you have braved the first two books, you face your biggest challenge yet with the third. Trust me...

THIS BOOK IS NOT
GOOD FOR YOU

IBSN: 9781409583844

There also exists a fourth, fearsome book that tells of time travel, treasure and dark secrets. But BEWARE...

THIS ISN'T WHAT
IT LOOKS LIKE

IBSN: 9781409583851

And lurking somewhere in a far-off dusty land, with tales of tombs, mummies and all manner of secretive dealings, there is a FIFTH book. But really...

YOU HAVE TO STOP THIS

IBSN: 9781409583868

ALSO AVAILABLE AS EBOOKS